Understand This

Understand This

Jervey Tervalon

WILLIAM MORROW AND COMPANY, INC.
NEW YORK

It is the policy of William Morrow and Company, Inc., and its imprints and affiliates, recognizing the importance of preserving what has been written, to print the books we publish on acid-free paper, and we exert our best efforts to that end.

Library of Congress Cataloging-in-Publication Data

Tervalon, Jervey.
    Understand this / Jervey Tervalon.
        p.   cm.
    ISBN 0-688-04560-X
    I. Title.
    PS3570.E76U5   1993
    813'.54—dc20   93-16360
                                          CIP

Printed in the United States of America

First Edition

1 2 3 4 5 6 7 8 9 10

BOOK DESIGN BY BARBARA N. COHEN

In Memory of Marvin Mudrick

Acknowledgments

I would like to acknowledge the support of my
wife, Gina; my parents, Hillary and Lolita Tervalon;
and Bob Blaisdell, Oakley Hall, Joy Harris, Thomas
Kenneally, Rose Marie Morse and Max Schott, for
helping me get this thing together.

1

François

■

The ball. When is that fool gonna throw the football? Been standing here so long the streetlight flicked on. "Doug, I'm boning out!" Ignores me, waves me off like I'm his bitch. Shit, Rika's the bitch. Too stuck up to say anything to anybody but Doug. Doug leans into the car and yells right in Rika's face. Here it goes. He hauls off and kicks the car door, rocks that Jetta. His car too. Kicks a big-ass dent into it. But she's still gonna talk head. Looking crazy, she pokes her head out of the window and says something. Gets him more pissed off. Yanks her halfway through the window and shakes the shit out of her. Doug turns away and throws the football but it sails way over my head. I run it down but it rolls under a car. Got to squat to tip it out then I hear it, two caps. Jerk around to see Doug falling. A little burst of white from the car, another one, Doug rolls away, flips on his back. Rika tears out, runs a stop sign and poofs. I get there before I know what I'm gonna do and see that shit. Fucked up for real. No way he's gonna live. I don't want to touch him. Side of his head looks caved in. Blood running crazy. Hole in his neck. Still alive, twitching and talking, saying silly shit . . . "No mama . . . I ain't . . . fuck this . . ." Take off my shirt, ball it up and press it on the hole in his neck. Don't want to touch his head. A crowd. Didn't even hear them come up. Somebody screaming. I'm screaming, "Call the fucking ambulance!" Nobody's listening. "My baby! Oh, my baby!" Doug's mama. I hear her through all that noise. Somebody went down there and told her. Shoving to the front. "Look at my baby!" she says slapping herself. She's so big, clears out people next to me. Squats and looks at him, then springs right back up, screaming, "My baby, my baby!" Don't even see me pressing on that hole trying to keep blood from running out all at once. No chance. Shirt is a big red sticky ball. I want to vomit. Homies come up, "Aw check that out! Who fucked him up?" I'm crying, crying. How long I've been out here? My hands are tired. Blue lights, red lights, police, ambulance rolling on the scene pushing people back. Knees and feet move around me. Policeman pulls me up and pushes me away and white suits cut Doug's clothes off. Ain't this the shit . . . walk away up the street to my porch, clothes soaked with blood. Is it drying? Can't go in the house like this. Mama'd go nuts, get blood on everything. Turn on the hose and hose my hands wishing I had some soap. Look at my jeans in the dim porch light. Fucked-up stains. Can't get that out. I sit back on the porch and try to cool out. Down the street the crowd looks like ants, circled around the yellow tape. Doug's cold as a fish. Coroners load him up and get around to driving him away. No rush.

The police stay. Black one takes the walk over to me.

"You saw anything?"

I shake my head.

"You hurt?"

"No."

Knows I'm not going to say anything.

"What's your name?"

"François Williams."

"You live here?"

"Yeah."

He's not going to sweat me.

"Thanks," he says and returns to the crowd. Probably be back tomorrow with more questions nobody's gonna answer. Sit there on the porch until it gets cold. Thought somebody would come up and ask me about it, some of the fellas, but nobody sees me like I'm a ghost. But I don't want to talk no way. Might as well go in the house.

It got quiet about eleven. I should call Margot, let her know what happened before she hear about it from somebody else and think I

got shot too. But I don't want to talk. Mama's gonna be home soon
and she'll know straight up that something happened. She'll know
like that. News ain't saying a damn thing. Don't know why I got it
on. Oh yeah. Here it comes. Stupid-ass reporter standing in front of
a 7-Eleven. "Nine shootings tonight, two fatally wounded. Shooting
earlier tonight took place behind me . . . gang-related shooting on
Fifty-fourth Street. Doug Goines, a twenty-one-year-old college
student, killed in a drive-by shooting . . ." That's it. That's all. Got
took out and all you get is a five-second mention that's all fucked
up. Doug a college boy? Joke. Wannabe high roller got gotted by
his G. That's how Doug would say it. Turn the station, flip it
around, more shooting but nothing about him. The door. Somebody
knocking at what, eleven something. Everybody knows Moms be
getting home and don't like people over. I cross over to the picture
window and peek out. First I can't make him out, dressed to bang,
baggy Pendleton cut off at the sleeves, baggy khaki pants, baseball
cap to the side. Ain't nobody but Ollie. Open the door just wide
enough to slip out. Don't want him to see what he don't have to
see. From the dim orange of the streetlight Ollie's face looks harder
than usual. Doug must have meant something to him after all. He
waits there, hands in pockets, looking at me. His lips kind of twist
up and he says, "Rika did it."

"Yeah?"

"She did it. Don't have to see it to know it's coming. Last
time I saw them together she kept saying she was gonna shoot him
and he took that. He told her to stop but she kept on saying it. I was
going to slap her if he didn't. She kept right on saying it."

"Yeah," I say keeping pace.

"She moved. Me and the homies were gonna do her but some
meskins live there. Doug tell you where she moved?"

"Naw, he didn't," I say and Ollie spits between his feet and
turns and stares out toward the street. He looks sort of silly. Skinny
and short sporting Popeye arms from curling. "Okay, homey. We'll
find that bitch. Later." I watch him walk off without bending his
knees with his shoulders back trying to fill out those baggy-assed
clothes.

*   *   *

Must have passed out on the couch. Mama's standing in front of me, looking shocked.

"Why do you have blood on your pants?"

"Doug got shot out front."

"Douglas." Her voice sharpened like it does when she's mad. "Is he all right?"

"Naw. He's dead."

She looks upset but she didn't like Doug. Said he was nothing but a gangster.

"Who shot him?"

"I don't know."

"Was it drugs?"

She sits on the couch next to me looking pretty even if she is tired. Her white nurse's outfit looks clean and just ironed after ten hours at Killa King.

"Drugs," she says shaking her head, answering her own question. "Did Mary see it?"

"Naw. You let her stay over at Keisha's."

"Thank God for that. We got to move. Can't stay around here."

Mama gets up and goes into the kitchen. Gonna get a drink. I shouldn't have told her. Now she gonna be thinking about it all the time until the next thing happens, thinking that I'm gonna get blown away. Can't worry about that. That ain't something I can think about. I look at my hands . . . Got to get this shit off. I stand up and head for the bathroom, switch on the light, and look in the mirror. Gotta get the do edged up again. A knock. Door opens and Mama's standing there with a drink in her hand. Smell it, sweet gin.

"Yeah?"

"Did you see it?"

What's to say? What I don't want to say. Maybe if I don't say anything she'll go. No. She's gonna out-wait me.

"No. I just saw a car drive away."

"That's it?"

"Yeah. It happened too fast."

Finally she gets tired of looking at me and walks away like a old woman too tired to make it into the bedroom.

Should have got a edge last week. Take out a razor and start touching up around the temples but my hand's shaking and shit. Put the razor down. Don't know what to do.

In the bedroom, headphones on, lights out listening to what, what's this, night beat, love themes . . . not in the mood. Maybe I ought to go by Doug's house. Gotta go sooner or later and listen to his mama cry. Listen to Ollie talk payback. People coming over all night. Somebody'll start cooking and then everybody'll eat. After a while somebody'll turn on the TV. The kids'll watch till they fall asleep then the adults'll pass out. Only Doug's mama'll be up all night on the phone, talking about it. Waiting on the funeral.

Can't sleep. Keep thinking about Rika. I know where she lives. They moved to the jungle. Why didn't I tell Ollie? Should have. If she didn't want to be with him she should have left him. Not shoot him in the face, shoot him down in the street. Forget it. I can't sleep. Up and out the door, out of the living room, outside onto the porch. I see it again. Doug down the street yelling to Rika, slapping her. The caps, the flashes and Doug falling. Walk out there into the street, where the yellow tape is still on the ground. Bloodstained latex gloves lying where he got shot. By the curb blood's jelling, rolling slowly to the drain. Mr. Andrews'll hose it down in the morning with bleach and soap and a push broom and clean it off before anyone's out the house. Two people coming down the street. One's tall and walks with a limp like he's trying to pimp. The other is fat. Rock and Jelly. Don't want to talk to no baseheads.

"What's up, F?" Jelly asks.

"Who got popped tonight?" Rock says.

I hate it when these fools try to make me talk.

"Who?" I said.

"You don't know? Your homey Doug. Bet those Main Street niggahs shot him."

Stand there, nodding to whatever they say.

"You know," Rock says.

I don't say nothing. They weren't getting what they were looking for, shock value.

"What you got for the head?" Jelly asked.

"I ain't got nothing for your head."

Jelly frowns.

"Why you talking to me like that? We go way back."

"Yeah, we go way back. Yeah, we *went* way back. I remember when you had a job."

"Why you fronting?" Rock says limping toward me.

"Who's fronting?" Turn back to face him head up. He backs down, beat with a look.

"Why you be acting like you too good to talk to somebody?"

"You don't want to talk to me. I ain't got what you need."

His face goes blank. These brothers are bugs, fading in and out looking for that flame.

"Loan me a dollar."

"Naw. I ain't got it."

"You a high roller."

"I don't roll. I go to school."

"Oh okay. That's how it's gonna be."

Shrug and head for the porch and they walk off looking for it. Inside, the house's dark. Click on the light and turn and there's Mama by the picture window. She must've been spying on me.

"Talking to drug addicts?"

"No. I wasn't talking to them."

"I saw you talking to them."

"They were asking me about Doug."

Trembling, arms wrapped around herself, she looks like a girl ready to cry.

"What's wrong?" I said putting my hand on her shoulder. I don't want to touch her.

"I don't want you going outside. Why do you have to go out there?"

"I wanted to see."

"What!" she said, her voice rising. "What is there to see, where that boy got himself shot? Is that anything to see?"

Nothing to do. Too late to calm her down, nothing to do but listen.

"You know how many times a night I think about you. Think you might be out there on the ground bleeding to death. When they wheel bodies in and I got to admit them, young men like you, blown up, cut up like meat on a rack. I say to myself that could be François."

"Mama, nothing's gonna to happen to me."

"Oh, yeah. Nothing's going to happen to you! How do you know what's going to happen to you?" she says and heads for her bedroom. That's it. She's not coming out again. Gin'll kick in and she be knocked out. But I don't want to chance going out the front door. Go into my room and slam the door loud enough for her to hear, turn the TV up so she could hear that too, grab a jacket, open the bedroom window and slide outside. I walk fast cause it's kind of chilly. I got to tell him. He's got to deal with it, not me. From half a block away, I see the house. Lights are on, curtains are open. All kinds of people are over. Somebody's on the steps. Some other people pull up. A old man and a younger woman carrying a big pot. Bringing food over already. They say something to the guy on the steps. It's Ollie.

"What's up?"

He looks up at me. I can see from the porch light that his eyes are red.

"Gonna find that bitch."

"Yeah."

I want to say something but I don't. I stand there nodding. I form the words in my head, I can hear myself saying them. Yeah, she staying on Hillcrest over in the jungle. But I can't. Ollie stares at me like he expects me to come across with something, then after a minute of me saying nothing, he gets to slurring and mumbling but I understand most of what he says.

"Doug was sprung over that high yella stuck-up bitch. Couldn't tell him shit. Bitch was dipping into his proceeds. Stupid letting her get away with all that. Reason she had the Jetta is he finally got smart enough to take the Benz from her."

Funny listening to Ollie talk. Acting like he and Doug were close. Couple of months ago Doug kicked his ass cause he saw him slinging. He said to me if Ollie wanted to be a punk-assed gangster that was his business but he wasn't fucking up Doug's operation doing nickel-and-dime shit.

"How your mama's doing?" I say because I don't want him asking me anything about Rika.

"She's doing all right. Crying since she heard about it. Hey, where's your car?"

"I left it at the house. Don't want Moms to know I'm gone."

"Can you give me a ride?"

"Where you going?"

"I wanna go over Doug's."

Damn. Straight out I want to say no.

"Why you need to go over there?"

"I gotta take care of business. Do that for me," he said, talking like I ought to be impressed. Ollie looks up and down the street as if he was expecting to see somebody.

"All right. Let's go," I said. Guess I oughta give his ass a ride. I owe Doug that. He stands and stretches like he must have been sitting there on those hard cold steps a long time. We start walking, Ollie gangster-strolling, lagging behind me. We don't say nothing. I don't have anything to talk about because I didn't want to slip and bring up Rika. Ollie got his own reasons.

We get to my car and I beep off the alarm. Loud-ass bug. Got to get the muffler fixed.

"Ollie. Let's push this up. Moms hears it every time I start it." Ollie nods and I take it out of gear. I push and steer and get it going but Ollie's dogging it in the back. Either he's too weak to push or he ain't trying. He's got his head down pushing like those little guys in B football. Weak.

"All right. That's it," I say. He gets in puffing. "Where we going?" I never got around to seeing Doug's situation. From what everybody said he was living large.

"On Overland in Culver City."

Going to the Westside. We take the freeway and get there in twenty minutes. Ollie's looking out of the window, is he sad? For some reason I feel bad about having to ask for more directions.

"Where to now?"

"Left on Overland. Pull over. It's the big apartment complex on the corner."

I see it coming up. I roll to the curb and stop. The radio ain't on. First time I can remember driving without the radio on. Ollie opens the car door and turns to me.

"You coming."

Ain't a question. Feel like telling him to cut that shit out, talking to me like I'm his boy but I play it off.

"Why you want me to go?"

Ollie shakes his head.

"Just come on."

What the fuck. I get out the car thinking I should have stayed at the crib. I follow him to the entrance. They got it lit up like daytime. Got a video camera pointing at us and a security gate that looks like it goes twenty feet up. Ollie pulls out a key and opens it. Soon as we get inside we see a guard, must have been checking us out. Ollie walks by him without paying him any mind. I follow, glancing back to see if the guy's still watching. Yeah, and now he's got his radio out, talking to somebody. I'm getting nervous, picturing it, a bunch of nervous security guards with guns waiting to rush us.

"Where we going?"

Ollie keeps walking, not saying a thing, then points to a building about half a block up. This place is like something you see in a science fiction movie. Five-story apartment buildings on both sides and in the center where we're walking, hot tubs and pools and brick ponds, cool and blue in front of each building. Ahead I see tennis courts. It's like Disneyland. We pass two white people soaking in a hot tub, their conversation dies as we get close. Must scare them like hell. Pay all that money to live behind twenty-foot walls and they still got to see us. Ollie heads for a building, on the awning it says Sans Souci. He unlocks the glass door and we go in. On the inside it looks more like an hotel than an apartment building. Halfway down the hall he gets to a room, waves me back and puts his ear to the door. I see him pull out a nine and holding it awkwardly, stretching away, he unlocks the door. I'm backstepping, inching toward the exit. Fuck this. Ollie goes in and I don't hear nothing. After a couple minutes I creep up to the open door, poke my head in and see Ollie sitting on a big white couch, gun hanging down in his hand.

"Bitch ain't here."

"That's what you doing? You think you gonna find her waiting here for you?"

"She gotta get her clothes and shit."

"What you gonna do, shoot her in the apartment? Police be on you straight out."

"Fuck the police."

"Aw yeah. You must think this is a joke. That rent-a-cop saw us come on in. We're on that video camera. If the bitch walk in here and you pop her you gonna get popped."

Ollie sits there fingering the nine and I get a chill. He'd put her head out and worry about it later. Yeah, I'm standing here like a duck and if she walks through that door I'm going down with Ollie.

"All right. You ready to get on?"

"I ain't going nowhere. I'm hanging till she come home."

"I'll check," I say not trying to hide it that I'm pissed off. I turn my back to him and that gun and I'm at the door and almost out. He calls me.

"Thanks for the ride. Close the door," he says. I nod and get out.

Some silly shit. What the fuck is wrong with me. I start the bug and pull out, rushing it, looking for the freeway. Get on and crank the radio and floor this little pootbutt car to the limit, not even seventy. Can think now. Before I was too mad to think about anything other than smacking Ollie's silly ass. Got played like a joke. Ollie used me as backup and I saw it coming and still went along. It's about Doug. I owe him, cause not that long ago he watched my back, was down for me, wouldn't let me do stupid shit. Yeah, he did the stupid shit. Even though we stopped hanging out, I had to be there to see it.

Get off at the Imperial exit and go west. Too late to see Margot. Daddy's got the gate locked and even if he didn't he'd slam the door in my face and talk shit for a week. Have to settle for seeing if her lights are on. Maybe she'll hear the bug. Roll down the block doing fifty. Don't like some of the niggahs in her hood. It's about Margot. She don't talk to them more than hi and bye so if she's talking to me I must think I'm hot shit. Couple of them are sitting under a streetlight, drinking eightball, looking to sling. Low-rent niggahs. Don't have money, don't know money. In front of her house I gun the engine and coast to a stop. Yeah, her light's on. Hope she heard me cause getting to her door is like breaking into jail. Her daddy's got a five-foot-high brick wall around the front yard with glass and nails at the top. He did it so it's hard to see like he wants to trick some basehead into going over and cutting his hands up. I gun the bug again. If she's up she'll hear that, muffler so bad sounds like a shotgun. One good thing about her daddy is he sleeps hard. I walk over to the gate, he's got it padlocked as usual. Can't hop the gate, he files down the spikes. Fuck it. She must be dead asleep. I turn to leave but the front door and the security door open and Tyson and Ali come racing out of the house barking crazy like they're gonna kill something. Tyson flings himself against the gate but Ali recognizes me and sits down. Ali's got sense but I don't know about Tyson.

"Hey, hey, what's up, boy . . ." I said trying to calm his stupid ass then I see Margot backlit in the doorway. She's got on an ugly robe and her hair's wrapped up in a scarf. Then she turns on the floodlights and I'm straight out blinded. I hear her slippers slapping the sidewalk as she runs to the gate.

"What the fuck is wrong with you. You can't call somebody? I've been waiting around for you to call. Everybody's calling me saying shit, 'Oh yeah, F got shot. Doug's dead but F got shot in the leg.' "

"I wanted to call you."

"Yeah, but you didn't."

"Too much shit was happening."

Man, she's mad. I'm standing here, blinded by the light, blinking like a basehead and she's in my face popping gum, pissed off.

2

Margot

Standing there looking at me like I'm stupid. Maybe I oughta reach across the gate and slap him, make him take it serious, but instead I unlock the gate and he comes into the yard. "Too much shit? How's calling me too much shit? Don't know why I talk to you." What's happening with him, standing there with his jacket open and no shirt, must be freezing. Eyes watering, is he going to cry?

"Call you about what? Call you and say 'Yeah, Margot, blood was spurting out Doug's neck.' What's that gonna do?"

I want to tell him to get his ass on. I don't need to hear this shit. I want to tell him if you don't understand what I'm saying you're stupid but I don't. I shut up, stop myself. Look at him. Look at him with his arms folded, staring at the ground waiting for me to do something, tell him it's all right. I don't want to be Mama. I don't have a crumbsnatcher. She's got to worry. She's got to see visions of him dead. I don't want that. I know what I want. I want to slap him for being stupid. But I say the right thing, "How you feel; you okay?"

He looks at me. His sleepy eyes squinting from the bright light. He's pretty but he doesn't know it. He doesn't even know I know it. Like a boy looking at me but I don't want to be . . . Mama.

"What do you mean how I feel?"

"About what happened to you, what you saw. He was your friend."

"I don't feel nothing, what am I supposed to feel?"

That's it? He really doesn't understand. He wants to be hard but he just don't know. So we stand out there not saying anything.

Ali's breathing on my leg, Tyson's running around the yard chasing shadows. How long are we gonna be out here freezing our asses? Finally I break down and put my hand on his shoulder, and he comes closer like I knew he would and puts his head on my shoulder. Yeah, he's crying. Doug. Fuck Doug. He really doesn't understand. Crying over some stupid-assed woman beater, some wannabe high roller, some fool that never gave a fuck about anybody but himself. How could François care about a fool? I know what he's going to say, "We go way back."

Yeah, reminiscing about shooting hoops and snatching purses, amazing that F isn't in jail now. Probably more luck than common sense.

"I know you and Doug didn't like each other," he says.

"No, we didn't like each other." As soon as I had said it I knew I blew it. Stiffening up already, pulls away looking hurt like I've betrayed him.

"Why you got to talk about that now. Can't you just shut up and listen," he says.

"Shut up and listen?" Why should I listen? I don't say anything but I can't help looking pissed off, can't help not giving a fuck that Doug is dead.

"All right I'll shut up and listen."

He gets soft again, shoulders come down, eyes look tired, then something happens, it's not me. He spins around, looking for something, turns back to me and pounds his fist into his palm.

"Ollie asked me if I knew where Rika lived. I didn't say nothing, shook my head like I didn't know."

"So?" I say shaking my head, feeling sick to my stomach.

"But I know. Doug took me around there when he had to get something from her. Her mama was staying in Baldwin Hills with a cousin. Doug wanted me to go to the door cause her mama didn't want Doug coming around since they broke up and Rika went back to live with her."

I'm listening to F still shaking my head and he don't even notice. He's gonna run this down to me, all the details but I don't care. Is he telling me Rika shot him? So what. I know everything I need to know. Doug is dead and soon enough somebody else is gonna be. And looking at F telling me what's up, like it matters. What matters is he's in the middle of it.

"You listening to me?"

"Yeah, I'm listening. So what, you didn't tell him. Why do you got to get involved in it. Everybody knows those two were smoking."

"What does that mean? You think she ought to get away with it?"

"Get away with what? Did you see it? Why you got to worry about it. You ain't a policeman."

F looks right through me. Didn't hear a thing I said. That's not a possibility, doing something the easy way. No, it's got to be complicated. It's got to be stupid.

"I gave her the message. Something about Doug wants the key. I knew she was crazy cause all she did was look at me like I was crazy and slam the door. I went back to the car and told Doug but he didn't even seem mad. Said he was gonna take care of it. Then they got back together a couple days later."

What's he telling me this for? I know already, he's thinking out loud. Trying to figure it out. Who's right, who's wrong, who needs to get shot.

"What are you worried about. You think she knew what she was doing?"

"Maybe."

"What if she didn't? What if she was too smoked out to know what she was doing."

"I don't know."

"You know. You just selling yourself on it so you can drop that dime to Ollie."

F shrugs cause he knows I'm right.

"That'll make you feel less guilty when you hear about how they shot her up the ass or something." He shrugs again, looks away like I'm bothering him. "You know, François, if you run with dogs you gonna smell like a dog."

I say something my grandmama says cause it's easier than trying to explain to François that he's not thinking. That's all there is to it but he wants to make it into something more.

"Why you looking at me like I'm a fool?"

"I'm not looking at you," I say. "You think she set him up?"

"Yeah . . ." he says looking unsure, like he knows I'm gonna jump on him.

"Why would she shoot him if she was setting him up? If she was setting him up she'd get somebody to do it. She freaked out, lost it and shot him. You thinking like she got some kind of master plan to get his money and dope."

François shakes his head. Yeah, he's mad cause I don't just nod and say yeah you right.

"She just went crazy, that's it. She's a basehead. Doug was a basehead. They were always beating on each other. Don't take too much to figure out what happened."

"Fuck it. I'm going home."

He turns and walks to the bug without looking back at me. Ought to get that muffler fixed, car makes all kinds of noise. He pulls away looking straight ahead. Fuck it. Why do I give a fuck? He really don't know what's happening.

In bed, can't sleep. Got two tests tomorrow and didn't study for either one. My hair looks like shit. Oughta get it braided again. Gotta get it done. Get F to take me to Sharonda's but he's not gonna want to wait for five hours while she braids. What's wrong with me? I'm thinking like everything's the same but it's not. Nothing is the same. It's obvious. He's got to do the dumbest thing, the stupidest thing. Got to face facts if I don't want to be there and see it. . . .

See him floating in the sky, white and dead, a ghost. Looking for me. He wants me to see, to see him dead, a corpse in the sky. I'm hiding somewhere but he knows and he's coming.

Morning. Couldn't slept more than a couple hours. The door swings open and slams against the wall. Daddy's standing there in his construction clothes.

"Your mama said you were outside last night talking to your boyfriend."

"Yeah." I want to say so what, get out of my room. Maybe I ought to ask him where was he last night. Laying pipe?

"You know I don't want you in the street at that time of night."

"I forgot."

"Sure you did." He turns around. Maybe he's gonna leave without saying another stupid thing.

"I'm gonna give you a ride to school."

"I don't need a ride."

"You're not gonna be late again."

Now he leaves. Riding with Daddy. Gonna tell me how to live. See how he likes this . . . the powder blue jumpsuit, the lowcut skintight one and the black leather boots. Good to go. Make all the dogs bark, have the cows saying I'm ho'ing. I get dressed and head outside before Daddy's finish eating breakfast. I walk by Mama and him before they see me. Mama sitting at the kitchen table half asleep, wanting to go back to bed, up after working to nine at that stupid restaurant because Daddy needs his breakfast. He don't even talk to her. Reading the business section cause he's damn serious about making it. Joke. I go outside to the truck, sun hasn't been up for too long. It's cool and windy; glad I brought a jacket. Finally Daddy comes out, newspaper under his arm, wearing work clothes like a business suit. Businessman.

"You going to school like that?" he says looking at me like I'm a tramp.

"Yeah, what's wrong with what I got on?"

"You're not riding with me dressed like that."

"What do you want me to do?"

"Change into something respectable."

I nod like I'm gonna really do it and go back into the house. Mama's still sitting in the chair smoking a cigarette, with a coffee cup in her hand. She looks real bad in the morning. Hair sticking up wild on her head. I guess with a man like Daddy she really don't care about looking good. All he's looking for is a good meal. At first she ignores me like I'm not even in the dining room, then she looks nervous.

"You're not gone yet?"

"No, he wants me to change."

Now she looks really tired like I just jacked up the program.

"Go put on a skirt or something."

"Yeah," I say and walk by her and out of the kitchen into the backyard where Tyson and Ali are curled up like short hair fur balls. I peek around the house, down the driveway and see Daddy slap the hood of the truck and get in. Oh yeah, he's pissed off. Hate somebody keeping him waiting cause his time is money. I wait for him to open the gate and pull the truck into the street and slam the gate shut. Good, he's not gonna go into the house screaming for me to bring my ass on. Finally he drives away and I go back into the house. Mama's at the table with the same look on her face like she's going to throw up. I walk by her hoping not to say anything but I hear her clearing her throat.

"Is he gone?"

"Yeah."

She nods. In a couple of minutes she'll get up and go back to bed. Every morning the same thing. She's really looking worn out. Hair's gone almost completely gray. Not like Daddy. He looks younger cause trouble is water off his back.

"I should put a rinse in your hair. You want to do it tonight?"

She looks at me like she didn't hear me. Then she shrugs and stands up and heads for the couch. She's not even going to make it to the bed.

"Whenever . . ." she says and flops down. I go outside into the bright morning, unlock the gate and start walking. One thing is for true. I got to get the hell out of here.

I'm a couple of blocks away from the school when I see her. That tired ass hooker is already out. Must have AIDS the way she looks. Too skinny to be wearing a miniskirt. Maybe she's going home. Got a home? Must be the rockhouse. How she earn money? Who'd want her in the first place? Dogs. More dogs . . . Couple of burned-out gangsters yelling for me . . . "Hey Miss Thang, Hey bitch come on over! . . . Got something for you!" . . . I don't have to look over there to know some fool is grabbing his little thing. Long as they don't throw a bottle at me. I hurry it up into that big ugly blue jail school. Bolt Blue Angels. How to be an Angel: Don't shoot somebody on campus. Do it around the house. Seems like two hundred ninth graders hanging around the front of the school. I glare a couple of little horny ones out of the way. Think cause you're dark skinned and you got something wild on they can look and slap you on the ass. Get knifed fucking around like that. Bell's gonna ring in five minutes and I still got to get my books. There's Mr. Michaels standing by his classroom watching the halls and reading the paper at the same time. Man probably can't get the ink off his hands from reading the paper all the time.

"Hi, Mr. Michaels."

"Good morning, Margot," he says kind of slow like he's still sleepy and wants to go back to reading the paper, but when I come closer he does a double take. Knew he would.

"You're coming to fifth period?"

"Don't I always?" I say and laugh.

"I'm way behind and grades are due in a week."

"Don't worry I'll be there."

He's staring at me as I walk away. Guess he can't help it. The bell rings I'm late. Miss Flynn isn't going to let me into class. Doing chicken-shit stuff like locking people out of class, slamming the door in somebody's face. And she likes me. Weird-ass rules. Fuck it. I go back to Michaels'. He's still at the door waiting for some of the tenth graders. He smiles when he sees me coming in his direction. I smile back and slip into his room.

"Margot, I said fifth period. That's when you have service."

He tries to look stern. It don't work. Too young and too easy-going to pull that off now.

"I can't go to first period. Miss Bubble Butt won't let me in."

"Because you're late."

"Yeah, so why don't you let me hang out in here and study for my next class. I got a test."

"You know I can get into big trouble letting you ditch in my class," he says looking worried.

"Who's gonna know," I say and slip by him. Soon as I get into the room I want to go right back out, go get a hamburger then try to catch up for the test. Bunch of mangy, stupid-looking knuckleheads running around the room like this is junior high, knocking shit over. I wanted to sit in the back so I could look out of the window if I got bored of studying but I can't hang with these hook heads. I go to the front of the class and sit at the table next to Michaels' desk. Yeah, more quiet near the teacher. Couple of homely girls, a fat one, and a goofy one checking homework, and some of the Latino kids talking quietly in Spanish. I open my math book and try to study, what is it, vectors. Michaels comes in shooing the bad boys into the room, four or five of them, all with blue sweatshirts and sagging khakis. Standing behind them until the tallest kid sits down and then they all do. He hands the tall kid a comic and heads to the front. A light-skinned zit-faced kid says something to the tall kid. They're talking about me. Probably about me and Michaels got something going on. I stare at them, till they stop laughing, till they look away. Michaels sits down and opens his roll book and takes attendance. Why would someone want to teach English, specially at Bolt? He ought to go to where people want to learn. After I graduate no way I'm coming back to this dump. But I guess it works for him, five minutes into the class and he's got them defining vocabulary words . . . *avuncular, oxymoron, morose, glib* . . . guess he's getting them ready for the SAT but he oughta be getting them ready for McDonald's cause that's where most of them are gonna end up working if they're not in jail or at home watching the soaps waiting on that county check. Well at least he gets to read the paper in peace, got his feet up cooling out while the dummies flip through the dictionary defining what they can't read. The ugly wannabe gangbanger in the back is hitting up in a dictionary. Figures, what he can't read, he's gonna fuck up.

"Hey, Michaels," I whisper, "one of your gangsters is writing in a dictionary."

He looks up startled, like he's really gonna get mad and throw the little gangbanger out the door. He gets up and goes to the window behind him and opens the metal security blinds and looks out to the street. Half the students look out too, like they think he's seen something, an arrest, or that crazy old lady's acting up again and chasing the elementary kids around. Guess nothing really does get him mad. Then he goes over to a Latina. She's shy. Hardly looks at him, hiding her vocabulary work, I hear him say, "Stop writing your *novio cartas de amor*!'' faking like he's angry. All the Latinos laugh, and the girl turns red in the face. See, she likes him. Probably cause he's light-skinned and he's got good hair. Bet she thinks he's part Latino. He leaves them and goes to the back of the room and opens a file cabinet. Then after a few minutes he turns around and sees the ugly kid with a marker, slashing the dictionary. Michaels crosses over and whispers to him, takes the dictionary and hands the kid a note. The kid nods and his head drops, then he shrugs, gets up and leaves. Michaels comes back to the desk smiling, only the gangsters paid any attention. Pretty slick, got rid of homeboy without him causing a scene.

"What you said to him?'' I ask as he sits down. He laughs. "I said for him to decide if he wants to see his parole officer or the dean. He's got to have a note from either one to return to class. He'll probably never come back. I've been wanting to get rid of him.''

Michaels smiles like he's won something and then hands me a stack of photocopies. Something from a magazine, picture of a sad-looking black woman holding a skinny baby, next page, Latino baseheads in a rockhouse pipes in hand. This has got to have something to do with AIDS. Michaels seems to think since he's the only young black male teacher at Bolt he's got to do the right thing, save the race and all that yang. Only reason he thinks like that is because he's from the Westside and he didn't go to a school like this. People are stupid because they want to be stupid. Like how could somebody fuck without a rubber? You see these strawberries walking around with the shit, skinny as a skeleton, smoked up, dried up, sprung. You know it's not just from the rock. Lots of fat baseheads somebody feeds them. It's got to be AIDS. Michaels ought to teach English instead of preaching.

"So I want y'all to read this to yourselves, then sum up the important points in a couple paragraphs. You have twenty-five minutes.''

"Why we got to read this? I don't want to read about any smoked-out strawberries.''

Aw no. This has got to set him off. He's going to talk to the end of the period. He's smiling big.

"Suppose, Herman . . . what woman on TV you think is cute?"

Herman, another one of the gangsters, laughs and slaps the desk, stupid clown.

"Who I think is cute? I don't know about TV, but I think Derrick's mama is pretty cute but she ain't giving up none."

Derrick turns around like he going to hit him, but it's just a bluff. The whole class bust out laughing. Michaels tries to play it off but he's laughing too.

"Okay, Derrick's mama's cute but isn't there somebody on TV you think is cute?"

Herman sits there for a second like he's trying to think. He sure is butt ugly. Ought to get his hair cut, fucked it up trying to wear a Jheri curl with that rough-ass shit.

"That girl on *Married with Children*! Yeah, that's the freak."

"All right. So suppose she's like the girl on the show, you know, sleeping around with everybody. You're at a club and she's comes up to you and says you're cute."

All at once the class's choking and coughing. If he was paying he still couldn't get a date. Herman frowns cause he knows everybody is laughing at him, specially Derrick, who's twisting around and really acting a fool.

"Yeah," Herman finally says.

"She wants to get hooked up and have puppies for you."

The class is rolling again. Michaels is bagging on Herman and he don't even know it.

"Yeah, so what?"

"So what you gonna do, get hooked up with her knowing she's fooled around with the football team, the basketball team and maybe the soccer team?"

"Fuck the soccer team," Herman says and you know he's messing with the Latinos but Michaels doesn't go for it. He says a "don't curse" in his teacher voice and goes back to the subject.

"Are you going to get romantic with her and take your chances with getting the gift that keeps giving, and get big bloody sores all over your body, lose so much weight your head looks big as a watermelon, cough up a lot of blood, go nuts and die?"

"I'd wear a bag and tear that pootang up!"

The little mugwug starts laughing but only his buddies laugh with him.

"So right in the middle of you tearing that pootang up, the bag pops . . . and it's see you in the AIDS ward . . . and your mama's saying, 'My baby, my baby! Dying of some disease only homosexuals get!' "

The class nuts up again. Derrick's got his hand over his mouth, jumping up and down like it's the funniest thing he's ever heard. Herman's sitting back looking dumb. Michaels lets it go on for a while, enjoying everybody acting a fool.

Now they're picking up the article, looking inside it. Some of them look like they're really reading it. I flip through the article, nothing I don't know. Can't avoid studying any longer so I go back to trying to think. The class gets quiet. Ten minutes go by, I look up once and see Michaels staring at me. He looks away, embarrassed like I busted him, checking out my cleavage. Better put my jacket back on, I don't want to fuck up his wedding. There's a pounding at the door. A Latino kid opens it and steps back and in come Mr. O.G. gangster himself, Ollie's stupid ass. Slides into a seat in the back, hands empty, no sign of a book, pencil or paper . . . aw yeah, homey's hard, little punk. Got his baseball cap on at the angle, sporting a long dangling earring and blue doubled up shoestrings. Gangster, gangster, hope he get his ass shot. Michaels looks like he wants to shoot him himself. Michaels walks straight up and says something. Ollie pops out the chair and stares at him.

"You ain't got nothing to say to me!" Ollie says with his fists balled up like he's gonna swing. Michaels doesn't back down, leaning forward like he's ready.

"Get out or security'll take you out."

"Fuck 'em, I ain't going nowhere."

"You want me to make you go?"

"What's up!" Ollie says sticking out his skinny chest.

"You threatening me?"

"Did I say I'm threatening you!"

Michaels laughs and reaches for the intercom. He picks it up without turning his eyes from Ollie.

"Send security, I've got a disruptive student."

"What's the problem?" a stupid-sounding woman asks over the loudspeaker.

"A student is disrupting the class and won't leave."

"Send the student to the dean's office with a pass."

"He won't leave, send security."

Everybody hears the woman sigh like she's really sick of Michaels.

"Look, just send them!" Michaels said. He's trying to look calm but it ain't working. He's starting to smile as he walks over to Ollie. Ollie's smiling too. Something's gonna jump off and unless Ollie's carrying something, a knife or gun, Michaels is gonna take his little ass and toss him but I'm probably wishing. Michaels don't want to lose his job and Ollie don't want to go to jail I think but you never can tell about gangbangers. Ollie's leaning on a bookcase with his arms folded across his chest.

"Thought you were going to throw me out?"

"Did I say that?" Michaels says and goes back to his desk. It's over. All that's left to see is if Ollie actually stays until security comes. Nothing happens for a few minutes. Some students actually go back to reading the AIDS article. I can't concentrate so I don't even pretend to try to study. What the fuck is Ollie doing here. Gangsters don't go to school specially for first period unless they're looking for somebody. What, he thinks Rika's gonna show up at Bolt? Just so the little pootbutt brother can find her? Naw, he's probably looking for François. Thinks François is lying or something. I'm out of here. I stand, see Michaels looking surprised, grab my books and I'm out the door, almost down the steps when I hear the door open behind me, it's Ollie. Fuck.

"Hey, Margot, hold up." He walks to me strutting like I oughta be impressed.

"What up?" I say to see if he's smart enough to see I'm fucking with him.

"What up?" he says looking at me all funny. "Where's your man?"

"My man? François? What about him?"

Ollie looks me up and down like he just remembered I can't

stand him. Two men walk past us and go to the bungalow. Michaels opens the door before they get to it and points to Ollie.

"That's the one!" Michaels says. The security guards, two fat ex-football players, turn and watch Ollie trot off, running with his elbows held high, laughing. They don't bother to chase him. One pulls out a walkie-talkie and radios somebody. All I hear is "west campus" and "ten-four." These guys are jokes. Where's the Latino campus cop. He'd have caught Ollie's ass. I walk away, heading for the main office where François has service but halfway down the dark hall, somebody busted out some of the lights again, and the windows stay boarded up so they won't get busted out again, I see François at the phone, beeper in his hand. I stand back and watch him, talking like he's a businessman. Yeah, he's a business-man. Finally he sees me and waves for me to hold on. I don't. I turn my back and go to class.

3

François

■

"Margot! Where you going?" Why she walking away pissed off? Aw shit, it's the beeper. Got the beeper in my fucking hand. I put it away hearing Tommy screaming into the phone.

"Yo! Yo! Why you leave me hanging?"

"Tommy, I got to go."

"Go? This is business."

"Yeah, I know that. I'll come by your crib tonight."

"Come by early. Nine or something cause I got a date with a freak."

"All right. Later." I hang it up and trot down the hall trying to see where Margot's gone. I run out into the quad court, gone. Then I see a bright blue ass going into the building across the field. How she get over there? I sprint, running, shooting past two teachers carrying cups of coffee. Hear one say, "Slow it down mister!" I speed up and cross the field in a five count and make it into the building in time to see her in front of a class, getting ready to go in.

"Wait up!" I say and she ignores me and reaches for the doorknob. I slow up, fuck it. Then she turns to me. She looks real good today but I don't know about her wearing that skintight, freaky shit to school like she's trying to get on *Soul Train* or something.

"Think you're so slick. Saw you on the phone with your beeper. Who you talking to? Your mama?"

"I was talking to Tommy."

"Oh yeah. Your business associate. I told you about that. I said straight out, I don't want to go to no funerals. I don't need gold-plated chains, I don't need to ride around in a Benz or any of that shit. I got a daddy to buy me all of that I can stand.''

Oughta just turn around and walk away. She's been acting fucked up for so long I forgot how it is when she's acting cool.

''Look, you've been running me down for the last two weeks. What you wanna bust up with me? I can understand that, if that's what you want to do.''

Oh yeah, she's calming down. She just looks like she normally does, pissed off.

''I don't know if I want to bust up,'' she says like she was considering it. Like it just might occur to her to do it and get it over with. I shake my head, feeling cold inside cause I don't want to bust up. I don't want to have to deal with carhops, squeezers and bitches. I can't say nothing cause if I say something she's gonna know I'm bluffing and if she knows I'm bluffing she's gonna nut up again and I really don't want to hear her going off again.

''See, like I said, you don't understand. You don't think. I went looking for you to tell you Ollie was looking for you and I see you on the phone and I know what you doing.''

''What you talking about,'' I say. She laughs at me. I hate that. She knows she's got my nose open.

''See you don't want to break up with me so don't be talking head. I'm not the one that's messing up. You're the one, and you know it. I told you from the get go about how I want things and that's how it goes,'' she says and I stand there like I'm talking to my mama, listening cause that's all there is to it.

''I got to go to class. Got a test. I'll see you at lunch.''

''Yeah.''

That's it. She goes into the class and I'm stuck looking stupid. Yeah, all this shit cause of Ollie. I walk back to the gym. Coach is gonna be looking for me. Out on the gym-field looks like half the school is ditching second period. I walk by the basketball courts where the Latinos play and the Main Streets hang on the bleachers.

''What up, F!'' I hear as I'm heading into the locker room. Ollie.

''Yeah,'' I say and notice as he's running up he's got on a

watch. Looks like a Rolex. Must be packing if he's wearing some
of Doug's jewelry.

"You hear anything about the bitch?"

"Naw, not yet."

"You gonna let me know, right?"

He's not asking me a question. I look at him and see that he's
not sad, nothing like that. He's smiling. I guess getting into his
brother's bank cheered him up.

"Yeah, I'm gonna let you know."

"Coroner's got the body and they got to do a autopsy so we
don't know when the funeral's gonna be. My mama wants to know
if you want to be a pallbearer?"

"All right." I can't think of nothing else to say so I nod.

"I'm moving into Doug's apartment. I'm gonna be running the
show. Somebody's got to take care of business. Come by and I'll
hook you up."

I nod again, "Yeah, I'll do that," and head into the locker
room.

Got to do five today. Everybody's looking but that's cool. Think
I'm crazy running laps in the hot sun but I don't care cause I'm
gonna play ball when I get out of here. I'm gonna be in shape. It's
the rhythm. I used to hate it but playing ball and having to do it
every day got me liking clocking the miles. I used to be able to
think running. Where I wanted to play ball, did I want to go away
to school or stay in L.A., if I wanted to get a new car. Now, all I
think about is Margot. Maybe I fell in love with a bitch I can't stand,
pissed off about everything. About her daddy giving her stuff, about
the school, about me. She don't want nothing from me. All she
wants is lunch. Take her to get a hamburger. That'll work. Check
my watch, ten minutes late already. I trot, cooling down off of the
field and head to the front of the gym. See some youngsters hitting
up on the side of the building, spray-painting a big, six-foot-high
green hand, fingers spread, pointing down. One sees me and flinches
like I'm gonna get after him. I turn the corner and see Margot
surrounded by a sea of heads, Latinas and homely black girls and

all the nerdy guys eating lunch in front of the gym, next to the campus police. Margot's got her hands on her hips, head sweeping back and forth, looking for me. She looks so good to me but why she dresses like that, boots and tights, and a top so low and tight you can see half her tits. I sneak up behind her and wrap her up.

"Who!" she says spinning around to slap somebody. She sees me and still swings. I duck and grab her again.

"Why you late!?" she says and looks at me, sweating in a black rayon running suit. "I'm supposed to be eating with you and you're all sweaty. You got to be joking."

"Come on," I say and put my arm around her and lead her to the parking lot. I kiss her on the cheek and she turns away but she likes it. "We can go over my house and I can take a shower and then we'll get the hamburgers," I say and open the door of the bug for her.

"Yeah, you just want to get some. Hah, way you've been acting, ain't no haps on that."

At the house, with Margot standing behind me, I unlock the door and we go inside. Smells musty in here. I open the curtains of the big living room window and see sunlit dust swirling around.

"Don't y'all ever vacuum?" Margot says. I shake my head.

"Mary's supposed to vacuum but my mama can't make her do nothing. That's her baby."

"Why can't you clean? See no man's gonna live with me being a slob."

I slip off my top and flex. "Men don't vacuum."

"Boy, go take a shower," she say swatting at me but I'm gone. I hurry up and shower and put on a pair of shorts. She's in a good mood and I don't want it to change. I go into the living room but she's ain't there. I hear music from the bedroom. She's on the bed and she's out of that blue freak outfit. Tiny black panties, tiny bra, don't want to get too excited seeing her. I sit down next to her, she's looking at the *TV Guide*, ignoring me. Lie next to her, unbuckle the bra, still ignoring me, slide down her panties, still . . . "You got a rubber?" she says finally looking at me. "No," I say. I hate fucking rubbers. "I got one," she says and opens her purse and pulls out a big white plastic square. I put it down and kiss her, try to get her excited so she'll forget about the rubber. She kisses me like maybe she is, then she stops and pulls away, sits up, reaches across me and picks up the rubber.

"You gonna make me wear a rubber?"

"I ain't gonna wear it," she says smiling, then she leans against me and I feel her breasts and she kisses me. She opens the rubber and slips it on me like she always does and pushes me back, slides on top of me and works it in, riding me. Looking at her face, so fine, sweat beading down from her forehead. Does she like it? Is she doing it for me? Gasping, losing it. Don't want to come. Cause I'm in her. She's here with me and nothing's gonna go wrong. I can't. I push her off of me and she looks surprised but not angry.

"I want to come inside of you."

Margot shakes her head.

"Why?" she says pulling me on top.

"Because I want to . . . we'd have that together."

"What? You still want to give me the big belly?"

I can't say anything.

"You want to be a daddy. I don't want to be a mama."

"No. I feel like that's what we should do."

She shakes her head, looking sad. She kisses me again, harder than before and this time I know I can't stop. Soon as I come, everything's clear. It's so fucking stupid. She's leaving. Without looking back, she gets up and goes to the bathroom. Not a word, nothing to say. She sees it, how I feel, and it don't matter. Toilet flushes, shower starts and stops and she comes back into the room drying herself, beads of water on her stomach, her legs. Finally she sees how I am. She drops the towel and sits next to me and holds me. I'm crying. Losing it. Why can't things be right.

"What's wrong?"

I can't answer.

"This isn't about a baby."

She pulls me close and looks into my face.

"Doug meant that much to you?" she says shaking her head.

"I don't know."

"Why are you crying?"

"Doug was fucking up but he was there like he had been since I can remember. You leaving, everybody's going."

"I'm not leaving. I'm going away to school."

"It's the same thing."

Shaking her head, looking at me without the mean in her eyes. "No, it's not. I got every reason to get out of here. I can't stand this fucking dump. You don't have a fool for a mama. I got a stupid fool for a daddy. If I stay around here I'm gonna kill him or somebody. Go off like Rika."

"Don't mention that bitch," I say shoving her away. Why she's got to bring that up?

"See you don't understand. You don't know what it's like when somebody has it over you. And uses it, grinds it into your face. Treats you like a dog and wants to make you like it. That's the kind of man my daddy is. He did it to my mama and he tries to do it to me. But I'm not gonna be around for him to try to fuck with my head. Make me crazy like he made Paul crazy. Always talking about money, making money, getting money. Made my brother leave cause of that. I don't know Rika but I do know if I was with some niggah like Doug I'd shoot him."

I shake my head. I'm not mad anymore. Margot's tripping, talking about me not understanding. I know she's smart, but she don't know what she's talking about. Rika shot him, straight out shot him, took him out in cold blood. Margot looking at me, wondering what I'm thinking. Let her wonder.

"So you mad at me for telling you what I think?" Margot says.

"No, I didn't say that."

"What's the problem?"

"Nothing's the problem. Everything's fine."

Margot nods and gets dressed. I know she don't believe me. But's that okay. It don't matter. Rika fucked up. She got to pay.

I dropped Margot off at school after we got hamburgers at McDonald's. We didn't say much but the whole time I caught her checking me out. Looking out of the corner of her eye, almost like she was scared for me or maybe of me.

Football practice went quick. Coach had me helping out some

of the new first-stringers. Showed them some things, and ran wind sprints with them. Kicked their asses, nobody came close to me and I wasn't running that hard. Coach wants me to hang out and take care of silly shit, making sure pads are put up and the sleds are locked to the goalposts so some fool don't try to steal them. I put the pads away and cut out, I ain't getting paid so why should I do it. Halfway to the parking lot and I start thinking, yeah Coach is cool with me, so I run back and do all the nonsense he wanted me to do while watching the rookies running sprints. Sun is starting to go down. Sky is orange and red, streaks of white clouds curving to the horizon and I'm starting to cry again. What's wrong with me? Sprint to the car and get the hell out of there . . .

At home I see the lights are on. I open the door and Mary's sitting in the living room with three of her friends from Catholic school watching *Oprah*. Girls look so silly with those uniforms on. The light-skinned, moon-faced one got a crush on me, dumb little eighth grade girl. I walk by waving my hello. Mary's following me.

"Tommy called. He said come over. He's waiting on you."

I nod. Mary stands there waiting for me to say thanks. I don't. She calls me again and comes closer.

"What wrong with you," she asks.

"Nothing's wrong with me."

"Why your eyes red?"

"Nothing," I say shaking my head.

"Your friend? Somebody shot him?"

Can't hear a word she's saying. Her mouth's moving but nothing's reaching me. Sweating . . . She's touching me, pulling me with her to my bed, pushing me down . . . Good. She's back with a wet rag, puts it on my face and closes the door as she leaves. I'm not sweating, tears. Crying again. Must have embarrassed her, big brother crying in front of all her friends. It's kind of funny. I lie there awhile trying not to think, cooling out. I realize it's my breathing. I'm not breathing right. Too fast, that's it, that's what making me freak out. It's like I'm running lying down. I work on it, breathing slowly like when I'm running for distance and I start to relax, almost fall asleep. Then I think about Margot. See her naked, on the bed, waiting for me, but she gets up and goes away. Can't control nothing, not even a fantasy. I get up. Now my breathing is all fucked up. Might as well go over Tommy's.

Baldwin Hills . . . Where you live if you're a rich negro but not that rich. Show your kind you got it going on. City lights all the way to the Hollywood sign. See just about everything from the front door. Tommy's house is on the highest hill, got the best view, at least that's what he tells me. Finally he gets around to answering the door. Hear him unlocking, swings the door wide, stands there filling up almost the whole door. Six-five or six, two-fifty, always on a diet and lifting but he always looks like the poppin' dough boy. Got a ponytail now, and a baggy MC Hammer outfit on. Strictly Hollywood.

"My brother!" he says shaking my hand. We go inside and I'm amazed. I've been over his house a couple of dozen times but it always makes me shake my head. Living room looks Japanese, screens and low tables and chairs and the far wall is glass so you get the same view inside. Upstairs they got a French room and they're working on a Spanish room. We go downstairs where he stays. Nothing fancy but a big fifty-inch TV and a pool table. His daddy owns a couple liquor stores, got ducats for real. Tommy clicks on the TV and hands me a beer. Lakers are on.

"Time to talk business. So what we gonna do?"

I can't look at him. I'm watching Worthy post up and spin around some punk.

"Your eyes are red. You been smoking?" He sounds nervous, hoping I'm smoking bud and not rock. I wave him off. "Not smoking a thing."

"What's up?"

"Doug got popped last night."

"Yeah, he dead?" Tommy says, fake concern in his voice.

"Yeah, I . . . don't know who did it," I say knowing that's going to be his next question. I do not want to talk about that shit. Don't know why I mentioned it. Not like Tommy gives a fuck.

"Oh yeah, how's his bitch, fine-ass freak."

I smile. Yeah, Tommy's a cockhound.

"I don't know."

"You and him used to be tight, right?"

"Yeah," I say feeling like I'm losing it again. Tommy looks at me and stands up and leaves the room. I'm thinking I oughta go, go home and do something, anything, when Tommy comes back with a big tumbler of fizzing soda.

"This'll fix you up, rum and Coke."

He hands me the drink with a big smile. Most of the time I don't like drinking. Don't take much to get me going. I'm a light-weight and Tommy can put it away. I take a sip and look at the game again, Magic turns the ball over and gets it right back.

"So what do you want to do about Santa Barbara."

Santa Barbara. He's still talking about that.

"I don't know," I say shrugging.

"Come on . . ." Tommy says making a pyramid with his fingertips. "Couple of months we'll make some real money. You can have cash to go to school with. We won't need to do this nickel-and-dime shit."

"Why don't you do it. You don't need me."

Tommy laughs and points at me. "What you gonna do, get a job managing at Micky D's?"

"Don't worry about me. I got options."

"I ain't saying you don't. I know you want to play ball and all that but sometimes you got to have a backup plan in case."

"In case of what?"

"In case it don't work out."

"Something'll work out."

"Just think about it cause you can go to West L.A. College anytime."

"All right," I say wanting to cut out but the game's getting good and the rum and Coke is kicking. I sit back and for the first time in the last few days start to chill. Tommy makes a call to somebody, probably one of his women. Can't hear Chick's play-by-play but that's cool as long as Tommy's not bugging me about going to Santa Barbara to do business. He's the businessman. He's the one with the cash. It's his money that he puts up, it's his thing, I just keep him company. Tommy hangs up.

"Baby wants me to bring her over here so we can drink champagne and watch videos. Got to pick her up."

"Yeah, all right."

"Finish your drink."

I do. Already feel light-headed, shit was strong. I gotta drive. Shit.

"Maybe you oughta watch the rest of the game. You look too buzzed to cut out."

"I'm all right," I say laughing at a stupid "Vern" commercial. Fool gets kicked off a ladder.

"Go out this door when you leave. Press that button to set the alarm. My pops hates when I forget to do it. Later," Tommy says and makes a exit. First I'm worried, what's his father gonna say when he sees me stretched out on the couch, or his mother or anybody. Tommy did say that they never go downstairs, that it's his thing. What a life. Big TV, big bed, car, his family just about gives him everything. Don't have to do a damn thing. Why he does what he does is beyond me. Guess he needs to feel like he got it going on. Why I do it? That's the question. Margot'd answer it by saying I'm stupid and small-minded and greedy. Maybe I am. I don't know. I just want to get over, just a little bit, to have something. Margot don't know, don't see it or she doesn't want to see it, what I have is because of what I do, and if I didn't have it, if I was a scruffling, half-assed fool working at some bullshit job she wouldn't gone out with me. My mama works hard for money. She don't need me begging off of her. In this world you gotta get up off of it, gotta get your own, work for it and not be a fool. I'm not a fool. Tommy's a fool cause he needs too much. I only need a little.

Game's over. Lakers won and Chick's bitchin' about defense. I'm not so buzzed now. Oughta go home. Can't see Margot, she's braiding heads tonight. I should study for history. Moore's gonna be sweating us. I feel it again. Sick. Breathing so fast. Gotta get air. Want to get out now. Tommy said press the button. I do and I'm gone. Outside's better. Cold air's calming. Feels like I'm gonna have a heart attack. Feel it again. Scared, then I'm not scared, just mad. Her uncle's house ain't but a mile from here, around on Don Diablo near where it dead ends. She's probably there right now,

sitting in the dark, thinking about what she did, thinking about going
on a mission to get another Five-O so she can get rocked up enough
to forget about what she did. Bitch! So mad can't get the key in the
car door. Shit, got the car alarm on, don't want to set that off in
this neighborhood. Finally get going. Do a U-turn, city lights roll
by, blinking to the mountains and I start up the hill. Takes some
time cause all the houses look the same, big Spanish boxes with
security doors, the higher the nicer. I think I'm there. Park and get
out . . . make sure . . . look at it for a while. No, that's not it. I go
to the next one over, with the orange and green lawn lights. Yeah
. . . that's it. Walk to the door. No security gate, just a floodlight.
Another fucking motion detector. Standing there blinded, suddenly
feeling stupid, I want to run back to the car and leave, but I stay,
finger paused over the bell, thinking of what to say if it's her. Should
I drag her out of the house and take her to Ollie, yeah right . . . or
get on the phone and drop a dime to the police? No, I just want to
see her, look in her eyes then I'll decide what to do. I press the
button and wait to see, see Rika. How she gonna look? Like a
model, good hair cut short, thin and tall, lighter than most white
people, green eyes, no contacts. Her face, stone cold, hard but
pretty. Not a bitch, but evil, something vicious. I hear somebody
come to the door, probably peeking out at me through the spy hole.
How's this gonna go? The door cracks just a little, what are they
worried about? Standing behind a metal door ought to do it.

"Who do you want?"

It's a woman, all I see is a eye and a pale cheek, maybe Rika's.
I can't tell. "I'm looking for Rika. I'm a friend of hers."

"Yes, I've seen you before."

A pause, she don't say anything. Looking at me. She opens
the door wider. Looks enough like her but it's not.

"I'm Rika's mother, Mrs. Jordan."

The way she talks and how she looks, she's got to be white.

"Why are you looking for Rika?"

"Just came by. Wanted to say hi, that's all." Stupid. Don't
know what to do. What if she slams the door on me? I just want to
see her. Mrs. Jordan looks at me not saying a thing. But she wants
to say something. I can tell.

"I don't know where she is."

"That's okay, I'll come back later."

"No. That's not it. She hasn't been home for two days now."

"Yeah?" I say wondering if she knows anything, what her daughter's done. Woman looks worried. Runs her hands through her hair. Hair's long not like Rika's, good hair too.

"She went out Tuesday. Didn't say where she was going. She never came home."

I shrug.

"She's probably back with that boyfriend of hers. I hope to God it's not true," she says.

I feel sorry for the woman. Picture it, when she finds out. Daughter's a killer. Gonna break her up.

"Do you know him, this Doug guy?"

"Yeah, I know him."

"He's not good enough for her."

I nod. Maybe I should tell her. Doug's dead. I could tell her that . . . No.

"I oughta go."

"What's your name."

"François."

"François . . ." she says as if she's trying to remember it. "If you hear anything about her, could you call me. I want to hear anything."

She turns from the door, goes somewhere and returns with paper and scribbles a number.

"Really, call me. Rika's not well. She's gets . . . she has a problem . . ."

I nod. Yeah, she's a basehead, I want to say. I wave goodbye and walk to the bug. Lady's kind of nice. How she looks worried for her daughter. Eyes sad like she's been crying for a lot longer than a few days. She just don't know. Her daughter ain't worth crying over. Time to go home and forget about this shit. Kick back and get ready for Friday. But, even as I get into the car, start it up and put on the radio, before I even get onto the freeway I feel it coming back. Maybe I'm gonna suffocate. Gun it, push the bug, blow by something slow moving, get off, get back on, head out.

Take the streets till I see it, black strip of ocean stretching along the horizon. Pull into the parking lot and beep on the alarm and I'm out and gone. To the sand. Run this shit away. Heart's racing to its own beat. Gotta keep up with it. Sprint a hundred, jog a hundred, sprint a hundred . . . See how far I gotta go, how long it takes . . . to calm down. I pass lovers doing it on the beach, maybe it was a couple bums keeping warm, waves pound the sand, run up to me but I dance around them, kicking spray. I know it now, Doug's back, haunting me. Like I got something to do with this shit. Like it wasn't his business. Why I wouldn't have much to do with him. His own fault. I can see him staring, looking at me, squinting like he's mad as if he's really got something to say. He doesn't. He doesn't know a thing. What would he say? What is he saying?

"She used me."

"You used each other," I say.

"You don't know. She used me. Turned me out."

See him looking at me with his arms folded, serious. Over and over it runs, image of him saying, "She used me." How far I gotta run before this is over. Five miles stretch to ten still . . . I hear it . . . his voice . . . I stop, grab my knees, gasp for breath, drop to the sand. Catch my breath . . . see the night . . . stars. Calm. That's it. I can think about it now. Him dying, dead. What was that about? Rika? Did she have to have something happen because that's all she could do . . . feel trapped in her life and doing something was all she could do. Am I thinking of me, is that me? What do I do? I don't do anything. I half-ass everything so nothing is me. That's it. I do a little of everything because I don't want to be . . . have all the cards on the table. A way out . . . if that don't work, some other thing might. But why is that so hard? Why was it hard before Doug got killed and harder now? Doug's simple. Easy to see . . . even dead. He always wanted to be something, gangster, gigolo, high roller, worked at it till he got good at it, all those things. Got what everybody wants, high life, money, the women. Then . . . Rika. She knew it wasn't nothing. She could see what it took to take him apart. Make him stupid and soft. But that's not it. That's what he wanted to believe. She only showed him how. He showed her how. How to get together and take each other apart. Fucked each other over because that was something too, something to work at and they couldn't do it alone. Couldn't walk away from it because they liked it, felt good. Remember how Doug first started hitting the pipe. Couldn't believe it, cause he was too hard and smart to do something that dumb. Looked at me when he lit the match, face red with the flame.

"She got me doing this shit."

They were both doing it, to each other.

Margot. She doesn't need me. Really isn't all that crazy about going out with me and probably pretty soon is gonna drop me. Thinks I'm doing all kinds of crazy shit, stuff that I've never done, like I'm Doug or Ollie. Both. But I guess it's better for her to think that. She knows a lot. Maybe more than I do. Maybe I don't know what I can do. Maybe that's it.

Sun's streaming in the window. Up. Where the fuck . . . Still on the beach. Six-thirty. Straight to school. Can't fuck up no more in first period. Lucky. Got enough gas to get there. Probably be on time.

4
Michaels

■

Amazing. Give a test, something where they have to look up facts, and everybody shuts up and gets to work. Ought to give more tests. I'd get through the newspaper faster. No one asks questions because everything is right there, the last five pages of chapter thirty-nine. Fill in the blanks. What did Kino do for a living? Who sings the song of life? I like how the Latinas in the corner keep looking over each others' shoulders. Might as well let them take the test jointly. Not just them, everyone's doing it. Looking for that little advantage. Herman's got his neck at such a weird angle he's probably going to hurt himself. And why is he looking at Murphy's paper? Big mistake. Murphy doesn't know what a passing grade looks like. Wonder what he's writing down, really should get up and pat him on the shoulder for trying. Can't though, I'm too relaxed. Made coffee this morning, not too strong so I don't go on a talking jag. Newspaper's good today. Metro section has three good shootings. Should read this one about the fourteen-year-old murder suspect to the class. Supposedly, he killed someone over sneakers. What I'll do is say it's not over sneakers but the kid's boxers, silk boxers. Try to make them believe it. Stupid thing to do, but it's kind of fun. "Kid shot this other kid over his silk drawers!" Sounds good. They'll listen to that. Have to get up. Falling asleep. I start my purposeful meander with Sally. She's a good student. See she had her hair done last night, new tight braids, oiled and beaded. She's found all the answers. Doing biology homework now. She looks up at me, narrow eyed, with an expression of pretend irritation.

"Go away, Michaels, I'm trying to do my work."

"Yeah, yeah," I say, and head elsewhere. What a great job. Captain of my own ship on the sea of education. Herman's got some kid's paper, copying fiercely. Close the distance and grab both papers.

"Herm dog, you just don't understand. You don't even know how to cheat right."

Class laughs and I return Linda's paper. Another quiet girl. He probably just reached over and took it from her. She looks a little scared. Herm's pissing me off.

"Herm dog. Let's go outside." I open the door and watch him squirm in his seat. Finally, after shrugging, and various fake angry moans, he gets up, smiling. Follows me outside. Catch his eye. Smiling. Probably likes the attention.

"Why you gonna do me like that?" I ask.

"Do what?"

"Dog me."

"I dogged you?"

"Yeah, you dogged me. Cheating. I thought we were cool. We go way back. Then I see you cheating with Linda's paper. You know Linda didn't give it to you. You just took it."

Still smiling. He knows I know. Who knows what evil lurks in the hearts of men or the goofs in B-2?

"I thought I was gonna do you up, give you that strong D on the twenty-week report card. Now, I don't know."

"Huh?"

Herm looks alarmed. I know he's counting on receiving that easy D.

"I'm gonna probably hafta give you a flag."

"Aw no. You not gonna do me like that?"

"Herm, you did me like that."

"I won't do it again."

"You won't?"

"No. I'm gonna be cool."

"All right, cool. But if you do it again, I'm gonna have to mess you up."

Give him the eye of death, squinting into his face, exhaling coffee breath deep into his lungs. He laughs and goes back into the class. Dart ahead of him to see who else is cheating but I'm a split second too late. All the boys and girls are back in place.

"Don't close that door!" I hear from behind me. I know that voice. At first I pretend to close it, just to see what she's going to say.

"Don't even play," she says and yanks it open. Angry today. Must be a tardy sweep. She strolls defiantly to her usual seat, at the table next to my desk. As if she thinks it's a good idea to keep an eye on the freshmen. What does she have on today? Baggy black pants, a short jacket and that edge, a bright yellow Body Glove bikini top with a two-inch plastic triangle window that wonderfully reveals a fraction of breast. To my eyes she is the class of a sorry act. At this school where a basic blue monochrome is *the* fashion statement, she wears what she wants. Even daring the occasional red blouse or skirt or jumpsuit. Disregarding what the bravest and the dumbest pay some heed to: Wearing red can get you shot. I linger over shoulders, peering blankly at looseleaf paper, wanting to return to my desk, to start a conversation with Margot, catch a glimpse of cleavage, hear her go on about François, her father, or some jerk stupid enough to come on to her. Slowly I make my way to the front, pull headphones off José's head, and a quick "Put that away." And I'm there, back in the seat, in control, ready to talk to the light of my day. I smell it, onions and grease, chili cheeseburger. I turn to see and there she is, biting manfully into a Bolt Booger Burger. Available a hot jump from the school at Chin's SoulMan's Food Palace, doesn't taste half bad, just smells like hell and the chili sort of resembles baby poot.

"Margot . . ." I say tentatively, not wanting to pull her from a meal.

"What, you want some?" she says, cutting her eyes at me. "You can have some fries."

Pushes the bag toward me like I should dig in. Embarrassed, that she could think I'm hungry, hitting a student up for fries, I take a few and pass them back to her. Rosa, a Latina, fresh from Mexico, smiles at me like I'm the biggest joke of the morning. I smile back.

"Margot, you can't eat in here. The vice-principal might walk in. She hates me already."

Margot slowly rolls half the hamburger up into the wax paper, chews thoughtfully and gets around to looking at me.

"You scared of her?"

"Damn straight. I got a car note."

She swallows and smirks. Approval. Likes my humor. To her I'm the outsider who occasionally makes a joke worth the time to listen to, the visitor who comes for eight hours a day. Doesn't matter that I did my schooling a few miles west, at schools just as bad, probably even more dangerous. I hung out with the fellas, and learned how to walk that walk, talk that talk. She's right. Doesn't matter in the least. My life is a million miles from here and about to double that.

"So what did Herman do today?"

"Same old same old. Cheating again."

She starts on the fries. Frowning as though they're cold. I'm looking at her with a little too much intensity. Probably'll think I want more fries.

"You still hungry? Here," she says and puts a half dozen soggy fries on a napkin.

"Late for fourth period?"

"Yeah, had to get breakfast."

"But it's almost lunch."

"So?" she says. Thinking about it, she's one unhappy eater. Food seems to be more a chore than a pleasure.

"How's the wedding coming along?" she asks.

"Fine. Costs more money every day. It's my own national debt, grows and grows."

She shrugs and finishes the fries, wipes her hands clean and opens a physics textbook.

"So why're you doing it?"

"Because I want to. I want to get married and hopefully so does Tina."

"Oh," she says, and pulls out a Hi-Liter. She has an opinion of my impending marriage. How flattering. Imagine what it would be like to be married to Margot. Kind of trouble you would get. Her moods . . . evil and introspective. Everything a masochist would get off on. François, the poor devil, doesn't have any idea of what he's up against. A babe in the woods, cannon fodder, all that and more, he just doesn't know. How does that Bill Withers song go? "Brother, if you only knew, you'd want it too." Guess I would.

"How are you and François doing? Still peaches and cream?"

What a glare! Knives and daggers straight for the heart.

"You know him. How do you think it's going?"

I shrug. "I guess it's going okay."

"What do you know."

"Oh."

"See you think he's cool because he's in school, doing halfway all right and got me for a girlfriend but there's more to it than that."

Oh no. I don't want to hear poison.

"He's always on the edge of doing something stupid. Kinds of fools he hangs around with. I try to tell him but he ignores me. You know his homey got shot. He went here about three years ago. Doug Goines."

I can see the knot of Latinas by my desk are paying attention to Margot's rundown. What time does the bell ring? Ten minutes.

"Better hurry up! Five minutes!" Always lie to them, I say. Now that they're struggling to finish their vocabulary I can get back to the story. Doug Goines . . . I remember the name. That's the guy who used to carry the cellular phone with him to school. Caught him listening to phone sex in class.

"Is he dead?"

"Yeah."

Margot unfolds the wax paper and starts in on the hamburger again. News must make her hungry.

"He used to be François' buddy. Now, François is acting really out to lunch, crying over that fool."

"Did the police catch who did it?"

"Police ain't looking. They don't even know who to look for and they don't care. Only person looking is Ollie."

"Ollie? That asshole I threw out yesterday?"

"Yeah, that's the one. That's Doug's little brother. That's why he was up here looking for François."

Margot sits back, folds the burger up again and tosses it into the trash. She actually looks sad. I've seen her amused, angry, angrier, pissed off, self-absorbed, but never sad.

"What's wrong?" I ask, knowing that I probably won't hear anything approaching the truth. She glares; I guess that's to be expected.

"Nothing. Why you think something's wrong?"

I look at her for a moment. She asked a direct question, something she hardly ever does. Demands yes, questions no.

"This business with François, is it bothering you?"

She laughs.

"No. I don't care. Why should I care what he does. It's stupid. He's a fool. That's all."

She quickly gathers her books together, stands, knocking the chair over, and somehow makes the noisiest exit for someone who isn't either running to or from a fight. Students are looking at me, smiling at my embarrassment. A long moment. Should I assign homework, something, anything to assert my control? I sit. The bell will ring soon. It does thirty seconds later. They rush out, knocking desks askew, jamming up at the door. I stay at the desk, not wanting to start for the cafeteria. Somehow, Margot managed to shake me out of a good mood. Replaced it with a vague feeling of embarrassment and something else—foreboding. That's it. That's what I see in her. That's what she feels. She feels it for François. Grieving beforehand. She's probably right to feel what she feels. That's how it is around here. You can see trouble coming but there's not a damn thing you can do about it. Here's to hoping that they'll be able to ride it out like surfers heading for the shore. Don't want to stay here in this dim room (when is the janitor going to put in new lights?) and think about it. Safety in numbers, distraction from the real, the numbers that add up to the facts. One in twenty-one wins the prize, bullet in the head. Better odds than winning five dollars in the lottery. Better to think of how dangerous Margot's shape is, how dangerous she is. Think of tying the knot, of moving on up, further out, so far out that I'll have to plan trips to the inner city to keep in touch. I go to the door, see scribbles that look geometric, mar that institutional beige. Herm's payback. Open it, bright light floods in and I squint in the face of it. Outside, the porch of the bungalow is crowded with kids spending nutrition by their next class, out of harm's way. I slip by them, ignoring their pleas for me to let them hide in my room. The green quad looks so beautiful in the bright noon sun, how the kids play, chasing each other like animals, improving dance moves, flips, splits. Not one desperate knot, the nucleus of a fight, calling them like a magnet drawing iron filings, to see some kid with his head split, blood tattooing a T-shirt, ruining the blue. Morning hunger disappears completely, course correction away from the cafeteria to the main building to see if Miss Bumpkins is in. Through the dark halls, to the second floor past the piss smells, kids hurrying by me, up to no good, hoping I don't throw them out of the halls. Hear the dean around a corner yelling for them to hurry outside. I see one big boy, no kid at that size, hurrying nowhere. Six something, must weigh three hundred pounds, filling the stairwell landing, hyperactive crowd encircles him, mostly girls. It's James, Panda Bear, Bolt's fattest gangster. What's that in his hands? I close in and see. It flutters, squawks . . . a chicken? He fakes a throw to a backpedaling girl. "No, Panda, I'm gonna tell," she says, heading down the stairs. He turns to another girl and does it again, the bird struggles, wings beat Panda's massive forearms but he doesn't let go, chases the girl up the stairs. This is what I mean, the kinds of things I'm privileged to see here at this outpost, this foothold of civilization in the vast barbarity of the inner city. I try to slip by them. Panda's not a bad guy. He might even return the chicken once he gets through tormenting the girls. I'm just about on the other side of the little scene when I hear Panda, "All right I'm gonna tear its head off!" I turn to see him lift the squawking chicken over his head and stretch the neck out like he's going to pop it like a rubber band. He's not going to do it. That would be disgusting, blood shooting everywhere. He is!

"James! Don't!"

Almost instantly he stops. His body that seems to have swollen even larger than usual, maybe bloated by the fake terror of the girls, shrinks back to normal. The voice of authority. He turns to the voice, my voice. I'm no authority from the way he looks.

"What up, Mr. Michaels?"

His expression changes . . . from irritation to embarrassment. His arms lower, the chicken dangles flapping by his knees.

"Where'd you get the chicken?"

"I found him," he says shrugging. "They don't think I'll wring its neck. I used to do this on the farm in Mississippi."

"Yeah," I say. He seems so reasonable. I wonder where he got the chicken. Who has chickens anymore? The girls seem to expect me to take the chicken and lead James to the dean's office. First of all, I'm not touching any chicken. I don't know where it's been. I don't even know how to hold one. I wish a security guard would come up and make the big decisions. Then Panda takes the bird and tosses it away, down the stairs. It flutters to an uneventful landing and hightails for the open double doors, disappearing into the brightness outside.

"I was getting tired of holding it. Guess I didn't want to break no neck no way," Panda says and heads up the stairs; the girls go off in various directions. I continue on my way thinking that this is a great school if you like weirdness like I do. Sort of the *Apocalypse Now* of South Central L.A. I come to the right room. I can hear the voices of teachers inside. I unlock the door and open it ever so slightly, peek in. My friends . . . I hang with the white devils. Oh no, I can't stay. They're being serious and all I want is one of those greasy, sugar-coated glazed donuts that Miss Bumpkins has on her desk. The three of them look bored. Bogger, the fresh-faced southerner, is quietly reading a Larry Bird biography. The conversation must be dying; D'Ambroise waves to me, must want me to join in. Miss Bumpkins, our dyed-blond, blue-contact-wearing queen devil, is wearing the shortest miniskirt I've seen a teacher dare at Bolt and she looks good, even if her substantial derriere is pulling in its own direction, raising the rear hem of her skirt dangerously high. She's a little irritated, probably something D'Ambroise said got her going.

"This school doesn't function because government workers don't worry about losing their jobs. Private enterprise would clean house here. Fire everybody and hire real workers who would be here for a dollar trying to produce the best students . . ."

Miss Bumpkins can't restrain herself, she blurts into D'Ambroise's monologue . . . "I'm conservative . . . I'm a damn good teacher, why should I be fired? I think we should all be held accountable, fire bad teachers but not the good."

Bogger turns to me. "What do you think?"

Oh no, I thought I could get away without having to say anything.

"I think I want a donut," I say and reach over and grab one and head for the door.

"You can't eat and run," Miss Bumpkins says and grabs my arm, holding me in place. For an awkward moment everybody seems to be looking at me. I wonder is it the "does the white lady got a thing for black men?" treatment? I pull away, smiling.

"I'm not running. I've got to see a student." I slip by her and open the door. She has her hands on her hips, giving me the teacher stare, then she laughs and throws her hands up and returns to D'Ambroise and the weighty conversation. Back in the dark hallways, I'm relieved. The last thing I need is to get in on that conversation. Most teachers at Bolt, black or white, don't want to be here; they feel more like rejects than the kids, and that's saying something. To the stairs and back down to the first floor. Halls should be cleared out by now. Empty of those quick-handed students who can ruin a freshly painted door or set a fire in seconds. Oh no, two students in the recess of a doorway, standing so close together that they're either getting high or trying to make a baby. I hope it's the latter, I hate filling out police forms. Oh, it's François and Margot. She is holding him very close, trying to catch his eyes but he's looking away. Oh well, I'll just go in another direction, really don't want to interrupt them.

"Where you going, Michaels?" Margot says, stopping me in midstride.

"To my class," I say, and start walking again.

"Come here," she says. She says it with the same tone as the older fellas in the neighborhood say "Come here," somehow establishing and reinforcing the pecking order in one breath. Impressive.

"What?" I say, staying put.

"Come here."

François is looking at me with sympathy, probably wondering whether or not I'm going to give in.

"What, Margot?" I say, looking bored.

"Don't play," she says, pulling herself away from François. Looks as though it's important to her to have her way so I concede a little and take a half step toward her. She looks a bit miffed but gets around to saying her piece.

"François has some business. I need a ride home."

I like how she makes statements, right to the point. "Sure," I say. She doesn't even bother to look at me again. Attention returns to François and I don't envy him a bit. I exit through a side door and hightail it outside, squinting in the bright afternoon sun, walking half blind to my classroom.

The last two classes went quickly enough. Juniors and seniors don't seem to have half the energy of freshmen. Basically, they just seem to want to coast to the finish. An empty class at the end of the day is such a pleasing sight. Straighten a few desks, clean off the plaques with a little 409, sweep up the gum wrappers and sunflower seed shells and I'm on my way. Where is she? Am I getting stood up? Might as well get a start on grading essays on *The Pearl*, what a great goddamn story. Where is Margot? I like to be off campus ten minutes after the bell rings, winging it to the freeway. But it's all for the best. Most of the nosey, good-for-nothing teachers will have already burned rubber out of the parking lot. I don't want to be seen with Margot. Don't need to start them talking . . . it's bad enough rumors are flying about me and Miss Bumpkins, and I'm supposed to be getting married. I'm now going against a school policy of not giving students rides home. Probably would help if Margot wasn't dressed so wildly. Just being seen near her after school is enough to get a note placed in my file.

> Mr. Michaels wantonly disregarded district policy and brazenly gave a female student a ride in his personal vehicle to her home.

Mrs. Rose would love that, getting something into my file. Where is Margot? Maybe I should go. Grab my things, my bag with to-night's work, and my coat, hit the lights and I'm gone.

"Gonna take off without me?"

I turn to the voice, wondering what took her so long. She's standing in the doorway, a silhouette. She steps back outside, turns and leans against the railing, her short jacket slung over a dark, bare shoulder. Picture of provocative beauty, if I had my camera . . . I'd shoot her and go to jail. She's looking at the after-school crowd; every day the quad fills up with practicing cheerleaders and the drill team and cockhounds to watch them. I step outside and pull the door closed behind me and twist the handle to see if it truly locked, no. It's spinning again. Have to work with it, spin the knob, lock and unlock it. Funny, Margot's not nagging me . . . There it goes . . . It'll work now. What a joke, custodians never do any work around here.

"Ready, Margot?" She's looking intently across the quad, not paying the least bit of attention to me. Then she whirls around, hands me her textbooks and runs awkwardly down the few bungalow stairs and sprints across the field, right through the elaborate formations of the gold and blue flag-waving drill team, scattering a few of the girls blocking her way. Now, I guess I'm supposed to chase after her and find out what's this all about because that's what teachers do. I'm not going to run, I'll walk, trudge after her like a stupid dog, carrying her books no less. She's stopped at a bench, standing, she seems to be talking to some girl sitting next to a few guys. Margot looks agitated. Man, I sure hope she isn't going to coldcock that girl. The girl is wearing the biggest blue curlers I've ever seen and she has on a fuzzy pink robe and pajamas and matching fuzzy slippers. Other than the fat curlers nothing too unusual for Bolt High, where kids come to school ready for bed. Margot isn't saying anything to the girl, instead she's staring. The girl doesn't seem to care. She doesn't look like a girl, more a woman but around here you see that often enough. She's got her legs crossed nonchalantly, leaning back, smoking a cigarette. The girl is very fair-skinned, much lighter than I am, and she is very pretty even with the curlers and the cigarette hanging from her mouth, moll-like. Margot seems to want to say something, her lips twitch on the edge of words but nothing comes out. I can't tell if she's mad or just shocked to see this girl. Maybe she's a relative, into the drug scene, something embarrassing. Margot shrugs . . . Finally, a word.

"Why" . . . another pause . . . "are you up here?"

The girl ignores her. I know the guys sitting alongside of her, big youngsters. They probably have been trying to hit on this girl, thinking that she must be drug-addled and easy to negotiate. Now they sense the tension, maybe a fight, a cat fight. The girl puffs on the cigarette looking at the ground, then up at Margot.

"Let me borrow a dollar."

A long moment. Eyes arch, glancing all around, a guy with a serious fade laughs into his sleeve. Margot isn't laughing.

"Give you a dollar?" she says, looking at her with so much disgust I start to feel like trash for her. Margot doesn't have an effect on the girl, water off a duck's back. She turns her eyes away from a very angry Margot to one of the guys, Murph, the football player.

"You got a dollar?" she asks. Her face softens for a quick moment. She makes brief eye contact with him, an alluding smile, then a return of amused attention to Margot. Murph leers to his buddies and almost cups his crotch. Margot's anger seems to be lessening. Now, she looks contemptuous.

"Are you a fool?"

The girl doesn't answer. She stares at the ground again, the cracked concrete, as though it has something to say.

"Why come here, you know the deal?"

This time the girl turns to Margot, her eyes seem intent, she doesn't look as though she is going to break into a laugh.

"Do you have a dollar or what?" she says.

Margot's arms snake up in disgust and wave off this girl. She's gone, striding as fast as she can toward the main building. I should follow her, but I don't. Instead, I stand there, watching this girl, this woman, like these knuckleheads, Murph and his pals . . . trying to figure her out. I shake my head watching Murph whisper to her, and her nodding. Then she looks at me.

"You got a dollar?" she asks.

Everyone's focused on me. She's almost smiling, amused? I take a dollar out of my pocket. I feel secure with the bill peeking out of my closed fist.

"What's this about? With you and her," I ask, nodding to a retreating Margot. She doesn't respond. Instead, she turns to Murph and whispers something to him. I shrug. Should I be trying to reason with somebody in a fuzzy bathrobe? Should just leave, but I don't, I stay.

"You go to school here?"

She looks at me as though the question irritates her.

"I graduated from Kennedy. I didn't go to a school in Watts."

Oh, she was bused. Big deal. Snotty. Sounds proper, like a Catholic school girl but no, she went to Kennedy.

"I got to leave. Are you going to give me that dollar?"

I hand it to her. It's a dumb thing to do.

"She thinks I'm stupid because I'm not scared. Tell her to worry about herself, she doesn't have to worry about me."

She stands up, tall in slippers, stretches and starts a slow walk toward the student parking lot, Murph dogging her heels. Soon enough she's out of sight and I'm left standing there thinking of a good reason why I wasted a dollar and drive time. Better hurry up, freeway is going to be horrible. I trot awkwardly out to the parking lot, trying to keep my briefcase and Margot's books from falling. There she is leaning against my car.

"What took you so long?"

She's looking at me almost like she did that girl. Now, I'm getting irritated.

"What's the problem?" I say, unlocking the door for her. I use my teacher-is-sick-of-you voice. I slide behind the wheel and see her looking at me, still giving me this death stare.

"What's the problem?" I say again.

"Were you talking to that . . . girl?"

"Yeah."

"Oh," she says.

I start the car and ease into traffic. Problem is when I take Margot home I have to go in the opposite direction. I'm going to be late for dinner. Tina's going to be pissed. I really shouldn't have agreed to this.

"You know that girl . . ." I ask.

"Yeah" . . . bet she's going to say that's my basehead cousin.

"That's the one who did it."

"Did what?" I wait for an answer as I dart in a lefthand turn lane and out again. Cars are riding bumpers because of the construction on the Harbor Freeway. Should have gone in any other direction. Hit a U-turn. Go back to Main and head north . . . might work. Yeah, traffic's much lighter. Stoplight, I turn to Margot, she's looking straight ahead, frowning.

"What's wrong?"

"Nothing."

"You said that before. So what did that girl do?"

"Nothing."

So surly and I'm giving her a ride home. Getting fairly close to her house, funny only a few blocks from the projects but the houses are so middle-class. Trimmed lawns, freshly painted, tract homes, a few nicely landscaped bungalows, even a two-story colonial. Maybe Tina and I should consider it as a potential area to buy a home in. Yeah right, Tina would take one look at the address and laugh. Live here?! You can't be serious!

"That girl is crazy, stupid bitch . . ." Margot says, muttering to herself.

"Coming to school dressed like that, she sure is," I say to be agreeable. But Margot looks at me like I should shut up and I do. Can't help but be glad her house is only two blocks away.

She points to a McDonald's in the next street.

"Stop at McDonald's. I want something."

"Margot, I can't do that, I'm going to be late."

She's looking at me with the usual irritation. Then it leaves her face, the hardness, the anger, what's left is the sadness from earlier in the day. I know it's about François. I'm at her house. Every time I see it I'm impressed. It's a hacienda garrison. It really would be an attractive house in any neighborhood, whitewashed walls, big picture windows with decorative, curlicue security bars and flower pots on the broad porch and a redwood bench to sit out and enjoy the breeze or the sun as though any right-minded person would feel secure in doing that, but who would with all the shooting. High, ornate wrought-iron railing should surround the yard, but in a concession to the reality of urban life he has an unmarred brick wall topped with barbed points and what, maybe shards of glass and two black pit bulls already at the gate, not barking but just the same menacing as they want to be. And banks of floodlights that I'm sure are truly blinding from the street. I've never met her father and that's something I'm thankful for. For some reason I suspect he's some kind of survivalist genius. The kind of man who can live next to a rockhouse and not be inconvenienced because he's the motherfucker on the block.

"Why are you staring at my house?"

"Me?"

"Yeah," she says, the sadness still apparent.

I hoped she would open the car door and leave me free to hit the freeway.

"It's not about McDonald's. I want to talk."

"Talk?"

"Yeah, talk."

"At McDonald's?"

She shrugs, I shrug. Instead of hitting the freeway, I hit a U-turn, and head back up to the El Segundo. I want to go to the drive-through so I can get on the road but Margot points to a parking space.

"Park there so we can see your car."

"Oh," I say. I park and look around. We walk in together and Margot says she wants a McChicken sandwich and a large order of fries. I guess I'm supposed to pay. I nod and stand in line. I thought we were going to be talking. I order what she wants and get myself a coffee and some fries. I'm going to be an hour late easily. I come back to the table and she's gazing out of the window looking for all the world like a sensitive young woman.

"You get ketchup?"

"No," I say and return to the counter. I come back with the ketchup thinking that if she were butt ugly I'd probably be home by now. All of this because I'm smitten with too vivid fantasies. She's eating, no, she's concentrating on eating, chewing. Methodically knocking off fries.

"So what's this about?" I say in the hopes of speeding things up.

"What's what about?" she says.

"You said you wanted to talk."

She shakes her head, then nods.

"You won't understand."

"Understand what?"

"How to shut up."

"I know how to shut up."

Her mood brightens as she confuses me.

"Just cause you know something you can't just do what you want to do. Sometimes you can't do anything."

"What are you saying? You think if you tell me something I'm going to turn you over to the principal?"

She shakes her head, mutters "Stupid," and looks at me. "That girl you saw me talking to, she . . ."

"Maybe you're right. I don't need to hear this."

How did I get into this . . . looking at me like I'm a total idiot.

"It's like this. If I hear of something that has to do with child molestation, drug abuse, anything like that I've got to report it to protect my ass."

"Oh yeah," she says, cutting her eyes in my direction.

"Really. I'd be dead."

She rolls her eyes.

"I knew you'd say something like that. The only way you'd get into trouble is if I say something and I'm not saying a damn thing to anybody but you."

"Oh," I say. She's perfectly right. Why would she say anything? Unless . . . she was trying to blackmail me. No, I've got nothing to worry about . . . except blackmail.

"Okay, so what is it?"

"You sure you want to hear this?" she says with the perfect tone to make me squirm. I shrug.

"Say it," I say.

"She's the one that . . ."

I must be frowning. She stops in mid-sentence, shakes her head. "What's it like getting married?"

I look at her, consider what she's saying. She didn't want to say what she had to say and that's a relief but I know I can't leave it at that. I've got to offer to hear even though . . .

"You don't want to know about this marriage thing."

"I do," she says firmly. Amazing how she can shift gears and be totally demanding on an entirely different subject.

"Why?"

"Because I don't know how you could. It don't make sense to me."

I'm curious. I want to take the bait and hear what she has to say, but I suspect she'll slip back to the first subject.

"How come you want to talk about marriage. What about that girl?"

Back to the fries. "That's not important. I figured it out. I said it to you, sometimes you can't do nothing, even if you want to. You fuck things up worse."

I nod, grateful not to know more.

"So why are you so interested in marriage?"

"Because I can't see it. You've got to trust somebody. That's not in my program."

"You're thinking of François. But he's too young, and you're not ready anyway."

She laughs sharply, evilly.

"François? Why would I be thinking of marrying him? I'm not stupid."

"Stupid? I wouldn't say you're stupid because you're serious about him."

"He ain't in the picture. You think cause we got something going on it's more than it is. He's not what I'm about."

"Oh," I say. Sometimes she sounds so cold. Time to go.

"Looking at your watch ain't polite," she says.

I guess we're leaving when she's ready. Maybe I can make myself angry enough to just get up and take off.

"François isn't going nowhere. He's going to hang around here."

"Sometimes you sound so mean. It's not too appealing."

She laughs good-naturedly, as though a frown and a word of disapproval from me is worth a laugh.

"You know I'm leaving for Santa Cruz in August. That's it. I'm through with L.A. and everybody in it. Got to deal with the future. Bet they'll be about fifty black people going there, and the men, probably'll be a bunch of men like you."

"Thanks."

"I didn't say that was bad, might be kind of good."

"How's that?"

"See, when I think about getting hooked up with somebody all I see is me getting dogged. But you're not a dog."

I see it coming, a grin appears on my face and I can't get it off.

"I know if I got hooked up it would be to somebody like you."

Wish she wouldn't have said that. I say nothing, think instead of everything, how angular her face is, how fine her lips are, how bright her eyes are. I know I must look too dopey, she's frowning into her orange soda.

"But if I was hooked up to you I'd probably do the dogging. I'd drive you crazy. I know that. It just how I am."

"You're so honest."

"Stop trying to sound so white."

How insulting, but I'm not insulted. I think, I know, I should go. But I have a question I need to pose. Now she looks as though she's ready to leave. She puts her uneaten sandwich in the bag and stands up.

"So we're ready."

"Yeah, François is supposed to take me to get my hair done."

"Great." She's going to be on time for that but me, my schedule is written in smoke. We walk to the car and soon as we're both inside I ask the burning question.

"So what would it be like to be married to me?"

Nothing, uncomfortable silence for the length of the ride. We arrive at her house and she still hasn't said a thing. Maybe it's better nothing's said. It certainly isn't very decorous for a teacher to be asking a student to imagine married life with him. I pull to the curb and turn off the engine and look at her, hoping for an answer. She pops the door open, nothing, then she turns.

"I dunno. It would probably be like being married. Thanks for the ride."

She leaves, walks quickly to the gate, deadlock to unlock, greets the pit bulls, onto the porch. There, she's inside the secure walls of the garrison. I drive off thinking of how that wasn't any answer. Of how well that tube top fit her, of how much of a fool I could be over her.

5
Ollie

■

"Okay, Mama, but he got a whole lot of stuff over here. I'm doing it . . ."

"You don't gotta stay. You can come back home. Help us get ready for the funeral. I don't like you being there. I'm gonna send your sister to help."

That heifer ain't coming over here.

"No. Mama, I can take care of it. Don't send Sally."

"I don't want you staying at that apartment. Ain't nothing but trouble there."

"Yeah. Mama, I know what you gonna say. I heard it. I gonna go now."

Stupid trying to talk to her. Like I'm gonna give it up. I'm here to stay. They might be putting Doug six feet under tomorrow but I ain't going out like that. Turn the phone off, don't need to hang it up, can carry it around. Stretch out on Doug's big white leather couch, click on the thirty-inch, check out another video, I ain't seen none of these. Aw, this one's it, that wild-looking bitch with the nose ring, she be hitting. Yeah. This is it. I gonna go get me some head. Doug really had it going on. I'm gonna get it going on too. Doug would be saying "Boy, you don't know shit, you nothing but a saggy-assed wannabe gangster." Look at him now, dead cause of a bitch. Look who fucked up. Who's the fool? I'm gonna be bigger than him, got my boys working for me, holding down the hood. Oughta get out and check on how it's going, collect my proceeds cause I ain't trusting nobody. But first I need to count the stash again. Step over piles of clothes, mostly her shit. He bought her all kinds of shit. Got it in the dirty clothes basket, wrapped up in a shirt, a shoe box filled with twenties and fifties but that's it. He must have more, maybe in some account. Mama'll have to get that out. But that's all he had at the apartment. Tore this place up looking for more but nothing. And the rock I found I already got Smoot and the rest clocking it. Smoot say we gonna have enough money to get three keys then we gonna make big bank. Kick back on the Cal-King bed, all this is mine. Pay the rent on the first, what is the rent? Gonna have to ask somebody. But I do want to get rid of that bitch's shit. Give it to Sally to sell, that'll give her something to do. Maybe she'll shut up and stop trying to tell me how to live. What she said, "You ain't smart enough to do what Doug did." Fuck that, she don't know. Phone. Must be Smoot.

"What up!"

"Who the fuck is this?"

Some niggah with a deep voice.

"Who? Who's you?"

"Who's you? Look niggah, you know who this is, and I know who you are. I know you been driving around in that Benz. That Benz is mine. Doug owed me twenty thousand. I'll take the Benz, I don't want you fucking it up."

"You must be smoking. That Benz was his, I ain't giving it up to nobody. And who the fuck is this?"

"This is Cowboy!"

Oh, yeah. Cowboy the high roller . . . yeah I heard all that. Like I'm supposed to be scared of him cause Doug was. Fuck that.

"Bring the car to Fifty-eighth Street and Dinker. One of my boys give you a ride home."

Ain't this a bitch, talking to me like I'm a stupid ho. Fuck that.

"I ain't giving you shit. The car's mine."

Niggah's laughing at me.

"Fool, your brother was right about you. Said you were stupid. I can drop a dime and get your simple assed smoked. But your mama has enough to cry about. Get that car to me before I send somebody over to collect."

Punk hung up, think I'm supposed to be scared, give up the

car cause he say give it up. Got a ·Uzi by the bed, a nine on the coffee table, let him try to fuck with me he'll see who's gonna get smoked. Now I got two fools I'm gonna show what's up.

I turn the corner off of Main and Ninety-first and get out of the fucking sun and this kid comes running up to the Benz. I got my niggah killa by my leg, finger on the trigger.

"What you need?" The kid is selling.

"Hands off." I point to his hand on the door and the kid knows I ain't buying or playing.

"Where's Smoot?" I ask.

"He getting something to eat."

Kid sees a basehead roll up in a truck, beats it over before the window rolls down. Yeah, make that money, that's my money. There's a fat kid leaning against the wall, what's he, a lookout? See my homies working it by Bolt Burgers. Wheel the Benz around and crank the system. There he is, Smoot's on the phone, can hardly see his black ass at night. He hangs up and runs to me.

"What up?" I say and he hands me a fresh forty-ounce.

"Money," he says.

"How the flow?"

"We doing it."

Smoot's grinning in the window, gold tooth glinting. I pull back the paper bag and start knocking out the beer. Be tasting good when you feel like you got it going on.

"Gonna have to get more product, Mother's Day, just about got us sold out."

"County checks."

Both laughing at that shit, bitches giving up the proceeds for the rock, on the first and the fifteenth.

"Somebody saw that bitch, what's her name, Rika, up at Bolt today."

"What!" Soon as I hear that ho's name I go off.

"Who saw her?"

"Pootbutt Ronnie."

"He said anything else?"

"Yeah, he said he saw Margot, F's G., talking to her."

Smoot's checking me out, seeing how I'm taking it. I ain't showing shit.

"All right. I'm gonna be back. I gotta go take care of some business."

I hit it, pull out in front of somebody, horns blow. I give a finger and keep going. Nobody want to fuck with me. I'm rolling seventy down Main but where I'm going? I hit a U and fly back. Where Margot lives? Yeah, now I remember, in that slob hood. Glad I ain't got on colors. Yeah, look at them niggahs on the corner, trying to flag me down, trying to clock to a hustler, fools. I roll by them laughing, wanting what I got, but they can't hang. I see her house. I park the Benz close as I can get it to her door, put on the alarm, would put the bar across the wheel but I ain't gonna be here long. How am I supposed to get to the door, big-ass gate and pit bulls, glad I got my nine, might have to shoot one of them bad-ass puppies. There she is, coming out the door, don't see me yet, what she doing? Turning on the water sprinklers. Don't look so good when she ain't made up, baggy sweats make her titties look small. That's all she got going, black ass tramp.

"Yo!"

She looks up and sees me. There she goes fronting like I make her sick. She turns the water off and walks to me, slow so she can waste my time.

"François ain't here."

"I ain't looking for François."

"What? You need your hair done?"

She's smiling at me, playing me off.

"You saw her."

"Saw who?"

"Don't play stupid."

She turned her back like she can't stand looking at me. I'm really starting to hate this bitch.

"Don't be coming over here calling me stupid."

"I ain't got time for this. Yesterday somebody saw you at school talking to that bitch, Rika."

She's looking at me . . . just staring like I'm a dog or something. I want to hop that fence and yoke her ass.

"You dressed to impress. Stopped sagging? Oh I guess everybody's a businessman now'days."

"Bitch! I told you."

I'm grabbing the fence about to hop over, I'm gonna get her
but both those fucking dogs come running snarling and shit. One
looks like he's going to get over the fence, I jump back and almost
fall on my ass.

"Ollie, really, you oughta chill before you get yourself hurt."

She wants to laugh at me, but she don't.

"I'm gonna kick your black ass!"

"Go talk to your ho's like that. It don't move me."

I'm shaking my head cause I know I'm gonna get her. Fuck
F. He shouldn't oughta be with a nasty-assed bitch like Margot,
disrespecting somebody.

"Stop acting like the ignorant niggah that you are. Be serious.
Why am I gonna tell anything to you? Come over here like you
think you gonna pimp-slap me because you driving your brother's
Benz. Some of your homies was there, why don't you go ask them
what went on."

I spit on the ground between us, let her know what I think
of her.

"Ollie, I know you been drinking eightball so I won't take this
personal. Next time . . ."

Still talking head, but I shine it on and get into the Benz. She's
still laughing at me. That's all right cause she won't be doing it for
long.

It's dark by the time I get back to the hood. Smoot's still across the
street watching the wannabes sling. I pull up and beep the horn and
turn down the system, rockin the fuckin hood. He gets in holding a
brew in each hand, looking so fucked up he might throw up or
something.

"Watch the leather."

He smiles like I'm joking.

"I'm watching it. I'm a clean niggah, not like your ass," he says and hands me a Cisco.

I laugh but I'm serious. Smoot know I don't be playing.

"One of Cowboy's homies came up. He wants to know if we need a key."

"Yeah, and what you say?"

Smoot takes a swig of eightball. "I told him I gotta talk to you."

"Yeah." I can't believe this shit. Sending somebody around already.

"What you think. He got a price we can work into our program."

I look at him to see if he got some game on, but Smoot smiling like he always do. Niggah ought to dress better, take off that Jheri juice–stained T-shirt and get into something else.

"So what you think?"

"Naw. They just gonna dog us out. Get us selling their shit, working like we their boys. Ain't nothing to say cept nod and get punked."

"Aw, Ollie, it ain't like that. Cowboy used to do business with Doug. Why you sweating him?"

"Fuck Cowboy. He nothing but a mark."

Smoot coughs like I must be smoking, got him choking.

"What? Cowboy got you going?" I say, but Smoot keeps jeffin and shit. "Fuck Cowboy, I got something for him." Smoot sees the nine and nods cause he knows I don't play.

Smoot turns the stereo to KGFJ that oldies shit. We just chill in the car, watching Bernard and Fred and the little pootbutts work the curb. Some ugly little niggah comes up and hits up on the wall, some T-Zone shit.

"Yo-Yo, come over here you little buster . . ." Smoot bust out the Benz almost knocking beer all over the car and catches the slow-running fool by the T-shirt. He jerks him back and fires up his ear, gets him down but the buster gets back up. Smoot grabs him again and throws him into a fence and stomps him a few times. Says something to him . . . boy comes out with a little bank and hands

it over. Fucked him up and stole his money, that's it. Smoot comes
back huffing and puffing.

"Yeah, I been after that little punk. Nikki's little brother,
claiming T-Zone. Told her I'm gonna kick his little ass."

Smoot takes the beer off the dash and starts drinking.

"You coulda spilled that shit chasing after that pootbutt."

"So," Smoot says laughing, "you drinking that Cisco, getting
fucked up too."

"It ain't about that. It's about this, this is mine."

"I know that."

"I'm serious, don't fuck up the car."

"Chill on that. Ain't nobody gonna fuck up your car."

"Nobody gonna get their ass kicked, if they don't watch out."

"Oh, it's gonna be like that. You doggin me. Nobody gonna
be fuckin me up. Somebody might get fucked up," Smoot says.

He looking straight ahead, at the boys working the corner,
clocking the cars rolling up. He don't want no part of me.

"I'm just fucking with you. It's about that Rika bitch. Get me
mad. Then I went over Margot's she got snotty and shit cause I'm
asking bout Rika like she down with her."

Smoot's nodding like he knows what's happening.

"It's cool."

Yeah, it's cool cause he don't want me to kick his ass.

"You got another beer. I wanna get a buzz."

"Yeah, I'll get you one. Got em in the back."

Smoot walk to his truck, finally got out that banged-up shit into
something new. He stops and then turns around like he's checking
out a ho. Oh, yeah, she's a ho. Dress ain't covering shit, tits falling
out. Smoot trying to talk to her, niggah don't know shit about
bitches. I beep the horn, lean out the window.

"Come over here!" I yell out to the bitch.

Ho sees me in the Benz, runs her ass over. Big tits too. Bitch
is gonna give me some head.

"What you need?" I ask her straight out, see what she say.
Bet the bitch say she want to get rocked up.

"I wanna ride in your Benz."

Ho is missing her front tooth. She sure enough is gonna get on the head. I ain't fucking nobody without a tooth. But this bitch damn sure got a body.

"Get in." She run around and get into the car. Slide in the seat, dress go way up her ass, bet she ain't go on no panties. She better not have crabs.

Smoot's back at the table at Bolt Burgers with a fresh Cisco. Probably pissed off cause I didn't tell him to come along and get his dick sucked. I get my dick sucked alone. I don't like no niggahs watching. I cruise around to the dead end of the street, where they got a lot of old people. Dark too, cause the streetlights always be shot out.

"Here?"

She trying to sound surprised. Ho probably do it in a trash can.

"Yeah, here. What's wrong with here?"

"Don't you wanna be in a motel? Snooty Fox is right down the street."

Can't believe this shit. Wants me to spring for a motel. Must think I'm rich.

"Look, I ain't got all day, what this gonna cost? I'll give you a five-O if you good."

She ain't gonna get a five-O. Shit, she better be glad I just don't kick her stupid ass.

"All right, that'll work."

I find the buttons that lower the seat and tilt the steering wheel up so she can get to the head. She gets my pants open in a hot second and pulls me out.

"Hey, don't let none get on my pants or the car seats. I don't want shit on nothing."

"Huh?"

"You heard what I said."

"What? You don't want me to get none . . ."

"That's what I said."

She gets down, slurping on it. Yeah, this is it. This is living large. Getting your dick sucked in a Benz.

"Take your time. Do it right. I ain't in no rush."

She says something, gurgling. Yeah, if a niggah got the money

and he down for his, he can get what he wants, what he needs . . .
People be acting like I can't get over, like I'm stupid and Doug was
down but it ain't like that. Doug was weak and soft over a ho just
like this one sucking on my bone.

"What's what, baby, you getting soft."

"I ain't getting soft. What you talking about?"

Shit, what's up with my dick? I thought she knew what she
was doing, but she can't suck shit.

"You supposed to know how to do that!"

I jerk up. She touching me, trying to play it off but I ain't going
for it.

"I can get you hard but this ain't no good place to be doing
it."

"Look, I told you I ain't paying for no motel. Just get on it
and do it right or I'm gonna go off on you." I yank her weave and
snap that head back to let her know who running this show. Push
her face back down on it. Make her choke on it. Knock her fucking
teeth out, see how she suck after that. That's it. I got it back. Yeah.
Couple more keys, make that dollar. What I'm gonna get, gonna
get myself another Benz, naw, get me a Jeep, yeah, that be bumping.
Gonna get some more suits, get a leather one tailored by that Chinese
fool be doing Doug's. Shit, now she doing it . . . yeah, I'm gonna
shoot all over her face. Bitch got it going. Must think I'm gonna do
something for her, treat her like she some kind of queen . . . shit
. . . soon as I come, yeah, I'm gonna throw her ass out the car.

"You hard now, bet I got you about to bust."

"Yeah, yeah, keep it up."

Shove her head back down on it . . . I'm gonna get me that
ring, big-ass diamond and that cable at the gold mart, sport that shit
around with the boys, niggahs think I'm rolling for real. Yeah, can't
wait to catch up to Rika's ass. I'm gonna fuck that bitch in the ass,
cut her fucking head off. Naw, I'm gonna make her suck dick then
cut her head off. Aw shit . . . can't stop.

"Quit! You pulling my hair."

Shit, I was almost there. Slap this bitch. Twack!

"Get back on it before I get pissed."

"All right, you don't got to go off on me."

Ho's scared. She gonna work it now . . . Gonna get me one of them CD Walkmans, shit I can get that now. Get me one of them Levi jackets with me painted on the back like I'm muthafucking star. Get T-shirts with the same shit on it, with Gang$tar O.G. Owl-E topping it. From the street to the bank—mo money—then I'm gonna get me a bitch like Rika but I'm gonna have her acting right. She'll know who's running the show. Step out of line, twack! "What the fuck! Who's opening the door!?"

Bam! Somebody got me good, blood is running in my eyes and the bitch is screaming, "Don't shoot!" Somebody got me by the neck, dragging me out and down into the street. Two of them, both got gats. One bends down and swings again with the butt. Konk!—head goes konk—stars! I see them like in a cartoon, circling in front of me. One of these punks rolls me over, goes through my pockets; the other one is laughing about how only fools get caught with their dicks out. I squirm and get free and start running the three blocks to Main.

Get Smoot and come back and jack these niggahs. Street's dead. Nobody. Nobody's working the corner. I cross the street and go to Bolt Burgers. No Smoot, no boys . . . nothing. Beat. I got punked. No Benz, no nine. Got set up. Smoot's gonna pay. Got a whole lot of payback coming.

Walking. Fuck walking. All the lights on. Bet Mama's up. Shit, Sally's here. No keys, no keys to the apartment, to the house, to the car I ain't got. Gotta knock. I know what they gonna say. Porch lights comes on. Sally's big ass opens it.

"Didn't hear you drive up."

Wanna walk by but her big ass fill up the whole doorway.

"Step aside," I say trying to push her back. She shove me out the door.

"Lord in heaven who been beating on you?" she say like I ain't got a head or something.

"Ain't nothing wrong with me."

"You not coming in the house looking like that. Mama ain't gonna have a heart attack cause you too stupid not to go get your butt beat. The day before they gonna bury your brother."

I oughta punch her ass.

"Boy, you bleeding."

"Nothing wrong with me."

"You got to go the hospital."

"I ain't going nowhere but get my gun and shoot some fools."

"No you ain't."

"Open the door so I can come in."

"No. I'm gonna go get my keys to take you to the hospital."

She ain't gonna get out of my way so I bum rush the door. But she push me to the wall and all of a sudden I'm falling, slipping down on the porch. I'm bleeding, she's right. Fuck. She goes back into the house to get the keys. I feel like I'm gonna pass out. Shit, did one of those busters knife me? Porch feels good, like a big-ass bed. Fuck I ain't gonna stay down here, gonna get up and go take care of business. Yeah, I can go around the back and get in through one of the windows, get the gat and go take care of Smoot's ass. I put one foot down one step, now the other foot. Shit, I'm losing it. Going down. Somebody's grabbing me, Sally. Pulling me up like a fucking fish. Lift me up and put me over a shoulder and carry me to the car, Mama's raggedy Rambler, and toss me in the backseat. She start the wagon and pull off. The first turn I throw up clear shit, must be the beer.

"Where you taking me?"

"King."

"King! Fuck, I don't want to go there."

She's laughing at me. "Where else you gonna go?"

"I don't need no doctor. Take me home." She don't say nuthin. Turn up gospel shit, just like Mama, think they can make a fool good listening to that shit. Try to get up, lift my head, and I'm throwing up again.

"Throw up out the window."

I'm tired of taking shit from her but I'm spinning like I'm on one of them big fuckin roller coasters at Magic Mountain. Yeah, those marks got me good.

"You know I don't shed tears for you and Doug but Mama don't understand. She don't know what y'all about. Just trying to get to the grave soon as possible."

I wanna tell her to shut the fuck up but I just listen to the fools on the radio howling about Jesus. It must be Sunday.

I must have passed out cause Sally's looking at me through the side window, big-ass ugly face staring at me, now she opening the door, nurses with her, but it's Sally lifting me out the car and putting me in the wheelchair. Nurse wrapping my head up, too tight, wanna yoke her ass but Sally got my arms. I wanna get up and get the fuck out of there, nobody want to go to this fuckin hospital. It's where you go if you too fucked up or too poor to go somewhere else. Nurse wheels me into the nasty-ass waiting room. Mostly meskins with their crumbsnatchers, couple cholos and one gangster bent over holding his stomach. The real fucked-up ones are in the hallway, behind the nurse booth, the niggahs that got shot and shit. Where they had me when I got capped on. Don't feel so fucked up now. Probably can get up and bone out but Sally watching me. Fuck, my head hurts . . . What they gonna give me? Probably tell me to hit the pipe and smoke my hurt away. Waste of fuckin time. Head hurting more, spinning too. When is somebody gonna come and check me out?

"Hey, Sally, what the fuck I'm doing here, these fools ain't gonna look at me." She just shake her big head and go back to reading the Bible. What she be seeing in the same book she been reading all her life? Yeah, I know, save her soul and all that hoopla. "Get me a fuckin nurse, my head is hurtin big time."

She look at me like Margot do, like I'm some kind of roach. Then she stand up like it the hardest thing she ever done and take her beach ball ass to the nurse's station. Nurse's shrugging and shit, pointing to all the people in the waiting room. Shit, if I was feeling right I'd go up there and tell her what's up. She can't be talking that yang to me. "Hey, my head is hurtin. Get me something. Y'all got fuckin aspirins!" Bitch ignore me and keeps talking to Sally. Yeah, I'm gonna go over there and get me some respect.

6
Ann

■

Oh no. Bone tired and now here's the last, positively the last thing
I need to see, some little hoodlum wheeled in here with his head
bandaged up, shouting like he's going to kill us all. My Lord, that
woman he's with is huge. Maria better control her temper and not
get that woman upset. Security would have to handle that. I'd better
talk to the boy before this gets totally out of hand. He's trying to
stand but he can't, falls back into the wheelchair and shouts, "Tell
that bitch to give me something." The woman he's with clamps her
hand over his mouth and tells him to shut up. I've got to quit and
soon. Anybody can call you any old thing and you must be civil.
He doesn't see me come up. I cough so as not to surprise him. From
the look of it, a thoroughly beaten young man with a Jheri curl and
an almost expensive suit, another one of our young men having the
typical troubles.

"Young man, is there a problem?"

"Don't I look like I got a problem. Got a goddamn bandage
wrapped around my dome. Bleeding and shit, and not a goddamn
one of you comes over to see how I'm doing."

He shuts up a minute, his head must be hurting again. Probably
has a concussion . . . No, this is the child that used to come by and
play ball with François.

"I think you know my son, François."

"Yeah," he says, looking at me like he has no idea of what
I've said. No, he leans over and vomits, spraying my shoes even as
I skip backward.

"Hold on, I'll see if I can get someone to take a look at you."

Walk away fast. I've got to get a grip . . . bad enough . . . bad enough to see this every day . . . and it just gets closer. There he is, Jeffries, looks worse than I do. Head on the water cooler, coffee cup in his hand.

"We've got another one, a teenager with a probable concussion, vomiting, disoriented . . . you want to take a look at him or should I have him X-rayed?"

"I didn't hear you, what's the question?"

I explain again and he looks at me. Glassy eyed, fatigued, and before he can ask me to repeat it one more time, I do. Why did I bother to ask, just send him to the lab for the X ray. So tired, don't want to think, I want to go home and have a tumbler of Tanqueray and collapse. This isn't no way to live . . . seeing more and more Françoises in the emergency room in various states of dying, some slowly like this new customer, others dead on delivery. Again in the noise of the waiting room and the ugly brightness, everyone looks ghastly, the perfectly healthy Latin girls holding their ill babies, concerned men sitting close to sickly women . . . it doesn't matter, everyone who comes here looks like they could drop dead at any moment. Well, that huge woman with Maria looks like she'll be here, outliving us all. They're talking civilly. Oh, a good sign, the big woman has a Bible in her hand. Maria comes to me. The boy is holding his head between his legs, looking worse than before. Maria looks happy to leave the big woman and comes to me.

"Ann, she says she doesn't know exactly what happened to him and he isn't saying."

"Go with blunt-force trauma and get him to X-ray and have a three-sixty done."

Maria shakes her head. "It's crowded up there."

She's right, I should just shut up and let her get it done when she can. At another hospital it would be a priority, here it's just another case, but I can't let it go at that.

"I know him . . . He's a friend of my son."

Maria, now long-faced, nods, knows the story, hears it when I have the energy to tell it, probably hates having to hear it; my constant worry about him. Now this kid, about as likable as a vicious dog, is François too. She smiles, pats me on the shoulder. She'll take care of it for me. Squats next to him, taps his shoulder and he turns with a balled fist, ready to strike someone. She recovers and talks to him, smoothly. Her words sound almost pretty like when she speaks to young mothers in Spanish, calming them. He jerks away, not going for it, but Maria isn't unnerved, slips around and steers his wheelchair to the elevators.

Finally got out of there. Driving home with the sun coming up makes everything easier. Seems as though nothing truly horrible happens at six in the morning. Never did see that boy come back down. He's probably back out on the street searching for the guys who jumped him. Wonder if François is awake, getting ready for school? I pull into the driveway, house looks so calm. All the houses on the street look calm. Cut across the dewy, overgrown lawn, maybe it'll improve on the coat of vomit that kid sprayed my shoes with. The door opens before I get my key in. Mary's already turning away, she says, "Hi, Mama," trailing off. Already dressed for school, uniform ironed, hair braided perfectly into two big schoolgirl braids.

"You had breakfast?" I ask, knowing she hasn't.

"No, Mama, I've got to get to school early."

"You always have to get to school early."

She grabs her book bag and comes to me smiling. She looks just like I did when I was twelve, even down to the Catholic school uniform, the everlasting blue-and-white plaid.

"I can get breakfast on the way."

"Oh, yes, you could if I gave you the money."

She holds her hand out. Really, the only thing that's her father is her smile. If she wouldn't smile I'd be glad to give her the money.

"Do you always have to smile like you're pulling a fast one on me."

"Me?" she says and I give her the money.

"I'll pick you up at three."

"Okay, I might be a little late."

She's out the door. The morning walk to the bus is fine but the afternoon is a different story, thugs and cute young boys. My God, she vacuumed the floor and coffee's on. I've got a daughter. Never worry about her, good grades, judgment, actually she's stuck up. Thinks she's better than what's out there. And I've got a son, cutting the lawn is too much to ask of him. Almost everything that I think about. I never thought I would be like this. So hopeless, like I don't have a life. My life is his. Stuck in some groove I can't get out of. Bedroom door is open, cracked. Sleeping like a dead man, on his back, arms close to his sides, barely breathing. Is he breathing? Almost in a panic, I walk into the bedroom. His smooth dark face contorts. He twists around onto his stomach.

"Baby, you've got to get ready for school."

"Girl, get out the room."

Thinks it's Mary. She probably tried to get a few extra dollars out of his pocket. On the floor, near his pants, is a roll of twenties and the beeper he tries to hide from me. And I feel it coming, hopelessness, rolling in like storm clouds. I won't ask anything because he won't say. I just want him to get up. A boy . . . when he was a boy, it was so simple. At the edge of the bed, I touch his shoulder. Shake it, wondering what will he do, ball his fist like that Ollie . . . will he see me?

"What! I told you!"

"It's me, Mama."

He stirs now, squirming because I'm here.

"You've got to get up."

"I am," he says, his voice halfway between anger and a whine.

"Missing all of that school. You were going to graduate but now . . ."

"Mama, I'm awake."

He is. Twisting into an awkward upright position, pulling the sheets to his chest, modest suddenly, then waves me out. I'm glad to leave. Maybe it's me, seeing Earl in him. Knowing how he handled things, how much of a man he was. I don't want to see that in François. Fix myself a cup of coffee, sweeten it with a taste of gin, make it biting and hot. Is that boy out of the bedroom yet? No . . . going to have to go back in there. There he is, bare chested, sweats for pajamas, same sweats he wears to jog. Looks so much like Earl.

"Want breakfast?"

He ignores me and goes into the bathroom. Not so much as a nod. Will it get worse? Had to be like this, didn't it, the boy getting tenser and tenser. Ready to jump at something, whatever it is, whatever gets him going. Like his daddy, fragile goods . . . something sends him off, no telling how far they're going to go. Out the bathroom, standing in the hall, towel slung across his shoulders, short hairbrush in his hand, runs it along the side of his head and calls to me.

"Mama, Douglas' sister called, wants to know if I want to be a pallbearer."

"Yeah," I said, nodding my support. It's obvious he doesn't want to do it. "So, are you?"

He brushes his flat top, stares at me, brushes the back of his head.

"I don't know."

"Why?"

"I don't know if I want to . . . I don't even know if I want to go to the funeral."

"You've got to go to the funeral. You two were close. It'll mean a lot to his family."

"I'm sick of funerals. Ministers saying the same thing, people going to be seen."

I knew he'd get this way, every time something bad happens . . . he gets so sullen. As though he can't stand to deal with anybody.

"I'll go."

"Go where?" he says frowning.

"To the funeral."

"What's that gonna do? You didn't even like him."

"Is Margot going?"

"Naw, she ain't got time."

"You should go with somebody. It'll make it easier."

"How is going with you going to make it easier? Whole thing is stupid. Makes me think about how things are. How people be tripping thinking they got all the time in the world to get things done. But it ain't like that."

I shrug, hearing it, the viciousness in his voice. I know he doesn't want to talk to me, cut everything short and get me out of his way. I say what I don't want to say.

"Ollie was in the Emergency, got himself beat up pretty badly."

"What? Yeah." Francois looks sort of amused, shakes his head.

"When is it?" I ask.

"When is what?"

"The funeral."

"Today, at four."

"I'll drive. You really don't want to take your bug with that bad muffler. Wouldn't be appropriate in a cemetery. Everyone would be staring at you."

"You think Ollie's gonna make it or is he too messed up?"

I shrug. "If he doesn't have a bad concussion I think they'll discharge him."

He shrugs, and goes into the bathroom. I hear the shower running. He'll be on time to school. What if I worked the morning shift and left before six? He'd probably never get out of bed. I wait by the bathroom door sipping coffee, listening to the shower and his stupid music. Shouldn't have bought that water radio. The door opens, at first he's startled to see me, waiting . . . must have thought he was rid of me. Turns and starts walking to his room.

"Don't take your car. I can drop you off at school. Pick you up at three-thirty, we'll have plenty of time to get to the cemetery."

He looks at me, water beading down his face, doesn't he dry himself? What's he going to say? He sighs and leans against the wall. Looks like Earl did when I told him I was pregnant with François. Like, Damn! No way out of this, guess I got to go along.

"Okay, Mama. I'll meet you in front of the school."

I'm grinning. Shouldn't grin. Don't want him to realize why I really want him there. See it again, even if he's seen it before. What I see every day at King. Maybe it'll sink in.

"Are you going to bring a suit to change into?"

He shakes his head.

"What are you going to wear?"

"I'll wear something."

"Oh. That's good."

I sit on the couch to wait for François to get himself off and open the newspaper to the Metro digest, check on yesterday's murders, drive-by shootings. See if it's someone who's come through the emergency room. Douglas didn't make the *Times*, just the *Sentinel*. François's ready or as ready as he ever is for school, comes into the living room, looking very unhappy, one thin Pee-Chee folder in his hand. The black, hooded sweatsuit he's wearing doesn't help.

"That's what you're going to wear?"

"Yeah," he says and heads for the front door. I watch for a minute until I realize he'll be late unless I drive him. I catch up to him as he's going down the steps.

"I said I'd give you a ride, school starts in ten minutes."

He shrugs. I feel so tired, like I've been climbing uphill for too long. It's a short drive to the school, I take Main and at a stoplight, I can't help but stare at the broad green outline of a hand with the middle fingers folded. "Main Street," François says without looking at me.

"What? You know them?"

"Just a bunch of fools."

I pull up to the front of the school. No one's going to class and the bell should ring any moment. If I had the money then I certainly would have sent him to Catholic school. Oh yeah, he would have really gone for that, priests telling him how to live, that would have really worked out. He sees her the same time I do. Blue miniskirt, boots and black tights . . . miss shaditty. Girl's always polite but sometimes she just rubs me the wrong way. He walks up to her, and right from the start they're in it, not a kiss but seriousness. She's talking to him like I would never talk to him, in his face, talking hard, lips just about sneering. She sees me. Damn! I don't want to talk to the child but it's too late. Her face, still hard, changes, looks younger the closer she gets.

"Hi, Mrs. Williams. You going to the funeral?"

"Yes, I'm going to drive François."

She looks relieved to know I'm going.

"I thought I should go, but I hate funerals. And I didn't get along with Doug anyway."

Too tired to look away or come up with a fake smile. I nod and tell the truth.

"Yeah, I understand. It gets hard."

Looking into her eyes, she knows how I feel, how I worry about him, the weight of it.

"I talk to him. I talk to him all the time. He listens sometimes. But most of the time I get too mad."

I take her hand. Her hand tenses, as though she wants to pull away.

"You're going away soon?"

"Yeah, I'm starting at UC Santa Cruz the fall quarter, get a head start, find a job."

Crying. I'm crying and I can't stop. She's watching me, afraid, afraid of me crying. The child pulls away, looks for François.

"Margot! You keep that up. Doing good for yourself."

She nods, pushes past a few kids and walks by François and goes into the school.

Went home and slept. I mean slept. So hard I woke with a headache and less than an hour to get ready. I'm so grateful to be able to sleep like a log. House gets so hot and musty having to sleep with the windows closed and curtains drawn, got to be so damn careful and those Latinos next door playing that salsa like it's the middle of the day, instead of the late morning. They just don't get it. Iron my uniform, hot comb a few curls in my mess of a head of hair and run for the door. Make good time to Saint Elizabeth, but Mary's not out there waiting like she's supposed to. I double park and get out to look for her. No, just plenty of brown and black faces and blue-and-white plaid. It's already three-fifteen. François's liable to get antsy and just give up on the whole thing and disappear. Thank God! There she is walking with her little Latina girlfriend. She's gonna get her behind spanked, wearing her dress hiked up like it's a miniskirt.

"Mar!" Here I am waving for her and she's still talking, Miss

Important. See about that. Must get to her before she comes when she wants to come. Big eyed, her friend sees me running up. Mary turns too late, jerk her good.

"Come here! Late already and then make me wait on you while you finish talking!"

Open the door and push the brat in. I get in and drive away without looking at her. I don't need to see what she's doing, slumped against the car door, head hanging down. Next comes the whines.

"What did I do so wrong? Just talking to Lilly and you come pulling me like I'm baby. Everybody's gonna be talking about it, embarrassing me in front of everybody."

I don't say anything because I don't want to fight. Plus the traffic to Bolt is bad enough to deserve all my attention.

"Where are we going?" she says bitterly.

"Pick up François."

"Why we got to pick him up? He's got a car."

"Girl, you can speak better than that, why we *got* to pick him up? I'm driving him to Douglas' funeral. We're all going."

"I'm going? Why do I have to go? I have homework to do."

"You're going because I say you're going."

"You're so mean to me. You don't treat me anything like you do François, because he's a boy and he's always getting into trouble."

"I treat you the way you deserve to be treated."

"I don't deserve this, you oughta be talking to François cause you know what he be doing."

I don't say anything. I want to correct her about that *be doing* business. But I can't because in a way she's right. What am I doing jumping all over her and I can't bring myself to say anything to François. How does it go? Raise the daughter but spoil the son. Guess I'm doing that. Mary starts flipping the radio. Know she's trying to find that one song I'll just hate, because she knows I won't tell her to turn it. She's won this one, got me thinking. Closer we get to Bolt the more squirmy she gets, twisting around to watch the boys walk home. We get to the school. She sees him first, kneeling, hands folded, hood over his head, next to a campus policeman. He walks slowly to the car. He comes around and lets himself in.

"Sorry we're late."

"It's cool," he mumbles.

Mary seems scared of him, not even a glance to the backseat. I can't bring myself to say anything either. Maybe he shouldn't go to the funeral. Maybe he needs to get away.

"Honey, you sure you want to go to this?"

"Yeah," he says, and that's it.

I turn onto Century hoping that Mary will keep quiet, not for some silly reason decide that now is the time to tease her brother. I've never seen him like this. Face so lifeless it looks like a mask. So somber he's scaring me into silence. What he reminds me of is those Latino gang members who show up in the ER. Ask a question with no trace of emotion, "How's Jamie?" then they sit back and wait for hours, wearing an expression that isn't a scowl, more like cold blankness as though at any moment they could kill you, could be thinking of killing you and you can't tell what they're thinking. Emotions frozen somewhere behind their eyes. I'd rather talk to the meanest, stupidest black gangster than one of those blank-faced cholos. I pull into the cemetery and I'm immediately directed by a policeman to a parking spot, I see a few more policemen, all black. Must be so expensive hiring all those policemen. We get out and in the distance I see a fairly large crowd beneath a green awning, most sitting but quite a few are standing, surrounding the proceedings. In the front row I see the big sister I met at the hospital, sitting on the end, probably for comfort's sake, looking very regal in a black embroidered dress that she had to have sewed herself. The minister, a dapper but small man, is squatting alongside the grieving mother, holding on to her hand, whispering to her. Everything looks so expensive; the coffin, gold and huge and covered with white roses, and the wreath, so large and shapeless it seems to be a clump of various white flowers. I guess the family can afford it. That boy, Douglas, had to have money set aside for it. Taking Mary's hand I lead us away from François, truth is he's embarrassing me, dressed like he's ready for a track meet, not a funeral. Well, at least he's not like these other kids, so many of them in blue T-shirts with RIP on their backs. I see two open seats on the end almost to the front, we head for them but this old bald man pats the folding chairs, smiles, taken. The funeral's getting ready to start, I lead us back to François, Mary's sighing behind me, irritated about everything. He's still there, but now he's not at the end of the crowd, he's surrounded by funeral goers. So I get to watch him, arms folded, hood still over his head, dressed so stupidly for the service. God, I hope no one here knows he's my son. Mary hardly knows anything about Baptist churches. Not like the Catholic church we go to. Maybe I should take her to an AME church, let her hear real singing. The minister silences the crowd, stands in front of the casket, Bible in one hand, and prays silently. Then he turns to us and begins to speak, his voice booming from such a small body. At first I can't understand him, he's talking so quickly, then it becomes clear.

These days are filled with heartbreak. Only Jesus knows when a bullet will find its mark. So many of us have been touched by this evil; the cruelty man inflicts on his fellow man. But we've got to be strong and we can't be strong without Jesus in our lives. Douglas is going to his reward, his time on this world is through, he is with the Lord now. He doesn't grieve, he isn't troubled. He is finished with the shedding of tears. But look at your own life, are you walking a narrow road?

This is what I want him to hear, a man, a minister, tell him what he should know. Look at him, walks out of the crowd. Turns his back to the sermon and kneels the other way. Mary's pulling on my sleeve.
"What's he doing?"
"I don't know. Be quiet."
He's looking down the hill to where the policeman is directing traffic. A car is at the entrance. He seems to be staring at it. It's hopeless, I can't watch him act disrespectful at a funeral. Why did he come if he's going to turn his back on it?

Greed! Simple, blind greed brings our children to this, this drugged world! Our children sell it, young girls walk the streets to have it. Our young boys kill to have it! It's time for a change.

We've got to turn to Christ for the answer, for the strength to turn away from temptation!

Temptation rolls through the crowd, the older folks hold on to the word and echo it to the minister. I didn't think the minister would speak on drugs with Douglas having been so involved in it. I lean forward to see the mother's reaction, but I can barely see the pillbox hat she has on. She's leaning onto the shoulder of her big, sturdy daughter. Where's the boy? Was he that battered to miss the funeral? Alongside the mother and the daughter are a few older men, probably uncles and cousins, but the boy, I don't see him. The minister is reading from the scriptures, wrapping it up. Maybe we should leave now, beat the crowd out of the gate, I do have to get to work. I turn to look for François, he's talking to someone, one of the many young men in blue sweatshirts. This one has on a beanie and sunglasses. No mistaking his gang membership, his pants are pulled so low, I can see his blue underwear. I leave Mary behind me and go to them, walking stiffly as though my knees, my legs are frozen. They're still talking, François with that ridiculous hood over his head, nodding his responses, his friend's mouth is moving constantly as though he has too much to say in too little time. He stops only to spit. Then I see his face clearly, it's that child, what's his name, Ollie. He sees me first, stops and lifts his sunglasses and squints.

"How you doing, Miss Williams?"

I don't say anything, staring instead at his eye. His right eye is bloodshot, horribly red. He drops his glasses, covering the bloodshot thing, and spits.

"You ready, Mama?" François asks.

"Yes," I say and turn to look for Mary. She's lingering behind me, reluctant to walk up. I want to say something to this boy about his eye. I'm sure that eye should be bandaged. That beanie is probably hiding serious contusions, the swelling must be bad. Whoever got him, got him good.

"How are you doing? Did you get an X ray?"

"Yeah," he says, hands in his pockets, suddenly not so intimidating.

"Shouldn't your eye be bandaged?"

Nothing, he doesn't respond. He looks at François.

"Gotta get on. See y'all later."

He walks away quickly, but near to the funeral awning, I see it, the slight swaying, the hitch in his step. That boy should still be in the hospital or at least in bed. Mary is suddenly at my side, smiling.

"Who's the gangbanger?"

François doesn't answer, I frown but she's not paying attention to me. We make it to the car and beat most of the mourners out of the gates of the cemetery. I feel a little awkward about not having made an effort to give my condolences to the family and especially the mother. But it's probably for the best. I would have been just another face saying the same line. I feel for the woman, having a boy like Ollie. She'll probably be coming back soon enough to lay him down. Cold. Down to my toes running to my fingers. I look at him from the corner of my eye, head against the window, eyes covered by the hood.

"Are you okay?"

"Yeah," he says lifelessly.

"Mama! Let's stop and get a pizza," Mary asks.

At first I ignore her; then again, maybe's it's a good idea.

"Pizza?"

He shrugs. "I don't care."

I turn into the mini mall parking lot and find a spot in front of the restaurant and hand Mary a twenty.

"No pineapple."

"Aw, Mama," she says as she leaves. I watch her almost run to the door of the restaurant, with her usual excited expression. Nothing intrudes on her mood, if she's happy, she's happy. I guess he's the same way, if he's sad, it's going to last. Look at him, his large hands resting on his knees, the shiny black material of his sweatsuit, hood over his head. He really is in mourning.

"How do you feel?"

"I don't feel nothing."

I don't want to lose control of my words. Load up too much and jolt him into silence.

"It's okay to be upset. He was your friend."

He sighs, hands clutching his knees. Finally he turns his head and looks at me.

"I don't know about being friends. We weren't tight for a long time."

"Oh, then why are you taking it so hard?"

"I'm taking it hard? You think I'm taking it hard?"

I look into his face for some clue to what he's getting at. His eyes are shining as though he's going to cry.

"I don't know. You're upset. There's nothing wrong with that."

Now I've done it. Sounded evasive. He's my son. I should be able to talk to him without my voice cracking, or coming off like I'm trying to tiptoe around everything.

"I don't know what I am. I don't know what I feel. I knew him, that's it."

It's so obvious he's lying. Playing down four or five years of his life. How could he say that to me and expect me to believe it. I really wish Mary would hurry up with the pizza. Wanted to take a nap before work.

"I knew she'd show up."

"Mary?" I say, straining to see for her.

"No," he says, shaking his head, looking down at his lap, almost if he were laughing.

"Who?"

"It don't matter."

"Are you talking about Margot?"

"Margot wouldn't go the funeral if I paid her."

"Who then?"

"Rika."

"Rika? So? That was his girlfriend."

He doesn't say anything, just looking at me, watching my reaction.

"I didn't see her."

"She drove up and looked from her car."

Mary knocks on the window, François turns around and unlocks the back door. She slips inside with this huge pizza. It's hot but she won't put it on the seat next to her like she's worried that it'll get away from her. I back the car up and pull into the street trying to think of some way of keeping the conversation going.

"Are you sure it was her?"

"Yeah," he says flatly.

What now? What did he do, is he in the middle of this? At the funeral he had been looking for her.

"Did you tell Ollie? Wouldn't she want to sit with the family."

He shakes his head.

"No, why should I tell him. If he looked he would have saw her."

"Oh," I say. I look in the rearview window and see Mary's intent face. She must know how I feel. But what about him, how does he feel?

The house is up ahead. Someone is sitting on the steps. François bursts out of the car soon as I pull into the driveway. It's Margot and she's smiling. She meets him halfway and slips her arms around him. He looks surprised but for the first time he seems how he used to be. I try to linger in the car, give them another moment, but Mary rushes out of the car clutching the pizza.

"Want some?" she says to Margot. Margot looks at her and then at her hair.

"I better do your head, told you about always using that hot comb."

François unlocks the door and they go in except for Margot. She waits for me with that serious look on her face.

"Hi, Miss Williams. How did the funeral go?"

I smile, shrugging, not knowing how to answer, but so glad to see her.

7
Rika

■

Look at this. Wondered how many people would show up considering the kind of fool you were but you've got a crowd to bury you. I can't join them, you know. See how beautiful that casket is and the flowers. Picked them out didn't I. Because you knew what happened was going to happen and you didn't want some low rent funeral. You wanted to look good going down. I have taste. I took care of it. You just didn't think that I'd be the one. It's fine down here at the foot of Forest Lawn. I don't need to join the crowd. I know what everything looks like; the yellow and white roses and tulips, the gold and pearl casket. Not your colors as much as mine. You were always too much into purple. Couldn't leave the gaudy behind. I know your mother's crying, Ollie's cursing me out. I know your associate's looking my way, checking the car out, trying to see if it's really me. Wonder what he thinks. I'm not a fool. I can come back anytime—you're not going anywhere.

It's night now. Sitting in the car above the lights. Bet you wonder how I make it. How you used to talk to me, "Can't do a damn thing for yourself cept spend money." But it's not like that. I know what I'm doing. Look at the roaches walking by. The jungle is buzzing tonight. Roaches after crumbs. I'm tired of watching, see what you've done to me. They look just like me. Noses open, sprung. Looking for a blast. Drive further up the hill, not like I'm living down in the jungle or anything. I might not be staying on the Westside but Baldwin Hills isn't the projects.

Oh yes, my uncle has a beeper for a reason. He's an architect, blueprints cover the kitchen table. See, they have a marble foyer with a coat rack. Now, if I can sneak to the bedroom everything will be right with the world. The TV's on in the living room. Sounds like *Wheel of Fortune.*

"She's back."

It's my uncle's voice.

"Rika, could you come here?"

Oh no.

"What?"

Gotta get to the third door on the left. Lock myself in, wait them out. Here they come. Uncle Jack, gray-haired but quick, pushes me aside and blocks the way. Must have been playing tennis at Dorsey, still in his sweat-stained whites. Mother looks shocked as usual. My fat auntie leads us into the living room, nice view of the Hollywood hills but the setting sun is still too bright. I need my shades.

"You left again," Uncle Jack says.

"You can't leave," my mother says. Her eyes, red and desperate.

"Where did you go?" my aunt asks.

I don't say anything. I smile.

"Jesus! She's high again."

Mother stands and runs to the other side of the room and starts crying. I start for the bedroom but my uncle is forcing me down into a bean bag. I make a big sloosh as I land. He's so mad he's sputtering.

"Do you know what you're doing to your mother, us? We are trying to help you. And you go out in your robe and slippers wearing a rag on your head like you're some kind of cheap hooker on Normandie."

I don't look at him. Instead I look at my slippers. What's wrong with my slippers? They're clean.

"We took you and your mother in because she needs help. We're going to give her that help. If we can't help you here we're going to have to commit you. But you're going to get help."

He keeps saying give, get and going. Maybe I should get going.

"Don't you have something to say?"

I shake my head.

"Where did you go, to the jungle to buy crack?"

"I did not!" I say but a scream comes out. Everybody jumps. I try to struggle out of the bean bag but I tumble over. My mother rushes over grabbing me, holding on like I'm going to run.

"Baby, baby, were you with that boy? You weren't with him, were you?"

With him? Wow, I thought she knew.

"I saw him but I wasn't with him."

They're looking at me, all in my face.

"I thought you promised me you wouldn't see him after all he's done to you," Mother says, tears rolling down her face. She cries even better than before.

"I wasn't with him. I saw him . . . from a distance."

"I bet he's the one who gave it to her," Jack says, positively irate.

Auntie throws her hands up and goes for the phone. "I'm calling. There's no way we can handle this. This girl needs professional help."

Mama pulls me out of the bean bag, with one hand, just yanks me up.

"See, she's making the phone call. We can't handle this. We can't watch you twenty-four hours a day."

Funny, they keep saying the same things.

"Why are you laughing?"

"Me?"

Jack grabs me by the arm and drags me to the room I was trying to get to in the first place. He pushes me in, Mother watching.

"You're not going anywhere."

Mother comes in and gives me a hug. She's wearing Chanel. "We love you. You've got to try . . ."

I wait for her to complete the sentence. Fill in the blank. To get a hold of myself. To control myself. Not hurt myself.

"Jesus. She's laughing again. She's not listening to anything."

"I'm listening!"

Another scream. Mother almost jumps off the bed. Uncle Jack shakes his head and leaves.

"You really are sick," Mother says whispering like she doesn't want me to hear.

"I'm okay."

"You need so much help."

"You should get a cut like mine. It's very summery."

Mother draws back. Pulls my hand from her hair. She should get it dyed too, I don't care for all of that gray. Now, she's holding on to me crying again. Softly, so Uncle Jack can't hear. He's so full of himself.

"Rika. You got to promise me not to see that Doug again."

"Mother, I thought you knew? Doug's no longer with us."

"What?" she says, her blue eyes streaked with red.

"He's gone to his reward."

"He's dead?"

"Yes, Mother. They buried him today."

"And you went to the funeral in a bathrobe?"

"I didn't get out of the car. It was okay."

"Are you sure . . . ?"

Mother's so happy. She doesn't want to believe me.

"Yes, I'm very sure."

"Why didn't you tell us? It explains so much."

"I thought I did."

"Oh, baby. I really didn't know."

Again, she wraps her arms around me and cries, tears drip onto my cheeks. It's embarrassing.

"Mother, you should go and get some rest. I'll be fine."

She looks at me, what's the word? Forlorn, forlornly. I've made her so sad.

"I am tired."

She kisses me and heads for the door.

"If you need me . . ."

I nod. She tries so hard. I hear Uncle Jack at the door locking me in. I hope nobody's smoking in bed! What's on the tube? I turn it on and turn down the sound. Who needs the words and lie back. What time is it? Eight-thirty. Much too early to go to bed. But I am tired too.

*   *   *

What I don't understand is how I feel. Suddenly everything changes.
I don't feel good at all. Comes in waves, my good humor washing
away like sand castles. Isn't that it. That nothing lasts, nothing
keeps, specially a buzz. I'm not like you, though. You're the kind
of man that would make his woman sit in a car; yes, it was a Benz
but so what, and for how long? Once, I sat in that leather-lined
pimpmobile for four hot hours, getting out only once to use the
bathroom. Knocked on the door of that run-down house and there
you were, with your associates, four or five very dumb-looking
future felons watching a basketball game in a smoky living room.
Then it was only the smoke of the best Ses but soon we would all
be smoking the roach powder. You actually looked pissed as though
I had no reason at all for interrupting the festivities, even if I did
have to go in the worst way. You looked at me like I was the
stupidest, the ugliest bitch in the world but you failed to notice the
way your associates were ogling me. You saw me like everyone
first saw me, a fine, high yella bitch, who looked like a model with
good hair and green eyes. Wasn't I a trophy? I had to be stuck up,
I had the look of someone who had to be stuck up. And you had to
have it. You had to train me because I needed to be turned into a
obedient bitch, and because I have certain problems I went along
with the program. But you didn't know then, that because you made
me sit and fetch and wait on hot leather seats for master to bring me
a bone, that I wouldn't forget, that the bitch would bite that bone.

Let me turn out the light, turn off that TV, this room looks like
an ugly motel, cottage cheese ceiling, hot green, oversized couch—
where did they get this stuff? Better in the dark, cooler.

It didn't start that way. You came into the Speak Easy like you
were going to yank some girl off the dance floor and take her to the
car and do a Ted Bundy on her. I'm sure you thought you were the
most dangerous player there, bigger, younger, better looking. But
baby, baby, nobody was fooled. The girls there knew, knew you
had the wrong zip code, even if you have a fat wallet. Too, too wet
for a girl who wanted a legitimate money man, that's why you didn't
get much play. You were in the wrong neighborhood. I saw you

coming but you know, right then, you were just the thing for me, what I was looking for. I really hate to be bored. More than anything, more than getting slapped by a man who doesn't know he'd prefer a boy or driven up the coast and left to find my way home. See, all of that wasn't fun but baby, I wasn't bored and I got their numbers, paid them back in kind. So when I saw you, a young buck-wild businessman, I just knew you were the ticket to go places I've been and wanted to get back to.

"Are you with somebody?" is the first thing you said to me leaning back in your chair to show your thousand-dollar suit to its best advantage. "No," I said. And gave you a wet-lipped smile and, Douglas baby, you were sprung. I could have had it then, twisted you into the most vicious knots I could have imagined but I wanted to see, see how far we were going to go. Just how bad it was going to be.

Somebody's at the door. Probably Mother, wondering if I'm okay, or Uncle Jack wondering if I managed to slip out again. They think because it's dead locked I'm securely tucked away. Too stupid. Soon enough and I'll be making like a roach and bug on out of here.

Oh, how nice. I slept. At least three hours of beauty rest. See with you we never had time for sleeping; either we were chasing the rock or fucking or fighting. But now, since you've gone on to your reward, I actually find time to rest. That's why I look better, that haggardness is gone. Sleep is truly a wonderful thing. What's it like to be dead? Do you see me? Do you see me when I smoke your money and you're not there to share the happiness, the bliss. Do you see me getting on my knees and getting a high school boy the best blow job of his life for a couple rocks? Not that I have to do it, I still have quite a stash, but baby, I'm not being simply frugal, though frugality is to be admired, really, the kick is imagining you spinning in your ten-thousand-dollar coffin. How sweet!

I should go. I'm not getting any happier. Sooner or later I'm going to have to get back to it. The job of feeling good about myself, going on a mission to shake my money maker. It's distasteful. Compared to the creeps I have to deal with now that you're gone, you were the perfect gentleman. Even though you were inclined to punch and slap and burn, you did it with conviction, that's the kind of lover you were, resentful, mistrustful and destructive but we shared those qualities. But Douglas, to these young men, a woman is less than a dog, less than a shrimp plate at Sizzler. They have no idea what relationship is all about. It's like a woman doesn't exist other than for a fuck or to cut. Too simple for my tastes. But I have a taste for the burning white smoke, rolling into my lungs to restore my good humor for five good minutes, smoke it all, my five-O limit. I can exert self-control, something you never managed to do. See, I smoke so I won't be sour, I prefer anything to being sour. Remember when we smoked fifteen hundred worth, and you started choking, really, turning code blue. What was I supposed to do? Call 911? But that's not me, no. You laid there on your back gasping, vomiting, looking like you had bought it. I knelt by your side, saying "I told you nobody can smoke that much." Sure, it was after the fact, but did you listen? I don't know what happened because I had to leave, couldn't sit there and watch you expire. Just like I can't lie here and reminisce about the good old times. One has to live in the present.

What's a deadlock if you have the key? There I go being ironic, but you never understood irony so you don't get the joke. Outside my dark room the hallway is brightly lit, and in the kitchen, near the living room, is my Uncle Jack, dead asleep. I guess he thought he could find out how I do it, make such quick exits. The front door opens without a creak and I slip out. Oh, the sweet fresh air, how I love it. Slip into the auto, take it out of gear and coast downhill. Yes. And the land quickly changes. From the upper middle class split-level ranches down to the jungle apartment complexes. Not stopping, no, not for a stop sign, I'm on a mission. I got a surprise for the fat man. How unusual, no one is lurking in front of the Kona apartments but the yellow light is on. Where are they, the police? It would be stupid to just rush out and plunge headlong into trouble. But what the hey. Yes, the door is unlocked. Inside, I don't see anyone waiting to do something nasty to me. Are things askew or am I getting more and more paranoid? Guess I'll mosey up and see with my own God-given eyes the situation. The hard steel door hurts my knuckles but I knock sharply anyway. Someone walks to the door, must be looking through the spy hole at me. I put my eye to the cold metal of the door. ''Fuck'' is said and I hear the door unlock even through the noise of the TV. It swings open and there he is, Alton, Mister Tub O'Lard.

''Hey, it's Miss It. She's back.''

He grabs me by the arm and leads me into the little nut hole of a living room, nowhere to sit but a nasty couch.

''You got money, or is it gonna be the usual?''

I nod.

''What's that mean?''

I shrug.

He opens his ham-sized arms wide and gestures for me to see the almost empty room.

''We closing up shop. Too hot round here. Police be sweating a brother twenty-four-seven.''

He comes over, perspiring like he's drunk and opens my robe.

''Ooh, that bra is cute but you don't need to be wearing one flat as you is.''

I smile sweetly, as he pulls my bra aside and takes hold of my nipple and rubs it clumsily. Thinking of what the next few minutes will bring, I smile even more sweetly.

''Aw, baby, you should take better care of yourself. Bet you slipped out the house with them curlers in your hair, wearing them silly slippers to get a blast. You know, ya still pretty, you oughta slow down.''

Oh, how nice, fat boy is giving me the just say no line while he's leading me into the bedroom. I guess we're going to be doing it on the mattress. Doesn't look very sanitary.

''What's it gonna be? Do it like I like, two rocks, like you like it, just one.''

He pulls my robe up, forces me stomach down onto that piss-stained mattress. Down come my panties. I hope you're watching. I hope you see what he's going to do to me. He's grabbing my hips, trying to put it inside my ass, but I wiggle making him slip, hoping he'll just do it the normal way. He pushes me away, and I roll to the wall.

"You know how I like it. You don't give it to me I'm gonna take it."

It's gonna get ugly. Is it time for the surprise? He turns me over and grabs my hips again, and yanks my curlers.

"Don't you have oil?"

"Naw. I like the friction."

See, he's forcing my hand down again, trying to push it in. It won't go. I won't let it. Pull the cute little .22 auto out the robe pocket and point it at his big stomach. He stops crawling across the nasty mattress to me. Actually, he's backing up, smiling like a big fat Cheshire cat.

"Baby, baby, what you need? I must be scaring you. I got it in the other room, everything you need. Rocked and ready to go."

I smile. How sweet, he's begging just like a dog. I might be a crazy bitch but he's a begging dog.

"Pull up your pants."

"Baby," he says whining pitifully, he really thinks I'm going to shoot him.

"Kneel," I say, he does. We're both the same height now.

"Were you going to hit me?"

"Hit you? Baby, it ain't like that. You didn't hear me right."

"Didn't hear you about what?"

With my left hand, I pull up my panties, the gun feels light in my right. Wonder if it's loaded. I think I loaded it but now . . . oh well. We both kneel there a while, him looking at the gun then my eyes. I know, he's going to go for it. He stands up, big belly aquivering.

"Fuck you. You ain't gonna shoot me."

He comes toward me, then launches himself like a big, fat blanket into the air. His big hams stretched out for me. I squeeze the trigger three times. Three sharp cracks and he's flying in reverse, rolling to the wall, all bug-eyed, trying to scramble to his feet. He can't, must have broken a bone in his leg. But he's not bleeding badly. Look, he's covering his big bald head, must be afraid I'm going to crack it like a big brown egg.

"It's in the kitchen. Take it. You don't gotta shoot me."

"Baby, isn't that for me to decide?"

"Sure, whatever." His big eyes are tugging at me. Pleading for me to let him live. I bet he has a wife and a child at home or a old mother he has to support.

I leave the fat boy and go into the kitchen. Talk about dirty dishes, all kinds of filth. There's what I need on the table, still in the pan. Empty the cake into a plastic bag, and take my leave. In the living room I see Mr. Tub O'Lard's gun, it's a big one, something to have so I put it in my other pocket and go to the door. Shit, it's deadlocked. He's got the key. Back in the bedroom, he's out, slumped against the wall.

"I need the key."

Oh shit. He's out. He can't be dead. I don't touch the deceased. And he's bleeding. I hate the sight of blood. Ugh, must I push him over?

"I got it. Kaiser card's in the wallet."

Oh, he's not dead. Just delirious. Pants are too tight though. How I'm supposed to get the keys?

"I need the keys," I say sweetly.

"Key? Oh yeah, the keys." He reaches around into his back pocket, must be painful the way he's flinching but like the good boy he is, he comes up with them and tries a toss but they roll out of his hand onto the brown carpet that's quickly turning red. "Thanks," I say and cut for the door. Must be nervous because I fumble with the keys, takes what seems like hours to get the door unlocked. Can't be too hasty. Peek before you leap. The hallway is empty, but they're watching, waiting to see who comes running out. Police are probably on their way. I crack the door open. One light for the whole hallway. Point Tub's big gun. Have to use two hands to point this big thing. Smooth, that's what you said. How to pull the trigger. Boom! Boom! Plaster flies everywhere. The light still shines. Damn gun just about broke my wrist. Boom! Boom! Boom! There she blows and I'm in the dark. Drop the gun outside and run. The two lowlifes watching from across the street scatter when they see me coming but I bet they'll sneak over and find Fat Boy's gun before the police get here. It's worth a dozen rocks.

"They're shooting in there!" I yell. Sometimes it's good to

state the obvious. I get to my car, throw myself in and burn rubber up the hill. In the rearview mirror I see the red and blue strobes snaking onto Hillcrest. Good, Don Diablo. Who named these streets? I hit the garage opener and pull the car in. See, Douglas, it's not hard to get what you want if you know what you want and you're willing to work for it. Now if I wanted to die, all I would have to do is leave this car running and close the garage door and inhale. Sure, this Lincoln would have shit-stained seats but that wouldn't be my problem. But I don't have a problem, at least not right now. I've got cake in my pocket. Crack off a piece, a nice-sized chunk and fit it into the pipe and fire it up. The red flame turns blue and I can see myself in the rearview mirror. My eyes, pupils are wide as plates, couple of full-lunged hits though, shrinks them to the size of pinpoints. The buzz-expand-run-run-run-till the soft spot hums. Is that it? I try another and another and another till every part of me hums. How much do I have to smoke till I get enough? I don't know but we'll find out.

I don't sleep, just close my eyes but when I open them again, I see the pipe in my stiff fingers. Still lots of night left. I much prefer the night. Maybe that's what I am, a vampire. Sucking smoke instead of blood. I really have to stop this Douglas. There's no future in it. And even though you couldn't see life without the pipe, even you should be able to appreciate my position. I'm carrying your child. You wouldn't want ''it, the unknown'' for your first-born? Well, it wouldn't truly be your firstborn, but those poor, drug-addled tramps that carried your seed don't count. I count. Because I'm the queen of your desire or is it the bitch of your desire. Anyway, let's be honest. I'm going to smoke that baby to hell.

''Get up. You're going!''

Oh, it's morning. I'm in bed and here's Uncle Jack and the rest of his merry crew. He just yanks me up and marches me through the house to the car. And doesn't Mother look disappointed. She slides in next to me, Uncle Jack takes the wheel and my butterball of an aunt gets into the backseat. I guess it's time to go to where they put people like me. To the funny farm where life is gay all the time. The garage door swings open and we pull out into the bright light of day. Mother is crying again as usual but she wants to say something, gagging on the words.

"How could you? We trusted you."

"It's too bright. I need sunglasses."

"We aren't stopping so you can run off. You know where you're going."

They're really going to do it this time.

"We found the drugs. A whole pocket full. How much did it cost? How'd you get the money?"

"I got it for free."

"She got it for free, hah. What did you sell?" Uncle Jack says. Mother is crying buckets. What a callous thing to say in front of her.

"I certainly did not sell anything that you're implying. I got it for free. I have ways."

"My God, she needs help," Uncle Jack says.

And here's the hospital.

"Emma, you park the car. I'm walking this young lady in."

Uncle Jack slams the brakes, stopping us right behind an ambulance, slides out from behind the wheel and pulls me along, my robe comes open but he doesn't wait. It's like being on a roller coaster the way he's pulling, jerking me one way and then the other.

"What's the rush?" I say, digging in my heels.

He looks at me, his brown face wonderfully twisted in a perfect sneer.

"How could you bring that shit into my house."

"But, Uncle Jack, it's so expensive. I couldn't just leave it outside."

His hand flashes up and smashes me across the face. I spin out of his grip and run for the sliding doors. But he has me, carries me, squirming mightily to the nurse's station.

"We've made arrangements for this young lady."

He's in great shape. I'm twisting around like my dog Kona used to do, twirling against his chest, but his grip doesn't break. The robe opens all the way, my pink panties are for the world to see. The nurse looks embarrassed for him. Mother and Aunt Emma walk into the lobby and see me wrapped in Uncle Jack's arms, ass out, the robe all about my shoulders like a straitjacket, and are even more embarrassed. The nurse gets it together. I'm too tired to keep up the fight so I watch as the forms are presented and signed. And everyone looks relieved to be getting the paperwork out of the way.

"Wait a minute! They can't commit me. I didn't sign anything."

The nurse barely looks at me, instead she shuffles papers. "You're not being committed. This is a drug treatment program. They've placed you in our care. The doctor will be out shortly to explain to you how our program works."

I nod enthusiastically. "That sounds great. I can't wait!" I shout and the nurse flinches.

Oh, since the papers have been signed, two big men in white suits appear, and they have a wheelchair I suppose they want me to sit in. I wonder if I could make it to the sliding glass double doors. Wild on the streets once again. But don't I need this. Don't I need to find out why I'm the way I am. Don't I need to dry out for the baby's sake, don't I, Douglas? Isn't this all a pathetic cry for help? Yes, I guess it is. I'm one sick bitch. It's bright and sunny here in this lobby, with fine, sturdy, modern furniture in soothing pastels. It might be time for a change. The doctor, balding and thin, comes up. He's wearing running shoes. He extends his hand. I extend mine. I shove hard against his chin and knock him into Uncle Jack and it's off to the races.

8
François

■

"It was a stupid-assed movie."

"Yeah?"

"See, it's like shoot a whole bunch of people and that's the plot. What you think?"

"I dunno."

"Great, F. Don't you ever have an opinion?"

"No."

Shakes her head. Stands up and goes to the TV and pops out the video. Shorts are too tight. Be different if she didn't wear it out in the street.

"What you want to watch now?"

She flips through the stack of videos I brought looking pissed off as usual.

"Don't you watch something besides shoot-'em-ups? Almost every one of these is about shooting. I don't want to see guns. Vampires, monsters, a comedy. What's this? The original *Psycho*?"

She takes it out and slips it into the VCR. She comes back and sits closer. Smiling like she does when she wants me to hold her. I do. We kiss, but what's the point. We've been doing that all night. Blue Balls. I've got to go. Daddy's going to be home soon.

"I oughta get on."

"Why? It's not twelve."

"I got to work on the bug."

"You gonna work on the bug in the middle of the night? Stop lying. You got plans with Tommy. Clubbing, huh?"

"I got to change the plugs. Car needs work if it's gonna run."

She gets quiet. Looks at the screen like she's really interested in the credits.

"Why-you-got-to-lie. You just horny and since we here and can't do it, you want to bone out."

"Margot, it ain't like that."

"What's it like then."

"I dunno."

"Suppose I say I don't want you to go. What if I say I want the punk to see you here on the couch when he gets back."

Shit. All I want to do is go over Tommy's and see what's happening.

"So what do I have to do to keep you here. Want me to sit on your lap or something?"

"It's cool. I'm cool."

She comes closer and puts my arm around her. I hate this. I hate being around her pops. He's a fucking nut. Like this crazy fool, what's his name? Norman Bates. Except you can tell her dad wants to bury you. She can go away, leave me to go to *college*, but I got to stay here till that big nut's going to walk through the door, looking at me like I'm stealing his TV.

"See. You want me around. But if I talk about you leaving, you get freaked out."

She sips a soda and looks at me. It's not the worried mama look like she's been giving me since the shooting. No. It's back to the "what a fool."

"Is this really what you been thinking about? You've been sitting over here all night like a lump. Hardly saying a thing, and this is the first thing you got to say? Let's be real. I'm leaving to go to school. I'm not leaving you. I never said I was leaving you. Shit, if you wanted you could go to school at Santa Cruz too."

Yeah. Always trying to make me sound wrong. She knows it's not like that. I'm not ready for any more school. She knows that.

"You can come visit. I don't even know why you be bringing this up. You think it's gonna be 'Polly want a cracker'? You think I'm gonna fall in love with the first white guy I meet? What you so worried about?"

What? She looking at me like I'm really gonna answer. Like what I'm gonna say. I just don't want you to leave. How that's gonna sound?

"You know this never gets nowhere. You just get quiet and start looking dumb like I ran over your puppy. Really, this is too silly to be talking about again."

What's there to say? She's got all of the answers. Got a lot of nuts up north. Crazy white psychos like Norman. Probably soon as she gets up there she'll be thinking it ain't so great. Probably nothing but nuts and trees.

"What you so quiet about? You just start staring off and I'm supposed to just sit here and talk to myself. You know when we first got together you used to have a sense of humor. Now, it's like all you have to do is look deep and I should be happy."

She can say more shit with one breath than anybody I know.

"I was watching the movie."

"You've seen this. I know you've seen this. So why you got to get all righteous like this is the most interesting thing you ever seen on a TV?"

She don't even have to move her lips to talk. Words just roll out.

"I'm gonna go."

I say it but I don't stand. I just stare at her like the words ought to shut her up. She starts with that shaking her head like I need to be slapped.

"So what do you want to talk about. Me having your baby? Yeah, that's a damn good idea."

"See. There you go cause I tell you how I feel. Nobody likes to get left behind. Not even you."

Now's the time. Walk to the door slowly so it don't look like I'm running. But I can feel her looking at me. Staring at the back of my head like she got a gun to it.

"No. You ain't going. I said you're going to stay and you're going to stay!"

She's yelling and hopping over the couch and flies by me and blocks the door.

"What you laughing at," she says.

I'm laughing? Guess I am. How's she gonna stop me from leaving?

"Margot, get out of the way. Got enough problems without your daddy giving me more."

I try to push her aside but she gives me a two-hand shot in the chest. Then she drives me back to the couch and then over. I spin backward trying to catch myself.

"Quit it. Gonna wake your mama."

She stands over me, red striped stomach in my face. Fists balled up like she's ready to punk me.

"I told you, you ain't going nowhere. You gonna stay till he gets home."

"Why? Why do I got to stay here? He don't need to see me."

"I told you. You heard me. I don't like him walking around like he owns me. When he sees you it makes him think."

"Yeah? About what? Most of the time I think he can't stand me."

She sits down hard, heavy on my legs. looking in my eyes, daring me to get up. Norman's already killed the G. Pushed the car into the lake.

"Still trying to pretend you watching the movie."

She reaches over and gets a hold of my neck and bites. "Quit it, girl!" But she grabs me and tries again. Bites and sucks. No stupid hickies. I push her away again but she keeps coming. Yeah, she's hot. And I'm hot. I got the jerry cap but damn, what we're gonna do? I don't need no six-four, drunk-assed fool, trying to kill me because he catches us doing it in the bathroom.

"No, I oughta go. You know the kind of trouble this is . . ."

She's got me, pinning me down with her legs. Kissing me, forcing her tongue by my lips, rubbing me.

"You know he gonna open the door and see us."

"Fuck him. In a month I'm gone."

She's working it. What pocket the rubber's in? Do it right on this couch. Wait a minute, what I'm saying? Here? She stands up, pulls them down, twisting out those tight-ass shorts and panties.

"You better have a rubber."

I hand it to her and she pulls down my sweats and puts it on for me. Get to it. Fast and hard, making that couch squeak and slide. Rolling with it, let her work. Fuck it, I'm gonna come.

"Margot . . . I want to . . . let me take it off."

"Boy, be quiet!"

Puts her hand over my mouth and gets to grinding. Sprung. Coming.

"Ah shit!"

"Shut up!" she says clamping down my mouth. She's out and up twisting back into the shorts.

"Put it back in. Don't leave your little man hanging out."

"Little?"

She slides next to me and puts it in and gives me a kiss.

"See, I'm too good for you. You need excitement in your life, get you out that stupid state you been in."

Don't wanna move. Just sit there and catch my breath and listen to her talk that nonsense. Like I was some kind of basket case or something. I hear it before she do. The sound of the truck, truck big as two trucks, something only he'd drive. I'm flying, zipping and running for the door. Margot's gone. Left the room. She comes back spraying Lysol.

"Don't go! He's gonna know something's up."

Yeah, right. I turn, swing the door open get the hell out of there, Mr. Moore is pulling the truck up. He don't see me sprinting down the steps but the dogs do, beating it toward me snapping and barking. I stop dead in my tracks, call for my life.

"Tyson, Ali, it's me, boys!"

They slow up, eye me like meat, hold me there till that big shadow lit by the garage lights heads over. Walking slowly like he's enjoying seeing me stuck like a bug on a flystrip.

"Why you running?"

"I wasn't running. I was leaving."

"Don't lie, boy. I saw you. You were trying to reach that gate. You weren't trying to get away with something, was you?"

Fuck this! I'm supposed to sit here and listen to him talk to me like I'm some kind of punk.

"I know what you was doing in there. Don't lie. See if she

wasn't grown I'd put my foot so deep in your ass it'd see tomorrow. But let me tell you, if you get that girl knocked up you better be planning on getting married and I ain't playing.''

"Yeah."

''I don't really know why you got your nose so open. She's going away. What you gonna do then, follow her?''

"I dunno."

''Better find you something else cause your thing is about to play out.''

''Come on, boys,'' he says slapping his thigh and laughing that deep laugh and walks away, dogs playing around his feet like stupid puppies.

Beer's giving me a fucking headache. Music is too fucking loud and I've got to piss again. Too crowded. Can't even see the fucking dance floor. No asses just backs. This really ain't happening for me. Oughta drag my dead ass home. Margot probably called to get in my shit and I'm out in the street. Just don't like that Jim Brown–looking fool of a father.

''Yo, F. Got you another rum and Coke. These be kicking,'' Tommy says.

Always trying to get me drunk but fuck it, I'll down it.

''So her daddy just about caught y'all doing it, huh? Boy, you be living dangerously.''

''Aw, fuck him. I ain't worried.''

''F. You ain't got to lie. I been over there. I've seen him. You'd be stupid not to be scared unless you got a bat.''

''It ain't like that.''

''Oh, here comes the preppie boy.''

Can't stand this little pootbutt. Think he's MC Hammer. Baggy silk pants, silk jacket, shirtless and a big fake gold chain resting flat on his skinny chest. Probably get jacked soon as his feet touched the street but here he's hip.

''Cop a squat, homey,'' Tommy says almost shouting to be heard over the music. He pats the empty seat, smiling cause he knows he gonna make some money off this mark.

''What you drinking?'' Tommy asks still smiling.

"Got my own," Pootbutt say and pulls a paper bag out of his coat pocket. He hands it to Tommy who tastes it, and screws his face up and hands it back.

"Cisco? You drinking project juice?"

"Like the buzz," Pootbutt says smiling, swigging from the bottle.

"Yeah," Tommy says.

He don't look in my direction. Better not. It's like a fucking joke, way he crosses his legs and holds his chin like he's some gangster holding down the hood. Just wanna be seen with us to impress his frat buddies. Real niggahs from the hood.

"So?" Tommy says smiling at this fool like he's the stupidest mark.

"What?"

Oh, he want to hear the code. What we say to let him know we legit.

"What you need?"

"Some of that Ses," he says slipping Tommy a fifty. Tommy stretches his long arms across the table like he's gonna choke him but instead takes his hand and shakes it. But the fool lets the little bag of weed fall out of his hand and land on the table. He grabs for it but Tommy has it and slides back shaking his head, laughing. Then he leans forward and grabs the boy behind the head and whispers something. The pootbutt loses all that preppie cool, stands up quickly, almost in a panic and bones out.

"Yo, F. Why you staring at him like you about to slap him. Mess up the business."

"You the one who had him scared. What you said to him?"

"Told him not to be dropping shit. People be watching."

"That's all you told him?"

Tommy waves me off and gets back to getting seen. Standing and stretching, flipping his phony ponytail like he jumped out of *Miami Vice*. Latin girl with big tits comes over, gives Tommy a big old hug, smiles at me. She's buzzed already, whispers to him but I hear her. She wants Ice. That's why she got all them zits. Tommy's smiling, gonna get something more than paid.

"Look, F. I'll be back. Hold down the table."

"Yeah, sure," I say but he's already gone. Man, these squeezers are working his jock. Why I got to hang out here, waiting around
till he gets back from riding that G. Gonna have to tell me all about
it, how he did all the freaky shit. Oh no, another one of these black
frat boys. This one's a preppie.

"Hey, um, you got any of that . . ."

"What?"

"Buddha."

"No."

"Where's the guy with the ponytail?"

"He'll be back."

"Can I wait?"

"Hell yeah, you can hold down the table."

Fuck it. I'm outta here.

Outside, in the parking lot, it's damp and kinda foggy. The ocean
smells really salty like it's closer than across Lincoln, more than a
mile away. Never liked that smell, what do they call it, brine? It's
dead for a Friday night. Nobody's hanging by their cars trying to
be seen. Used to like all this, making a little sideways money.
Hanging with Tommy, getting paid for nightclubbing, watching his
back. But it's gotta end, it's gonna get . . . complicated. Something's got to happen sooner or later.

"Yo, F!"

Fuck. I knew I shouldn't parked under the light. Tommy's still
got the skeezer with him and leads her over with his arms all wrapped
around her tits, like this is the one.

"What? You boning out on me? What's the deal, B?"

"No deal. Just tired, been up early. Went to class."

"Oh yeah, you still got to get that paper. But look, you oughta
get with me about going up to Santa Barbara. My homey's in school
up there and said we could make some serious money at this club.
White folks who want to get fucked up and we got what they need."

Don't need to hear this. Heard all that yang before. Anyway,
it's hard to listen when the G is licking his ear.

"Really, F. You need to get out of town. Your baby's going,
you oughta go. Get a fresh perspective on everything."

"Yeah," I say sliding into the bug. Everybody's got advice. What they know? Tommy leans in the window grinning like a stupid Magic Johnson.

"Think about it. White chicks be on you, riding your jock for real."

"Sure you right."

Milks my hand, nods and keeps smiling.

"F. It ain't like that. You'll see. I've been up there. It's cool. You don't got to watch your back. Nobody's gonna be fronting you and we got serious backup."

"Who?"

"Cowboy's down with us."

"Cowboy?"

"Yeah. Says he needs to do business up there and I told him we'd check it out for him."

Can't believe this. Tommy don't know.

"You too big for me. You know that. You oughta find somebody who wants to high roll but I ain't with it."

"B! Don't be selling yourself short. Make some money, hang out on the beach, G the white girls."

"Tommy. Straight out, I don't want to do business with Cowboy. I don't want to sound like a punk but the brother is ruthless. What you gonna do if shit goes wrong? You ain't working for yourself. See you got this freak she ain't paid for shit. You can get away with that but Cowboy gonna be looking to be paid in full."

Her head is hanging down, Tommy's got to hold her up.

"You better lay her down somewhere cause she gonna be vomiting on you."

"F, you don't know Cowboy. I've been running with the brother for a while. He ain't nothing but a businessman. I want to do a little business. It ain't complicated. Your homey used to do business with him, what's his name, Doug. What he said? Did Cowboy ever burn him? Naw. He's legit."

"Cool. Hope it works out."

Start the engine and throw it in reverse, outta here. Then the skeeze leans over and lets it spray. He jumps back and she falls to all fours. Guess he's gonna have to send those pants to the cleaners.

*   *   *

Tommy don't know. Saw it with Doug. Think you running the show but the show's running you. Boogerburger ain't too crowded. Couple bums hanging by the curb and some Latino guys on the phone. Got a space almost in front. Don't even have to put on the alarm. Security guard look older than my dead granddaddy. He ain't scaring a damned thing. Shoulda brought my gun instead of leaving it in the car. "Wadda you want!" Korean fool screams soon as I get to the window, stinky breath all in my face.

"Give me a burger and fries and a big Coke!" Scream back in his face. See how he likes that. "Five-fifty," he yells back. Security guard lift his gray head off the table long enough to see me hand the fool a ten. Get my change and go find a seat. Aw shit soon as I get comfortable some fool in blue come walking in, cap hanging way over his eyes. Fuck! Just my luck, it got to be Ollie. Back to the gangsta life for real. Security guard still don't wake up. What they pay this geezer. I lean the other way, maybe he ain't gonna see me sitting in the corner. Don't want to talk to him, ever since he got jacked he been talking too much head about big payback and all that yang. Glance over and see him give a order and give the guy a twenty. Got some money. Must be jacking again.

"Smaller! Got smaller bill?!" Korean yells at him. Must be deaf, think nobody else can hear.

"No," Ollie says. Damn, I thought he was gonna go off. Ollie acting reasonable? Guess he got his ass kicked again. Shit, he sees me. Nods his head, get his change and comes straight over.

"Sup niggah." Smell the eightball. He's swaying. I know he gonna want a ride home.

"Going back to the hood?"

"Yeah, what you doing? You walked all the way over here?"

"Naw, one of my homeys dropped me off. But he had to get on. Gonna give me a ride?"

Shrug. What else I'm gonna do?

"You need one?"

"Bus ain't running."

How fucked up is he? Sweating on a cool night, eyes red as a rag. Looking me up and down like he wants something more than a ride.

Good. Food's up. Fool's waving like I'm too stupid to see him. Pick up the greasy brown bag and head to the door. Don't need to get seen with Ollie.

"Gonna be in the bug."

Get inside wishing, wishing I could just drive off and leave his ass but that wouldn't work. He'd run after me all the way home like a dumb-ass dog. Blow the horn make him think I'm gonna leave, hurry his ass up. Tape player is still fucking up, can't listen to that garbled shit. Listen to the radio, oldies station, "Atomic Dog" is on. Yeah, that's it. Crank it. Put the bass on, rock the bug. Margot likes to dance to this. Yeah, she was cutting up that time at the marina. That was before she got sick of seeing Tommy around and stopped going. She always got to have a problem with something. . . . What's that? Bang? Somebody's letting off?! Turn this music off. Fuck it, I'm gone . . . Ollie! Running backwards got a gun in one hand and a bag in the other. Pop! Shooting into the air, get to the car. Tries to open the door, I got it locked.

"Open the fucking door."

His face is pressed against the window, looks like he's smiling. Go! See myself pulling away and Ollie plugging me in the head. I lean over unlatch it and pull away, Ollie's falling out, don't have both legs in before I hit a turn on Crenshaw and the door flies open, and Ollie's grabbing to the seat, almost out again. I pull him in. He's laughing, yelling and shit.

"Got them muthafuckas!"

"Shut up!" I yell but he ain't listening.

"What I got here?"

I'm driving lost, what the fuck to do?

"Fuck, lots of ones! Oh, yeah, here's the twenties."

"Stupid fucking fool! Pull a jack and get in my car!"

Still ain't listening to me. Counting his money and grinning like the nut he is. Wanna slap him but he still got that piece in his hand. Where I'm going, out by the airport, driving by them blue and white Christmas lights. Man, I'm a fool. Got him with me, got the gun, the money, probably shot somebody. Murder one, armed robbery and he's grinning in the dark.

"What was you screaming about? Want some gas money?"

Put a fucking twenty in the ashtray. Yeah, that'll do it. Now we're by the beach, always getting lost around here. Pull over and reach under the seat. Got something for Ollie's ass.

"What you pull over for?"

His gun is pointing down at the floor so I show him mine.

"Ollie, you so goddamned stupid. Give me that!"

Snatch that stupid .22 away. Wish he would do something besides look stupid. Wouldn't mind plugging him. Deserves whatever he gets.

"Get your dumb ass out the car."

"Why you being fucked up? What I do?"

He got his hands spread wide, still grinning. Fog lights make his ugly face pale like a fucking movie zombie.

"You smoking. Hitting the pipe like your brother did."

"Naw. That ain't it," he says shaking his hands and that oily mess of a Jheri curl.

He puts his hands together like he's praying, gonna be a good boy or something.

"Get your ass out the car."

He does, slowly, trying to fuck with me. Turns around and leans into the window.

"Real fucked up what you doing. Thought we went way back. Dogging me like I'm some kind of punk."

Yeah, sounds like the old Ollie. Guess he's mad now.

"I'm gonna catch you slipping, see how you like it . . ."

"Don't say another thing."

Point at his eye. Another word does it.

"If I go down, if I get arrested I'm gonna find your ass, you ain't gonna have to look for me."

Smiling like the punk he is but I'm the fool. Toss his bag, with the burger and bills out the window. He bends over to pick it up and I hit a U-turn, toss his gun out too. See him in the mirror running across the street holding that hamburger bag to get it. Maybe I oughta do another U and roll him over, like a bullfight, bug against

bullet. Find the fucking freeway, San Diego to Century, no traffic
. . . get off, no traffic, but at the signal on Main is some fucking
sheriffs. Gonna have to pull next to them, they checking me out.
Looking me up and down. If somebody saw the bug, got the plates,
I'm as good as gone. Green, pull out slowly but not too slow, see
if they go ahead. They don't, change lanes riding behind me. Any
minute they gonna put on the spotlight, flash the strobes, have me
facedown, kissing the cement. Find my gun under the seat, at least
the weekend in the county. Fuck. There it go, backlit. Pull it over,
wallet on the dash, hands on the wheel. Can't see a damned thing.
Hear him coming up.

"See your license."

Hand that and the registration to him before he asks for it.
Running a check on me. Keep me busy then do the routine, pat me
down, then search the car, I'm fucked. Wait for the worst. Got the
luck of a fool cause I'm a fool. Up ahead at the signal, hooptie
blows through a red light doing seventy, another one right on its
ass, a lowrider deep with heads. Policeman drops the license in my
lap, both of them run for the car and burn out like Batman. Ain't
that a bitch. Got lucky.

Why is all this shit in the yard. Mama got all kinds of boxes blocking
the gate. How somebody supposed to get in the driveway. Move
this, move that, getting dirt all over my pants, bet I'm gonna smell
like cowshit moving bags, these big-assed bags of fertilizer. Light's
on. Mama? Yeah, peeking through the backdoor screen.

"What are you doing out at this time of night?"

"Nothing. Pulling the cars in the backyard."

"Now? At three in the morning?"

"I thought I heard somebody messing with them."

"The alarm would have gone off. Nobody was messing with
those cars."

"Go back to sleep. I'm taking care of it."

She just sitting there watching me work.

"You just put a twenty-five-pound bag of manure on my zin-
nias. Are you through?"

"Yeah, I'm through. I can pull the cars in."

"Great. So tomorrow I get to back my car out of that gate and down that narrow driveway because you decided it's a good idea."

Not going to say anything cause all we gonna do is argue. Drive mine in first then hers cause she leaves so early. Close and lock the gate. Damn, I'm tired. Why won't she go in the house. Walk past her, watch, she's got to say something.

"What's going on? Someone's looking for you? The police?"

"No, Mama, nothing like that at all," I say slipping by her. All I want to do is go to bed. She follows me through the house looking at me like I'm one of her patients. Get to my room with her right on my heels.

"Margot called. She needs a ride to the airport. Something about that school flying her up for the week."

"Yeah. Thanks. Good night, Mama."

I smile as I shut the door with her standing there, worried as usual.

9

Margot

■

"Is that boy gonna get here or do I have to drive you myself?"

Why don't he eat his grits and shut up.

"He's gonna be here."

"But when? Young men with no visible means of support don't have to be anywhere on time. They can just sit around and money comes calling."

Aw no. Not this. Do I have to listen to another speech. Where is he? He can't leave me hanging. This lunatic don't have to go to work for another hour. Only me to talk to cause Mama know better than to say a damned thing sitting there looking so ugly she blends into the woodwork. Today Mr. Big Stuff has on a new shirt and his good Levi's, looks like he's not going to be contracting, working on decks or driveways or any of that yang, just laying pipe.

"So what they flying you up there for? See what kind of inner city negro they giving their money to?"

"Yep. You got it."

Won't he shut up. He's gonna ask stupid questions till François shows.

"Baby, I packed you another bag with sweaters. It's cold up there. Take your coat."

She said something. That done it. Now he's looking at her, sucking on that pork chop bone like he's cleaning it so he can stab her with it.

"Don't you have better things to do than to be helping her pack. She grown enough to go fly away for the week, she grown enough to pack her bags."

Mama shrugs and looks away as she gets up from the table and starts to clear it. Still working that bone, he's looking at her. He is so ignorant. Staring at her like she look even worse than she do, like she's some dog on its last legs. If what goes around comes around, what did she do to deserve this?

"Clearing the table? I'm not finished."

Says it like he's that guy on CNN, trying his best to sound proper, like he has some class. Mama shrugs again and sits down at the table holding a saucer of butter and the orange juice carton like she don't want to put it down to have to pick it up or maybe that's how she messes with him. Looking like Whoopi Goldberg on a bad day and acting like she got a plate in her head.

"So, Miss College Student, what are you going to be majoring in? Something useful I hope."

"Useful?"

Smirks. Like he actually knows something. Must have heard somebody talk about it on the news before he flipped the channel.

"I don't know."

Smiles. Oh yes. He likes that. Likes thinking I'm too stupid to major in money. Maybe if I didn't live with the biggest asshole in the whole fucking city I'd consider it, but no, whatever pays the most is the best.

"Accounting. I could use an accountant. Bet a lot of people could use accountants."

I nod. He's thinking. Easy to tell, his mouth ain't moving and he looks unhappy.

"Sounds like a good idea."

I get up with him still sitting there looking glum. Bet he's thinking about me making more money than he makes.

"You know just cause you educated don't mean you can make a living."

"I know."

"Lots of educated people don't have a pot to piss in."

"Yeah," I say and back out of the room. And there's Mama, still sitting there holding the butter and orange juice.

* * *

She must think I'm going to be gone for a month. Two suitcases for a week? Don't want to have to ask that fool for a ride . . . but I might have to. What if François don't show at all? Maybe his car broke. Wait another ten minutes. Straighten up my room, kill some time. Here they are in the sock drawer. I know I'm not gonna need them, like who am I gonna meet that fast I'm gonna want to do it with. I'll take them anyway. Somebody's knocking, must be François but before I can open it, he comes busting in.

"Thought you was packed! That boy is waiting on you."

"I am packed."

Did he see them, the rubbers? . . . Yeah, so what if he did even if they are his.

"Let me get that."

Big fool takes both suitcases in one hand and tries to get through the door, bangs them against the wall, sending books flying off the dresser. In the living room Mama's still sitting there at the table resting her head in her hand while Daddy goes bumping through. François's outside the screen. Daddy wouldn't even let him in the house. Kicks the screen open and almost catches François. F's trying to help but Daddy pushes by, ignoring him.

"Bye, Mama. I'll call you."

"Have a good time," she says and finally gets up from the table and heads down the hallway. Guess she wanted to see me off. Outside, Daddy's already got the bags in the car. It's not the bug, it's F's Mama's new LeBaron and that fool's leaning on the hood with his arms folded, shining off F's glares.

"You better put a move on since your boyfriend's operating on colored people time. Y'all got about a half hour."

F waits to open the door for me till Daddy gets his big butt off of it. Figure I can slip in and keep the window rolled up till we get going. Just wave goodbye and that'll be it. Fuck. He's tapping on the glass. I crack it open. He's leaning over looking in. Checking out my blouse.

"What's wrong? What you looking at?"

"Button it. No reason for you to be walking around with your blouse open."

Fuck him. I ain't doing it. Let him be mad. François is looking straight ahead, looking like he's gonna run over the first dog he sees. Fuck it. I'll button it. Now's he happy.

"How much you need?" he says pulling out a roll of twenties, peels off four. Dangles them outside the window so I got to reach for them like I'm some kind of dog going for that goddamned pork chop bone he got dangling from his lips.

"I don't need money. I have some."

"You have money? You don't work."

Wonder if François got the gun under the seat? Shoot his ass.

"Mama gave it to me."

"Your mama don't have any money to give."

He sticks his big hand in the window and drops the bills into the car. I catch and crumple them and shove them out of the window.

"I don't need your money."

"Suit yourself," he says and picks up the bills and shrugging turns his back on us and walks to the house. F takes off tires squealing, shaking his head, muttering.

"I'm never coming over again. He's a fucking fool. Somebody's gonna kill him."

"Yeah." Too mad to say anything else like why the hell he's so fucking late. What he thinks we can get to LAX in twenty minutes? Guess he expects me to run like a fool to get on.

"What day you getting back?"

Conversation. Must know I'm mad.

"Late as we are I'm probably not going anywhere. You said you were going to be on time."

"I'm gonna get you there."

"Plane leaves in twenty minutes. What you gonna do, fly me to it?"

Shaking his head like I'm sweating him. But I ain't gonna say nothing. Look out the window and ignore him. Men are idiots. He's not going to get on the freeway. Gonna take the streets.

"Don't rush. Just wasting your gas. Plus the plane don't leave for an hour. I knew you were going to be late."

Cuts his eyes and curses. "Why you gonna do something like that. Lying to me."

"Because, baby, you don't want me going. You're late to everything you don't want to do."

He nods. "Really think you're the smartest woman in the world?"

"That's a question? I thought you knew. Anyway, do you got some cash. I didn't want to take any of his."

"What? It's still money."

"But it's not like your money," I say as he pulls into the airport parking lot and cuts the engine and looks at me, his eyes red, circles beneath them. Was out all night again.

"Am I your man or your fool?"

"That's a stupid question too and you know the answer to that one."

"What?"

I lean over and kiss him hard.

"If you don't know by now I ain't telling you."

He looks mad for a minute, like how could I say something so mean, then he laughs. "I'm sprung. I know I'm sprung. You know I'm sprung."

I pat him on the head. It's good to tell the truth.

I lead him to the restaurant and get us drinks and sit us next to this really fat, red-faced man so I can watch the clock. What we got, ten minutes? I want to look sad to be leaving, you know, cause he looks like hell and all. I hand him the soda and he won't even look at me. Cute how mad he is, like some spoiled boy. He sips the soda and he is a little boy, about to cry trying to play it off by acting like he's mad.

"I'm gonna be back Saturday. You gonna pick me up?"

"Yeah," he says swallowing. He's not gonna get emotional. Hope he's not. What's he gonna do when I'm going for good. He sits there, slumped shoulders, elbows resting on his knees, holding that soda so low it looks like it's gonna touch the floor.

"I am coming back."

"No, you ain't."

He looks at me, expecting me to get mad. The red-faced man is just staring at us. I stare back until he turns his fat head.

"I ain't gonna be sitting around here waiting on you to get back."

"What? I'm going for a week and you got some plan. You got some chick that want a piece?"

Check him out, saw that smile. So weak, all I got to do is throw a bone and he's jumping for it.

"Naw, it ain't like that."

If it ain't a girl, it's got to be money.

"I got a business deal going. I'm going out of town for a couple weeks and if it works out I might stay."

"Yeah? Guess I gotta get a ride from somebody else. Why you'd say yes if you can't do it?"

Shakes his head like I'm the one who's stupid.

"See, like I told you, you don't like somebody doing what they need to do, but it's cool for you to do what you gotta do."

"Oh yeah. That's what you call doing what you need to do, you and Tommy making a little run to the border to sell that baking soda?"

Now look at him staring at his knuckles like he wants to back-hand me but he knows better than that. I take a hand. "I got to get on the plane, but you'd better pick me up. Don't do something stupid to impress me."

"Girl, you so wrong. Make fun of me like it ain't nothing."

Rub his neck, kiss his lips . . . not kissing back but he's not pulling away.

"See when I make serious money then you gonna be acting different."

Now I'm the one pushing him away.

"No, I'm not going for that shit. I ain't like that. I ain't playing you for your cash. I'm gonna get mine. I'm gonna do for me!"

Got me mad. He's smiling all cute and everything cause he knows he played me out. Got me all upset. Likes that. So . . . I reach around like I'm gonna kiss him again and instead slap the back of his hook head. Pow! Sounds like a gunshot. He grabs me, all excited, eyes big from the sting. Playing like he does, carrying on like some kid who don't know what to do with a girl, strangle me or cop a feel.

"Shouldn't play," he says trying to act hard.

"Who's playing?"

Got his hands around my neck drawing enough attention another one of them airport cops start checking us out. Push through his weak stranglehold and kiss him again, stop all this nonsense. Now's he kissing back. People are staring. See them looking all shocked and everything like they've never kissed somebody in a airport. But it's time to go. Takes a two-hand shove to get loose.

"Better walk me to the metal detectors. Gotta go."

"Okay," he says glumly, brushing himself off like we've been making out on the lawn. I take his hand and squeeze it tightly, something I usually don't do. Guard is checking F out again like he's gonna cause trouble. F takes the bait, drops my hand and walks up to him like he's gonna walk through him, swaying his shoulders, sticking out his chest and all that. He stops short and glares till I reach him.

"Why you getting sore about him when you know it's about me," I whisper into his ear, standing so my breasts press against his arm. He smiles.

"Can't even get mad without you saying it's you I'm pissed off at."

"Yeah, that's right." I kiss him again but it's quick and he's looking all dazed. "You never did give me that cash."

His eyes clear. Like he knows he gotta be on his guard, women and money and all that. He reaches into his back pocket and comes out with a money clip, looks likes a half dozen twenties.

"Sixty. That should do it. Wouldn't want to take more than half your money. Don't want you worrying that you getting pimped."

He frowns and slips the three bills out of the clip and hands them over so slowly it's like the money is trying to stay in his hand.

"What's wrong? Don't want to give it to me? It's cool. I can do without."

Turn my back on him and start for the metal detectors. He grabs my shoulder from behind and spins me around.

"I didn't say I didn't want to give it to you. Here."

He hands me eighty.

"If you need more, call. *No problema.*"

"Thanks."

"You don't have to be so hard. I was gonna give you the money."

"Yeah. I knew you was. But I had to play you out like you played me out."

"What? About that money?"

"Yeah. Like I'm like that."

Looks at the floor, he really doesn't want to see me go. Nice for the ego to get all this attention. Finally, he looks up and wraps his arms around me so tight I can't breathe and kisses me and he's gone, leaving me gasping, watching him run through the airport until I lose him in the crowd.

Somebody's supposed to have picked me up an hour ago. Small little airport, couldn't miss me if they tried. I'm the only black I've seen since I left L.A. Suddenly I'm it. Catch eyes glancing at me, probably wondering what the hell I'm doing up here. Outside it looks like a fucking forest, green everywhere. Cold too, glad Mama said bring a coat. Probably going to have to catch a bus to the fucking school. Yeah, great, bout time, there's the damn UC Santa Cruz van pulling up, just an hour late. Must know he fucked up the way he's parking in the red and running in. Oh, a black boy, a freak. Ain't so bad having to wait if that's my driver. Wish he didn't have those little dreads in his hair, like he's a wannabe Whoopi or something. Comes in all big-eyed, blowing steam. Boy got on red biker shorts, big thighs and all, and a thick down jacket. His pretty butt must be freezing. He sees me and comes over looking really worried like I'm gonna sweat him.

"Sorry I'm late. They just got told me I had to pick you up and it's a forty-minute drive to Salinas."

Sounds just like a white boy. No problem I say and he bends to pick up my bags. Then he puts them down again and sticks his hand out. We shake hands.

"I'm Jamal. I'm on the staff."

"Margot, nice meeting you," I say but my voice sounds too heavy. Probably sound like a real ruffkin straight out the hood. He smiles, must not sound too rough, and finally lets my hand go and takes up my bags again.

"What you got in here, dictionaries?"

"Nothing, clothes, sweaters . . ." He sounds so white but not really nerdy.

He smiles again and turns away with the bags, lugging them, straining, all the way outside. At the van, steam puffing from his mouth, he puts them down and unlocks the door for me.

"You've got quite a few clothes in there," he says shaking his head, and then after a moment of sitting down on the suitcases, he jerks them up and flings them into the back of the van. What a drag, I knew I didn't need all that stuff Mama packed. Now the boy thinks I'm some kind of clothes freak. He gets inside of the van and doesn't look at me like he's really pissed or something. Puts a tape on as he pulls out. Some rock shit. Naw, that's got to be punk shit. "Kill your Mama" music.

"What's that you listening to?"

"Red Hot Chili Peppers."

"Oh, you like that?"

He smiles again.

"I'm listening to it, I must like it."

"Lots of people do stuff they don't like."

"Oh, I see . . . you must be a philosophy major." Sign says Santa Cruz forty miles away, forty miles of listening to devil music with some kind of pretty Oreo who's pissed off cause my suitcase strained his back. Fuck, ain't this the shit.

"Why are you so silent?" he asks and he's smiling again.

"I don't know. Just thinking."

"Hope I didn't seem too irritated back there but I got this groin pull and lifting those suitcases got it going again. Put me in a really shitty state of mind."

"I could have carried them."

He laughs and takes the tape out. Thank God. Sure and the hell glad he's through with that shit. Puts another one in, just as bad as the other one. Sounds like a radio between stations.

"What's that?"

"Sun Ra, pretty wild, huh?"

"Yeah."

"So you're from L.A."

"Naw, almost. I'm from Compton. Right on the border."

"You're from Compton? How is that?"

"What you mean, how is that?"

"Just asking. I'm from Westport, Connecticut. I've never been to L.A. I've listened to N.W.A. and I saw *Colors*. I'm just curious that's all."

Got him going without really trying. Thinks he can just keep talking down.

"I grew up in a pretty much all-white neighborhood, just one other black family. It was a pretty boring childhood."

Oh, so now pretty boy wants to know the real scoop on how black folks really live. I'm supposed to tell him about how so-and-so got shot and how Mary's a strawberry.

"You know, I stayed in the house a whole lot. So I'm not the one to ask."

"Oh," he said looking straight ahead and not bothering to glance at me like he was doing. This Sun Ra shit is worse than the stuff before, really's getting to me. Fuck it. Pop the fucking thing out.

"You really don't go for Sun Ra."

"No, not really."

"Got a N.W.A. tape, *Straight Out of Compton*." He puts that in.

"You know I don't listen to that."

"Why?" he says smiling.

"Why I don't listen to that shit? Because it ain't about shit. Supposed to be real, if that's real it ain't real for me."

Now, he's laughing. Thought he was through with me.

"Wow, you really are deep."

"What's that supposed to mean?"

He's looking at me again. "I know N.W.A. is sexist and all that I just mean you never answer anything straight. You answer with questions. What are you going to do in class when the professor asks you a question?"

"I'll answer it," I say and look out the window.

"You've got a real attitude," he says almost in a whisper like he really doesn't want me to hear.

"An attitude? I don't have no attitude. I just don't like how you want to hear horror stories about the hood. You said your neighborhood is boring, mine is too. It's boring watching your back and staying in the house after dark because of some fools who got guns. It might be exciting for you but it's boring for me."

Look at him looking all confused, running his hands through those stupid dreads.

"Okay, okay, maybe I approached this the wrong way. I'm sorry."

Look at him driving with his shoulders slumped, bulging his eyes like a real nerd.

"What you doing that for. It looks stupid."

"Oh, I was wondering when you were going to notice. I feel stupid."

Looking at me with those pretty brown eyes. Trying to run serious game. Oh, I see, we're there. Wants to make everything right so he can hit on me later. Like I'm going to go for that move. We roll by a whitewashed wall with UC SANTA CRUZ painted across it and cruise by a booth with a friendly-looking cop on a stool who waves us through. I'm here. Made it to fucking college. We keep driving, campus looks like a forest too. After five more minutes of going through the thickest part of the forest we get to a bunch of modern-looking white buildings. He pulls up to the dorm, it's got clothes hanging from some of the windows and longhair hippie-looking chicks and white boys are walking in and out of what looks like a hotel lobby. This nut roars right up to the sidewalk, tires kicking up gravel, and runs out like he pulled up, frantic as a basehead looking for a rock. Slides open the van door, pulls out my suitcases and opens my door and helps me out. Guess I should be happy. Couldn't get any farther from L.A. if I took a rocketship to Mars. Everything is green and white except this Oreo smiling at me like he ain't the biggest jerk in the whole world. Carries my bag into the dorm lobby trying to look cool, like it ain't kicking his ass. Inside it's all warm and new, comfortable. But it smells damp and

mildewy, guess it's always wet around here. What's his name . . .
Jamal walks to a counter where some older hippies are busy handing
out notebooks and keys to these really young-looking white kids.
One of the hippie chicks says something to Jamal and Jamal laughs
stupid, must not be funny at all, and she hands him a notebook and
a pair of keys. He comes back smiling like a damn pumpkin.

"Got your keys for you. See, now you don't have to stand in
line."

"Thanks."

"You're just in time for lunch. You're supposed to get settled
in your room and meet here to walk over to the commons."

"Cool, thanks . . ." I turn to the hallway, pull the cords and
start rolling my suitcases.

He follows me, then I hear him sighing.

"Has wheels huh?"

"Yeah," I say wondering when he's going to take his ass on.

"Let me do that for you."

Feel his hand on top of mine, taking hold of the cords. I let
go, if he wants to do it let him. Must think he's gonna get brownie
points. We keep walking down the hallway and I start to get lost,
twisting and turning, looking into people's rooms, white guys lying
around listening to that rock shit. See some girls lying up with some
of the guys. Haven't seen one black face except for Jamal and he
don't count. Seems like all the girls have their doors open and they
got big stuffed animals. Jamal stops and leans against the wall,
looking like he's really done something.

"Well, here it is."

"Yeah," I say and unlock the door and as fast as I can I reach
for the suitcases but he beats me to it and wheels it into the room.
Smiling again like he's so slick. Posing by the window, trying to
look good.

"So have I made amends?"

"Amends? What you amending?"

Shaking his head again, like I'm so dumb.

"I'm trying to make up with you."

"You don't need to do that. There's nothing to make up."

Shrugs like he's so tired. Like he's tried everything and nothing's working but he's still gonna try. All this to get some.

"You ought to let me buy you dessert. We could have coffee at this café on the beach."

Got to smile. He really ain't gonna quit. Like I'd be caught alone with him again. Wouldn't trust him to shoot him.

"Thanks, but I bet they got a lot planned for me to do. Nothing personal but I'm tired so . . ."

I open the door wide and stand there waiting to see how long it's going to take him to get the message. But he ignores what's right there in his face.

"Time to go," I say and finally after looking at the back of his hands he gets up and walks to the door. Then just when I think he's out, he stops in the doorway, milking drama, and turns, standing inches from my face, serious and sexy, playing his ace.

"I'm not going to stop until you forgive me. Give me a chance to show you I'm not . . . what you think."

Maybe it's the voice, or the move being so obvious, but I can't keep a straight face. Crack a smile.

"What do you think I think?" I say it but I don't know why. Must be slipping. Now he's never going to leave.

"You know, a jerk. You'll see. I'm not what you think."

He reaches for my hand and squeezes it, gives me a look, a look I've only seen on soap operas. Weak love daddy moves. And he's gone trotting around a corner. Seems like they always got to run off when they think they're up to something, getting away with something.

Bad enough she talks to somebody like they're stupid. Smiling and shit, some really dumb black woman wearing an afro, hair turning gray and all and she's wearing this jungle print thinking she's coming across like an African queen. Talking to us about how we have to study and have a sense of purpose and believe in ourselves and all that yang. Give me a summer job and an apartment and I'm cool. I'll take care of the fucking grades. What is it, two dozen of us, in this transition program, and just about all of them look like hippies, just like the white people. Go for the tour, see the campus, see the bay, see the trails, the trees, too many fucking trees, too fucking cold for June. Everybody seems so impressed. Like this is it. Like this is heaven, so "beautiful" I keep hearing. All these black faces I've never seen before. So soft, in their bell bottoms and tie dye. Straight out of MTV. Bet they've never even driven near the inner city. Not one of them said more than a "hello" to me but that's cool. Not too much in the mood for talking anyhow. Fucking black phonies.

Been coming here to the commons and having my dinner for a couple days now. Always take this seat as far away from people as I can get. Face the ocean. I can see it, the sun setting and it makes me think . . . what a big-assed mistake.

"What's it like?"
    "It's like Margot on Mars."
    "You like it?"
    "No."
    "Come on home."
    "Yeah, right. How am I gonna stay up all year if I can't stay a week."
    "I don't know. If you don't like it, why stay?"
    "Look, F. Why don't you just say it. You want me to come home. But I ain't. You know that. I don't like it here but I don't like it there either, so that's how it goes."
    "Any black folk up there but you?"
    "Yeah. Couple Oreos and some boozey bitches fronting cause they got cars and weaves and went to white schools."
    "You ain't got into their shit yet?"
    "Naw, it ain't like that. Just checking out the classes, seeing about work for the summer. But it's too dead up here. It's like somebody killed it."
    "Isn't that what you wanted?"
    "Yeah, guess so."
    "You miss me?"

"You? Do you miss me?"

". . . Yeah . . ."

"Then you better pick me up."

"I told you. I'm gonna be out of town. Business."

"Not that line again. You were supposed to be out of town three days ago. You better stay your ass home."

"Yeah. Right, Margot. Do what you say but don't do what you do."

"So you ain't gonna pick me up."

"I'm not gonna be here. I'm gonna be in Santa Barbara. What I'm gonna do? Stuff's happening here, I gotta go, you oughta be behind me on this. I'd tell you what's up but . . ."

"I didn't ask you all that."

Hear him breathing heavy on the other end like he's pissed for real.

"Don't try to talk like that, like you punking me."

"I'm not talking to you no way. All I asked for was a yes or no. You can't give me that?"

"I told you . . . what you want me to say?"

"Yes or no!"

"Don't talk to me like that."

"Yes or no! Can't you say it. If you ain't gonna do it you ought to be man enough to tell me straight out."

"Margot, you pissing me off."

"Yes or no!"

"Hell no. I ain't doing it. Get your own fucking ride!" Bam! Slammed that phone down. Guess I got carried away. But he's still gonna give me that ride. He's gonna change his mind.

Thought this was going to be a vacation. Do nothing. Maybe have fun. Yeah right. Already got us writing papers. "Gun Control: Right or Wrong?" Depends on who's got the gun.

Gun control is possible only when people in the community feel safe. Where I live nobody feels safe, everybody has a gun, and people keep getting shot.

That's it, that's all I got to say. Still got to bullshit for two pages. Therefore, consequently, furthermore, and in conclusion. Still short.

Knew I wasn't going to like this from the get go, getting naked in front of a bunch of women. Showering in a big room so everybody can look at your ass. Guys have to do that. Waiting till midnight and take my knife. Big bathroom is empty like a tomb. Cold too. Maybe I oughta just wash off . . . but no, I ain't gonna be stinking in class. Have somebody thinking that black bitch needs a bath. Get the water going, wish I could take a shower in the robe. One of those two-minute showers and get the hell out. Ain't even going to dry. Got all this shit in my hands, towel, soap, toothbrush, trying to turn the water off somehow the shower door swings open before I get my robe on and there's this pale-faced white girl by the sinks who looks shocked to see me and backs up real smooth.

"Have a nice night," I say to do my part for race relations.

Black hippie chick with a plate loaded down with salad passes me in my corner of the cafeteria. Saw her checking me out, actually smiling my way instead of looking down like most of these spuds be doing. See her going to the other side of the commons, sitting with that table of stuck-up B's with weaves. Oh well, back to the draft. Third paragraph:

> Some people wonder how the criminal element gets their hands on so many weapons? They steal them, that's how.

Stuck again.

"Hi. My name's Mandy."

The hippie chick is standing over me, smiling nervous. "Margot," I say and try smiling back. She looks like I'm scaring her.

"Why don't you sit with us," she says pointing to the table with the stuck-up B's.

"Thanks . . . but I'm trying to finish this paper for my class."

Girl's getting more shaky by the second looking everywhere but at me. Standing at attention, holding a soda like she's going to hand it to me. If she got something to say she oughta say it.

"You're in the transition program?"

"Yeah. I've seen you in the writing workshop."

"Oh," she says and pulls up a chair. She's got good hair, just wears it wild and she's wearing a Malcolm X button and a cross. Probably a Catholic school girl.

"Are you from L.A.?" she asks seriously like it's leading to something. More of the third degree. Sure bet somebody told her I'm from the projects.

"No. I'm from Compton."

She looks startled like the rest of them.

"I'm from Compton too. I went to school there. Sacred Heart before we moved to Pasadena."

"Yeah, I went to Bolt."

"Bolt? That's not in Compton. My brother graduated from Bolt about ten years ago."

"I live kind of close to Compton."

She don't even blink when she catches me in the middle of a lie. Being from Compton has more of a ring.

"You shouldn't be alone. Specially since you're coming here next year. Some of us are planning to be roommates. Some of the dorms have suites."

"Oh." She ain't going to leave. Should have acted deranged.

"I'm really behind on this paper."

"Oh, nobody's worried about that. The placement test is not till the fall."

"Oh." She isn't leaving unless I come. Going to sit there like a zombie. So, I take my notebook and my tray and walk across the cafeteria. Hate walking across the commons, all these eyes on me. People checking me out, checking us out. We get to the table and the weaves and hippies say hi. Table of bright-eye bushy-tailed black girls.

"I'm Margot," I say to all of them and look at my cold hamburger.

"We're all prelaw," the light-skinned weave says. A pretty girl sporting lots of gold bangles.

"Yeah, I like the law," I say and look down not wanting to say more. Rather figure out who's head weave and if I'm gonna be cool with them. Then Miss Diana Ross on the other side of the table calls to me. She don't have a weave just long straight hair like a Barbie doll. Lots of makeup too, like who's she gonna impress.

"We need another roommate. You want to share a suite with us?" Miss Ross asks.

Oh, I see. They need me for the all-black bloc in the dorm.

"Marcy asked me to room with her. I told her I'd think about it."

"Mandy," Mandy says patting my hand to correct me.

"So you're not sure? You need a place to live, so why not live with us? By the way I didn't get your name."

"Margot. M-A-R-G-O-T. You don't pronounce the T. By the way, what's your name?"

Lips want to make that *B* sound. Everybody's looking at me like I just nutted up on her. Guess I did but just a little bit. Miss Ross is all big-eyed looking at her friends, fake shock stuck on her face.

"I gotta work on this paper. Catch y'all later."

I'm up and outta there with all these eyes on me, black ones, white ones, all of them riding me.

"François, it's me. How you doing?"

"It's one A.M. What you calling so late for?"

"Cause I want to talk to you. Is that a thing with you?"

"If I called you at one you'd be bitchin about it being too late and all kinds of shit."

"When's the last time I got mad at you about calling. I don't remember doing nothing like that."

"Look! I'm just tired of you dogging me. See, it makes me want to do the same thing to you."

I ain't gonna get mad. I didn't call to get mad at him. Why did I call? Make up to break up.

"I was wrong talking to you like I was doing last time. I didn't mean to piss you off and sound like a bitch. It was wrong."

He's not saying a thing. Hear him breathing, thinking about it, considering what he's gonna say.

"Why you gotta act like that. Like you got to be evil if something ain't going your way?"

"What you want me to say? I told you I was wrong. Want me to tell you I'm a bitch? Okay, I'm a bitch. You want me to apologize, I apologize. What else you want?"

"I don't want nothing."

"Then everything's cool."

"Yeah, everything's cool."

"You still going to Santa Barbara?"

"Yeah, it's business. I got to go. Leaving tomorrow."

"What about school? How you gonna graduate?"

"I ain't worried about that. Just leaving a couple weeks early. Teachers say they're gonna pass me."

"You believe that? Something for nothing. They don't give breaks. Most of them just lie to get you out their face."

"I ain't worried about that. I got other things to worry about . . . I've got to go, get out of town. Ollie got me into something."

"Yeah, what, a bank robbery?"

"What's that's supposed to mean?"

"Nothing. I just don't understand why you need to go to Santa Barbara before you graduate."

"The police might be looking for me but it ain't nothing I can't handle just like I'm gonna handle Ollie if I see him again."

"Well, I hope you can handle all of that."

"What's that's supposed to mean?"

"Nothing. I hope you can handle it."

"I don't need your hope. I am gonna handle it."

"Well I just called to see how you were doing."

"I'm doing fine."

"I can see . . ."

"Why you got to say silly shit all the time."

"Am I being silly?"

"I don't know. I don't care. I gotta go."

"Oh, all right. But . . ."

"But what?"

"Are you gonna pick me up from the airport?"

* * *

"Margot, what do you think of 'A Rose for Emily'?"

Me? Why me? Eleven other colored people in here and she calls on me.

"I thought it was good."

Guess that was the worst thing possible I could have said from the way she's smiling at me like I need to check myself.

"Okay, you thought it was good, anything more?"

Back on me. Isn't she supposed to sweat somebody else after I made a fool of myself? Grinning, grinning like a pumpkin cause I can't think . . . Mandy is looking down, must be embarrassed for me, but Miss Ross the super weave is smiling like this is the floor show.

"Isn't this story, doesn't it strike you in a particular way? Is there one word to sum up the entire tone of the text?"

"It's sick." Why I'm mumbling? She's gonna ask again.

"Excuse me. What did you say?"

"Nothing. I was clearing my throat.

"Did you say the story's sick?"

"Yeah, I guess."

She looks down at a notebook and writes something. Her fingers are so big seems like it would be hard to write. She shouldn't be sitting at a desk in front of us. Her legs are so fat they're hanging off the chair. Ought to hide them things.

"Margot, you're right. The story reeks of perversion. But what kind of perversion? What has twisted poor Emily's mind to the point where she does these horrible acts?"

"Is it sexual?" Mandy asks in her Catholic school voice.

"Yes! And you'll know that. It's obvious. Think about it. Her father won't allow her to leave him so when he leaves her, she feels cheated because all she has is him."

"Did she poison Homer because she didn't want him to get away? So she could keep him like a stuffed animal? Seems like she's kind of hung up on bodies."

Ms. Bristol smiles her big smile. It looks good on her, like she's a huge Cabbage Patch doll. "Yes. She killed Homer not for the reasons a hunter kills a buck. She killed him because she needed to keep him. She needed to keep him there beside her in that bed for the rest of her life. She kept what she knew was there to claim, the corpse. The corpse wouldn't leave her, wouldn't abuse her, wouldn't prevent her from being what she wanted to be. The corpse wouldn't keep her from doing what she needed to do. It was enough for her to sleep next to a rotting corpse. Homer putrefying in the love bed was enough to get her through life.''

"Why?" I ask not knowing that I wanted to know. Least she's interesting, not like some of these classes I've had to sit through.

"Because love is strange," Ms. Bristol sort of sings with a big grin.

So this is what Michaels was saying about college. Said I'd meet people that liked to talk like him. People who have opinions about everything. Ms. Bristol takes a stack of papers from her briefcase and passes them around. When they reach me I don't really want them. Don't want to see the grade. But I take it, and already I'm depressed, look how it's marked up, scribbles everywhere on the first page. Bet the second is even worse. I turn to it and see more of the same and at the bottom, in the margin are all these comments and the only one I can make out is "*SEE ME!*" Yeah, great. Everybody is leaving and me, I get to stay after class and talk to the quarter-ton Cabbage Patch doll. Great, Mandy's at the door lingering, trying to see what's happening, then she's gone and Ms. Bristol puts her notebook down and looks at me.

"Margot, come over here. I want to discuss your paper."

"Okay," I say and sort of stumble into the seat next to her.

"Did you read the comments?"

"Yes," I say lying.

"Take a moment and look over them."

I nod and look over the pencil marks, scribbles, and try to make sense of them. A couple are obvious but most are just too messy to understand.

"Margot, I'll be frank with you. You're a very smart young lady. I found your essay about gun control compelling and original. You have a genuine sense of humor, something that I appreciate. I want you to understand what I'm trying to say. If you're going to make it here you're going to have to be committed. I marked up your essay because I want you to see how 'they' will see your work.

People who have no interest in seeing you make it. Any mistake you make proves them right, that you're another Affirmative Action failure. You've got to really work, really try to do your best.''

She's looking at me so sincerely it's embarrassing. Guess the paper was a total fuckup. "What grade did I get on the paper?"

She smiles that big-faced grin and shakes her head. "What grade do you think you received?"

"I don't know, a C?"

She shakes her head again. "Your paper was an A by my standards. But my standards aren't everyone's standards. I'm always grateful for a paper like yours."

"Oh," I say. I got an A so I guess I'll listen, be polite.

"I'm supposed to evaluate your work, help you to see where you are in relation to other students. But with you it's very simple. You are going to have to work very hard at your papers and no one will be able to find fault with your abilities."

I nod. I should be happy. "Thanks," I say and stand up to go. "Other students," yeah right, what she means to say is white students. Guess none of the other blacks and browns need a pep talk but me.

"Margot, you'll be in my section for English 1A."

Get out of there thinking maybe I don't need so much encouragement. See myself slaving over another fucking paper to please her, otherwise "they" will get me. That's how it'll be, living up to my potential. Maybe I oughta get pregnant, then I can rag to my baby about potential.

If I lie still long enough it'll happen. I'll fall asleep and I wake up and it'll be time to go. Why won't he answer? Rings and rings and rings and nothing. Guess he don't have the beeper with him. Yeah right, he just don't want to pick me up. He better.

Room's too fucking cold. Heater's on and ain't doing a damn thing. What I'm supposed to do, sleep in a coat? Rings and rings— where the fuck is he? Not going to do it, call that fool. François better be there, I ain't playing.

Punk ain't there. Just straight out dogging me. So what does he think's gonna happen? Gonna go deal to rich white people and fuck rich white girls and dress in silk suits and grow a ponytail like Tommy. Fools can't get over *Miami Vice*, think they would since it's nothing but reruns. I know what Tommy wants, some of that blond bootee. Think he'd go out and buy him some since he can't seem to get none with his mack daddy lines or his new clothes or his daddy's money. Don't know what François sees in that fool. Maybe it's a man thing. Maybe they like each other. Yeah, better Tommy than me.

"Who is it!"

"It's me. I need a ride from the airport tomorrow."

"A ride—calling at eleven? What's wrong with you?"

"It ain't late."

"Late? What you know about late. You ever had a job? A real job? Not just braiding nappy heads. Something where you've got to be on time? No, you ain't. And hell yeah it's late!"

Hang up hang up hang up! Listen to him breathing all heavy—drunk-ass fool. "So you gonna give me a ride?"

"I thought that hook-head boyfriend was gonna pick you up. He in jail or something?"

Fuck it, hang it up. Fuck him, hang it up.

"Don't worry about it . . . I'll get home . . ."

"Wait a minute!" hear him yelling before I slam it down. "I'll pick you up. What time?"

A question . . . fool's actually asking a question.

"Three. I get in at three in the afternoon."

"Three?"

"Yeah, it's flight 557 Delta."

"Got it."

"Okay, bye."

"Wait a minute."

"What?"

"You better be on time. I ain't waiting around."

"Yeah, right. Bye." All because of you I had to talk to him. Gonna pay you back. You'll see.

*   *   *

Who's knocking? Probably Mandy. Don't want to talk about no dorm. Probably never gonna come back to this fucking icebox. Open it expecting to see her looking all timid like I'm gonna slap her or something but there's Jamal smiling like I'm the best thing he ever saw. He squints and frowns.

"How's it going? Something wrong?"

"Wrong? Nothing's wrong. What's up with you asking me what's wrong?"

Shrugging like he don't want to get me mad.

"Your eyes are red; you've been crying. Something must be wrong and you've got that big coat on and the heater's blasting."

Got to be drunk looking at me like I need the attention. Like I need a shoulder to lean on.

"Yeah, so my eyes are red. Maybe I've been smoking. What you came by for?"

I step back from the door and he steps in, smiling. Must think he caught me slipping.

"I want to know if you'd care to go with me to a club in Santa Cruz. We could have dessert."

Oh yeah, he's fat and happy. Gonna be nice and spend a little money before he collects his pudding.

"No. I don't think so. I'm going home tomorrow. I've got to pack."

Look at him looking around to see my bags already packed like he caught me in a lie as if I give a fuck. Standing there blinking his eyes, probably wants me to dim the lights. Better stop smoking or drinking or whatever, cause the lights are staying on.

"I know you're leaving. That's why I came by to make sure you're leaving with a good impression of me so that when you come back . . . maybe we can be friends."

"Friends? I know what you mean when you say friends but they ain't gonna be no haps on that friend thing. I got a boyfriend and if I need another one I let you know."

"Friends? That word must be really loaded for you. For me it just means people who like each other."

"Yeah? Where I come from when somebody says they want to be friends they mean they want to fuck you and leave you at the motel to pay the bill."

"Me?" he says pointing at his chest with that skull with roses behind it T-shirt. Freaky devil worship shit.

"You've got me wrong thinking I want to put the moves on you." He blinks and bulges his eyes again, must be what he does when he's lying. "I'd be lying if I said I don't find you attractive but it's not about that with me. I just want to get to know you."

"Yeah," I say, softening just for a second to see what he'll do. See if his eyes are gonna bulge, bet they do.

"It's a nice ride along the ocean. It's a neat place. They play live music. I'm a gentleman, you don't have to worry about me." He stops and blinks his eyes and there they go, bulging away. Lying dog.

"Look, I know you, I don't care what you say, you're a dog and if you try something stupid . . ." I pull it out of my coat pocket and crackle it, blue sparks jump the gap to let him know it's got a fresh set.

"You come prepared," he says stepping back.

"Yeah, cause there's a dog behind every tree."

"Oh."

He stands there staring at the black plastic stun gun like he's never seen one.

"Are we still going out or do you want to forget about it?"

"No, I'm ready. I still want to take you," he says walking to the door backwards like I'm gonna give his little ass a jolt.

Outside, the cold wind off the ocean stings my face. Then I see what he's driving, a fucking little banged-up sports car and he's got the top down. Cold as hell and he's got the top down. I knew that this was gonna be a big mistake.

"Cute, huh? It's a 'seventy-six MG. I'm rebuilding it."

Grinning like I ought to be impressed. Got it parked under a light, with a lock on the steering wheel like somebody's gonna want to steal his shit.

"You gonna put the top up?"

"Top?" he says shrugging.

"It's cold. You gonna put the top up?"

"I don't have a top . . . yet. I'm going to get one next month. But I got a blanket. The heater works real well. And the moon's out. It'll be nice."

Boy just lies to me straight out. I'm gonna freeze my ass off. Ought to just turn around and go back in the dorm but I get in like a fool. See him grinning, happy, happy little boy. He pulls out, kicking gravel like he did in the van, fishtailing into the street. Soon as we get away from the dorm it's real dark, even with the moon out and the fog lights. Nothing but black but as we climb through gaps in the wall of trees along the road I can see the silver ocean.

"Listen to this," Jamal says and he puts in a tape. Can't even see his eyes, but I can see the tips of his mini dreads. Music comes on, lots of strings, and some guy singing falsetto. It's the Delfonics, "Didn't I Blow Your Mind?" Jamal comes in. At first he sounds really bad, like a nasally white boy, then he gets into it and he sounds sort of like the song.

The song ends and a new one starts and he keeps singing. I'd rather sit here listening to the engine roaring and the wind whipping by the car but I guess if it makes him happy. The blanket and the heater keep the cold off. And I know this fool is trying to scare me driving these twisting roads like it's some kind of ride at Disneyland. We come out of the dark into open road, driving along the ocean. I see lights, a small town or something. He finally stops singing when we get to the town. We drive right up to the beach and he turns up a road to where it's lit like a real city, 7-Elevens and shit. We pass some nice-looking places where we could get something to eat but I know he's gonna pick some place that's like his car, fucked up. Whatever part of town we're in now looks run down, tired old houses and trash in the streets, can't even see the ocean. He parks under one of the few lights on this street. I see a bar with some bums hanging out in front of it and a couple yards with construction equipment.

"So how does your boyfriend handle you?" he asks as we get out of the car.

"My boyfriend doesn't handle me."

"Oh. I didn't mean to get you mad. I just seem to get you so mad. Even my singing gets you mad. Maybe he knows how not to upset you."

"Don't sweat it. He upsets me in a big way."

He walks around the car smiling smoothly and takes my hand. At first I think about jerking it away but I don't, if it means something to him, gets him off, cause it don't mean a thing to me. We seem to be going into somebody's house, from the outside it looks kind of like a rockhouse, run down with bag people hanging out on the steps. We go inside the dirtiest club I've ever seen. Straw's everywhere, straw mats on the floor, coffee sacks on the wall, big painting of a lion is over the coffee counter and reggae is louder than when fools try to rock the neighborhood from their trucks and the grungiest-looking people, not anything like the hippies on campus. Some of the white guys got thick matted dooky braids for hair. And the white girls look so poor with their thirdhand clothes I'm way out of place with tights and a baggy top even if I did get them from the Crenshaw swap meet. Everybody's drinking big steaming bowls of something and smoking cigarettes. Got my eyes burning. Pull my hand from Jamal and point to what they're drinking. "What's that?" First he doesn't understand. "What they're drinking?" "Cappuccino, you want one?" I ignore the question like I don't hear him. He looks cute even with the braids, makes him look like he's got on a crown or a Jughead Jones hat. It's stupid standing here with everybody staring at us and then they're waving and calling to Jamal like he's Mr. Big Stuff. Almost all the tables are taken but Jamal finds one near the door, cause I can breathe a little bit and it ain't so loud. "You want a cappuccino?" Jamal shouts.

"Whatever," I say having to shout over the music. Before he can get up to go order one of the hippies with the dooky braids comes up, smiling at Jamal then at me. Too toothy for me so I turn my back but I see him shaking Jamal's hand, shouting into his ear. Jamal's laughing, not again. Don't want to see him laugh anymore tonight. Hear him, "Man, she's beautiful," Jamal slaps him on the arm and turns to me.

"Margot," he shouts, "this is Blue." He sticks his hand out to shake mine. Guess I got to, shake his hand and he leans over and yells, "You're beautiful!"

"Thanks." The boy is just grinning like he can't get over me. Jamal's shaking his head over how Blue's reacting, just enjoying it. It's embarrassing, dopey white guy and silly black boy acting stupid over me in a place like this.

Finally they go for the drinks. Man behind the counter making the coffees, a six-something beanpole of a fairy waves them to the front and shakes Jamal's hand. This is ridiculous like Jamal is king of the hippies. Bet he has a dozen half-white sunshine babies running around. Do I really want to spend the rest of the night around here watching Jamal lord over these nuts, listening to this weird-assed island music, looking at all these weird-assed people. Up in the front there's a little more room, a space cleared with amps and a drum set and keyboards and mikes and a couple of white girls in smocks are doing this stupid dance, looks like the Watusi, having a good, spaced-out time. Jamal's coming back with the drinks and Blue's bringing the white girls with them. The girls are beaming, all budded out. They just run up ahead of Jamal and Blue and sit themselves right in front of me, too curious to hide anything.

"Hi, Margot. I'm Jane and this is Anna. Jamal's been talking about you since you got here."

Jane chick has a tiny diamond stud in her nose and about six earrings on each ear. Anna looks pretty average except for the buzz cut she's sporting looking like Bart Simpson. Everybody is so happy. Too happy, these girls must be smoking only the best weed.

"Nice to meet you," I say and wait them out till Jamal comes up with the coffees. Blue sits between the girls smiling just like them. Happiest people ever. Jamal puts the coffee down in front of me and some kind of cake. "Try it," he says.

"I'm not hungry."

"It's good."

I smile cause I don't care what he says. I'm not eating anything from this place, probably got poison in the icing.

"May I try some of your carrot cake?" the Anna girl asks.

"You can have it."

"Really!" she says all excited like I've given her some money and she turns to Jane and they take the cake and start eating. Must have missed breakfast. I smile cause I don't know what to say. Blue turns to Jane and puts his arm around her. Guess they have a love thing. Then after a minute of cooling out Blue and Jamal and the girls get up and push through that sea of heads to the space where the girls had been dancing. They start tuning up looking too serious like they're counting money, whispering and making signs with their hands. So that's it, Jamal's in a band, that's why he's got the attitude and all. Blue's on the drum, Jane's on the keyboards, Anna's got the bass and I guess Jamal's gonna lead. The crowd quiets and they start, what do you expect, they sound kind of weak. They play all right but the singing ain't cutting it. None of them can harmonize. Weak. Some song, think it's called "No Woman, No Cry," and man, Pee Wee Hermanish. Crowd is into it though, bobbing their heads and acting like this is it. I can see me singing lead. Wouldn't that be cool, singing for hippies. Jamal starts to dance all stiff legged, with his elbows close to his waist, moving his hips, and with those shorts on he looks way silly. First song finishes and he points into the crowd, fuck, he's pointing at me.

"I and I going to dedicate the next song, 'Waiting in Vain,' to my special friend, Margot."

He starts that dumb dance, swaying side to side, and somebody turns a spot on them. He looks good but that hair, little dread spikes gotta go. What's he singing that song for, like I'm gonna be so impressed I'm gonna hop in bed with him. Must think I'm easily impressed. Pointing both fingers at me . . . "I don't want to wait in vain for your love . . ." I'm shrugging and everybody staring at me. What is this? Jamal's getting emotional, jumping up and down, straining like he's got to yank the song out, and he's singing like he's some kind of Rasta, I and I, my ass. Can't believe it—dropping to his knees and begging, moaning—Jesus, what he's begging for? He should have some pride about himself. Finally the damn song ends and everybody is up and applauding, solid noise. Jane comes up with a big floppy dread hat and passes it around and the marks are putting money in it. They really like this stuff. By the time it reaches me it's full with dollars. I put in a bill and pass it on thinking what a scam, money for moaning.

"How'd you like it?"

Guess he expects me to be blown away like I'm sitting next to God, in God's fucked-up little sports car, driving on the fucking darkest night of the year with one arm around me when he needs two to steer and shift.

"It was cool."

"Hope I didn't embarrass you but I needed inspiration."

Make the move. Fat-assed chance.

"I wasn't embarrassed."

"So what did you really think?"

"You asked me that."

"Aw come on, I'm not going to get mad. What did you think?"

"They pay y'all to sing there?"

"You . . . nobody says the kinds of things you say."

He goes off again, laughing like a fucking lunatic. I turn up the radio, rather listen to his crazy music than hear him laugh. He chuckles through a couple songs and finally when I'm starting to like this African-sounding stuff, he pulls his arm from around my shoulder and takes my hand.

"I know we don't sound so good. I don't mind admitting it now because we're going to get there."

Glad to hear the brother's honest.

He pulls into the driveway of the dormitory with all the drama of a car chase. Soon as he stops I'm getting out but the car is so small I have to kind of slide onto the ground.

"Get a real car," I say dusting myself off.

He looks at me all sheepishly, like I should lean in there and give him a kiss.

"Did you enjoy yourself?"

"Yeah, I did," I say after pausing to make him sweat.

"Well . . ." he says. He wants to come up.

"It's cold out here. I gotta get some sleep," I say and lean over and shake his hand and head for the dorms. He stays there, the MG idling, watching me unlock the glass door. I turn back around.

"It was fun," I say with conviction.

He smiles and waves once I'm inside.

It was fun, now that I think about it.

At the luggage carousel it's the same thing, rushing to get their stuff, to get the hell out. But I sit back and watch the suitcases fall. Maybe François will come running up ready to grab my bags and take me home but I don't see nothing but a bunch of people.

What'd Jamal say, "May I call you?" Just like a white boy. "I'll call you," I said so he wouldn't get to begging then he gave it to me, a small black box and inside, a thin silver chain, an ankle bracelet.

"So what are you giving me this for?" He smiled like he knew he was impressing me.

"Friendship," he said lying through his teeth.

I should have gone, just walked away and waved and promised to call but I didn't. I stood there too long and he leaned over and kissed me. A weak, friendship kiss.

"I'm looking forward to seeing you again. Maybe I'll visit."

"Yeah, if that's what you want to do."

"Yes. That's what I want to do," he said nodding his head.

Most everybody has already got their bags so I guess I ought to get mine. Daddy's gonna have a shit fit if I'm a half second late. I go to the carousel and yank off my big-assed suitcases. Why did I take all this shit? Pull loose the straps and wheel them away. Outside, I sit on one of the suitcases, high up and right on the edge of the traffic island so there's no way he can say he didn't see me. So fucking bright out here but can't find my damned shades so I got to deal with it. Why doesn't he come up, the bug booming making everybody look, and he'll have on that stupid black sweatsuit, and a black cap with the hood up over it and he wonders why the police be fucking with him. Dogged me out. Just fucked up forever. If he ain't about getting here it's over forever, never ever going to talk to his ass again. Dead as a doorknob. Be singing "The Love I Lost," like he just has to be a fuckup. Got a new fuckup, no more of his moods and his mistakes. It's all over. Here's the truck, so fucking big I can see it two blocks away, driving like he's gonna kill somebody. Sees the cops and slows it down and swoops into the passenger lane. Gets out in his pressed jeans and creased workshirt, fresh from a day of giving orders and eating donuts. Don't bother to look at me, takes the suitcases and tosses them like they're trash bags into the bed of the truck. I get in and he's already rolling. I hate F. He should have picked me up.

"Did you have a good time? Scare the white folks? What you're crying for? You pregnant?"

Let his stupid ass wonder.

10

Tommy

■

"Get off the bed. Get up and face the day my brother. Time's passing, time's money, get your lazy ass up!"

I do not have time for this. Do we not have the setup? Yes, we have the setup. Did I find us a too clean apartment? Do I not have the clientele, the connections, the product? Yes on all counts but my associate got a fucking love jones.

"Come on, get up, we got to go. See the ocean, the chicks."

Takes the pillow off his head, pissed off yet again.

"So why do you need me to go. Go on yourself."

"Well, seems to me we're in business together and this is business. What if something comes up and you're not there? What if I need you to watch my back."

"Nothing's gonna happen," he says and puts the pillow back over his head. This brother needs to check himself.

"How do you know that?"

"Because you're going to the beach, what happens at the beach?"

I don't say nothing. I'll just stand here until he understands I'm not going anywhere.

"Go ahead, you don't need to watch me. I'm cool. I'll be here when you're ready to go to the club."

Couple minutes pass with me leaning against the wall looking at his bookcase. Brother's going to do some reading, *Autobiography of Malcolm X*, and some other books I haven't seen before. Surprised he don't have the Bible up there. Margot gave him this shit. Man, she's trying to turn him into a Moslem or something.

"All right, if you're gonna stand there looking at me sleeping."

Worked. Bugged his ass into moving but I got to get him out of the black cause he looks like a sorry-assed gangster. Talk about a brother going through changes. Oughta thank God he's got a true homey like me looking out for him.

"Okay let's go."

"Yeah . . . but you oughta change, wear something cool. You look like you ready to stop and rob."

"Yeah, yeah, let's go."

Nothing I can do with him. Gonna get us stopped, rousted like typical niggahs.

"Let's take the bug, put the top down."

"Whatever."

Sure, the bug's ratty but I don't want all that salt spray fucking with the 5.0's paint job. Just got it done.

We get to rolling and it's cool. Top down, and radio booming, everywhere I turn fly white girls of every shape and size. Gonna get two of each.

"Check this out, F. We walk out to the wharf and get some fish and clock the freaks. Nothing to do till tonight cept kick it."

"Kick it? Thought you said this was business."

"Chill, my brother. You're just too too serious. Can't you chill?"

"Chill?" F shakes his head frowning like I'm wasting his time. Shit, this ain't gonna work, putting up with his attitudes but I ain't gonna say anything. Let him figure it out for himself that you don't dog your partners cause you got problems with your woman. I hand him the two dollars for parking and he gives it to the brother with the flattop working the booth. One of the few black faces I've seen up here. He's nodding at F like he wants to know what happening with us, but F is too much into his own thing to pay any attention.

"What's up, B?" I say.

"Ain't no thing."

"It's happening at the Inferno."

"Yeah? I'll check."

"Cool," I say, and F rolls us onto the wharf. He hooks it into a parking spot right next to the fish stand.

"What you want, shrimp and chips?"

"Yeah, that's cool."

I go up to the stand and check out the fish. Always like looking at fresh fish, specially black shiny catfish on ice, but I never get fish. I always get the shrimp and chips. When I get to the front of the line the white boy behind the counter is smiling at me like he knows me, "Two shrimp and chips." "Sure," he says and gets right to it. Probably thinks I'm a football player or something. But I like this, sun and surf and chicks and white boys serving me instead of some pissed-off, garlic-eating Korean. Two cops on mountain bikes ride up. I knew it. Think they're so slick, checking out F on the sly. Shit. They're stopping. The really pink one comes out with a radio phone and starts talking while still scoping on F. The Mexican-looking one rolls up to him. The boy don't know what's going on, just sitting there on the bench, staring out at the ocean like one of those black Hallmark cards. The cop cruises up in front of him to block that route to shore. Man, I wonder what homeboy's gonna do? I hope he don't nut up. The cop's talking to him, pleasant enough. Yep, got that stupid hood over his head with that fucking baseball cap. Stupid gangster-looking fool. Least he's not scowling. The cop says something and F hands his wallet over and the cop takes a peek and hands it right back. Guess it's no big deal. He says something else to F and rides away.

"Here it is, your order," the white boy is saying pushing the plates of shrimp and chips and the Cokes toward me like I can't see them. Guess he's been trying to get my attention but I didn't hear a thing. I take the food over to F and put it down in front of him but he just ignores it and shakes his big head.

"What the cops were sweating you for?"

"Same old shit, think they'd have something better to do. They see I'm not up to nothing."

I'm not going to say it. I'm not gonna say, I told you don't dress like a criminal. The brother's intelligent. He should know that. And he's got clothes, clothes in the closet, in his suitcase, no need for him to be dressing like that. Fuck it, I'm gonna eat.

"Hey, you gonna sit there or are you gonna grub."

"Naw . . . I ain't hungry. I'll . . . be back."

Well, if he ain't gonna eat, don't want it to waste. Big shrimp, in a nice batter, kind of spicy. Man, polished that off too quickly. Feels good, cooling outside in the Cali sun, couple white girls in bikinis walk by, oh yeah, just like a commercial. Getting sleepy . . . getting kind of chilly too, sun's going to be setting. Where is that fool? Maybe he killed himself. Jumped right off the wharf. Shit. Get up on the table and see for his stupid half-assed self. Nothing, just more chicks. Maybe he's waiting in the car or something. But before I get there, I see this freak standing by the railing with her bike, alone, looking at the ocean. Something out of *Playboy*, blond with a bootee, wearing a high-cut one-piece, split to her waist. Got to talk to that Tender Ronie. What I'm gonna say . . . hey, what's going on with you? Naw, that ain't gonna get it. How you doing, I'm from out of town, where's it live around here? Naw, that won't do. Fuck it. I'm just gonna do it. Slide in next to her, catch a peek, see if she looks as good from the front as the rear. Oh yes, lord. Let me get some of this. How do I look? I look good, all in white, got my baggy white shirt, and shorts, looking chilly. She's got to be impressed.

"Hiya doing?"

She turns and eyes me, smiles. Yes. This is one fine bitch.

"I'm new around here. What's the live nightspot?"

She turns to me. Oh yeah, she likes what she sees.

"You don't have plans for tonight?"

"No, no not really. I got something to do but I can cut out. Why, what you have in mind?"

"Here," she says and unzips a belt pouch and comes out with a pamphlet. It says *Life Firm* on the front. Guess she thinks I need to lose some pounds.

"What's this about?" I say and honey pie slips closer to me. "It's about realizing your potential."

"I'm down for that. What time should I pick you up?"

"We can meet there. It's a party. All my friends go."

"What do you do there?"

She laughs at me, her teeth are too white and her hair is gold curls. I know she don't have no damn weave. So what if I got to talk to somebody about diets.

"It's very important. You'll meet the warmest people there."

"And afterward?"

"Afterward, who knows . . ."

What a smile, she pats me on the shoulder and gets on her bike and kicks, her high ass just floating away. Fuck!

"What's your name?"

"Giselle."

"Tommy!" She waves and weaves the bike between the cars and couples. Oh yeah, tonight. What's the address? Right here on the pamphlet. Now where's homeboy? I get to walking, cutting through the crowd, keeping my eyes open. I get to the bug but he's not there, must be off the wharf, maybe he met a babe. Some white chicks probably go for that gangster look. I get beyond all the shops to where the wharf narrows before it drops to the beach and I see him, the only fool on the whole beach in black, jogging with that hat and hood. I met him on the sand but he runs right by me heading for the wharf.

"Hey F!" I yell and everybody turns and checks me out except for him. He just keeps on running up the wharf on the narrow wood curb between the people and the cars. Not even going to bother to try to catch him. He's gone. When I get to the bug he's leaning on the hood, bare chested, using the sweatshirt as a towel to dry the sweat from his face. The brother is soaked. Must have run miles.

"Where'd you go?"

"Running."

"I know that. You've been gone for an hour, where'd you go?"

"I ran. I didn't go anywhere."

What a fool.

"How far did you run?"

"I don't know. I ran for forty-five minutes."

He shrugs and puts that hot-ass sweatshirt on. We both get into the car. Man, I hope he gets himself together cause I can't be holding up his end of it. Acting like some moody bitch.

* * *

Back at the house he finally starts acting normal, actually put on something other than that black shit. He even looks happier, that run must have done some good for him. I got our shit together, some powder and a Baggie of stepped-on rocks and as much bud I could get bagged cause these white folks get off on that. Plus some of that Ice but I don't even like touching that shit. Feels like I'm a supermarket, carrying all this stuff, but Cowboy wants to know what's happening here and he's springing for everything. Guess we'll have to give taste tests, see myself saying, "Hey what y'all smoking these days?" I put the shit in the deep pockets of my leather full-length and check myself in the mirror, yeah, I look fly. See I got on black but a silk shirt, and baggy cotton pants and Italian toe sandals and with the full-length I look serious. I turn around and there's F looking at me checking myself in the mirror. Good to see the brother together, black jacket and jeans and loafers, looks preppie, and that's cool.

"You got the gun? Last time you didn't even bring it."

"So, what I need a gun for there? Who's gonna jack us?"

"You don't know. You don't know who's gonna come in."

"Only thing I'm worried about is the police. If I get stopped I'm not having anything on me."

"So I get to have all the yao and you don't even have to be strapped?"

"That's up to you."

"So if I get popped it's on me?"

"You know what's happening. I'm down with you but I ain't getting into that. That's you."

All I can do is shake my head. If he wants to be down he's got to be strapped. What I'm supposed to do if shit gets out of hand. "Wait up, my homey got to drive to the house to get the piece then I'll take care of your ass." Guess he's going to have to take his stupid butt home and live off Moms. He walks out of the room, shrugging like it's me that's got the problem. Phone's ringing, I'd pick it up but I got oil on my hands, trying to get this stupid ponytail to lay flat. Four rings and he still ain't got it so I pick it up.

"Yo."

"Hello, Tommy, this is Mrs. Williams. May I speak to François?"

"Sure. Let me get him, how are you doing?"

She says fine and I put my hand over the phone and scream for him. "Hey, F. Pick up the phone!"

The line opens and I linger a second to hear how he's going to play it.

"Hello," he says like he's knee deep in it. I hang it up. I know she didn't want him to come up here. Bet she's trying to get him home. Not like that's such a big-assed deal. Save myself two-fifty a week, what I need with backup that don't want to be backup. So I got to be the one to pack. I put on the ankle strap and slip in the auto. That should take care of any static. In the living room he's on the phone as hangdog as I've ever seen the brother. Moms must be reading him the serious riot act. Hope he can see I'm ready to get on. Want to stop by and check out the freak before going to the club.

"I know. I'm gonna take care of it. Did Margot call?"

He takes the phone from his ear, must not want to hear what she has to say. Voice changes up, high and tense—that's all he cares about. So what if she called? White girls all around and he's freaking out over one a hundred miles away.

"What? Why! When you're going to be doing that?"

Yeah, F's gone again. Real upset. She must have dropped a big bomb on him.

"I don't see why you got to do that. It's not over me. I'm doing all right . . . Yeah, okay . . . bye."

He puts the phone down like it's so heavy and stands up brushing his clothes like he can't wait to get going. Then he sits back down and picks the phone up and starts dialing but before he finishes he tosses it aside like it's a wet food stamp, my fucking phone too.

"What's wrong?" I ask heading for the door. Maybe if he sees me leaving he'll get the picture.

"Mom's moving."

"Moving?" I come back into the living room waving for him but all he's doing is standing there with his hands at his sides looking sick.

"Come on, let's roll."

"Oh, yeah."

The boy is dazed but he follows me to the car.

See if F had any taste he'd appreciate the kind of deal this is—it's
beautiful sitting by a big splashing fountain sipping frosty margaritas
and eating free happy hour stuff surrounded by white girls of all
shapes and sizes and I bet most of them have money. Rich and ripe
for the plucking. I know they're looking at me, wondering what
kind of a fuck I am. Gonna try to get around to each of them. Have
as many sunshine babies as I can pull. People'll be saying, "Look,
he got another high yella one. How many is that?" and all of them
will have rich mamas and I'll be set, large and legit. Look at him
not even drinking, hardly eating, still looking sour like somebody
shot his dog. Maybe he should go home to south central to all that
craziness and get his ass shot off cause he's . . .

"So look, what's wrong? You've been moping since you got
that call. What's the deal?"

"She's moving," he says sitting there looking at his hands like
they're ugly or something.

"Why are you sweating that? You live up here."

"She's moving to Atlanta. She wants me to come with her."

"That's the South. What are you gonna do down there? If you
get caught with a white girl you get lynched."

He rolls his eyes at me like I don't know. What does he know?
He ain't been down there.

"You're the one with the thing for white women. I might get
lynched but not about that."

"What you trying to say? You think I got a problem?"

"I didn't say that."

I know what he's doing, trying to play it off like there's something wrong with me, but that's not going to work. Nothing's wrong
with white chicks. They got the money, the looks. He's the one
missing out. Thinks if he walks around like he knows everything
nobody's going to call him on it.

"If you think I'm wrong say it."

"I don't care who you doing. That's you."

"But you wouldn't do it. Admit it, you think it's wrong."

"Just cause I don't go chasing them don't mean I'm running from them."

"So you saying I'm a dog chasing white girls?"

Stares at me like that's it. He's through talking. Guess I should be scared.

"That's all you ever talk about. Always got to be about women. You oughta be thinking about your business. Calling Cowboy and letting him know how's it going."

"I called him. Everything's legit. What, you think I'm not taking care of business?"

"I don't know, are you?"

"Yeah, I'm doing it. I have it together. It's all down on paper but see you wouldn't know cause you don't deal with it."

He shrugs like he's heard enough of what I have to say.

"Got to make a phone call."

"Yeah, to who?"

Nothing, just walks around the tables ignoring the chicks, not even looking at them looking at him, to the phones by the library. I know he's gonna call her, bet she hangs up on him. What's she's supposed to do, cheer him up, make him feel better about ignoring all this opportunity, and he doesn't see it. He acts like this is hard, like it's work. He just doesn't know.

Soon as we get situated Keith comes up. He's got to be the prettiest boy in Santa Barbara but I don't really know if he's a fag. Some of these white guys act like they go both ways. Got his long dark hair tied into a ponytail and his face is just like one of them models, what's her name, Cindy Crawford, and he's wearing MC Hammer kind of stuff. He always comes in with a gang of girls and after they get seated he comes over to us. He's sitting closer to F even though he usually acts kind of scared of him.

"What you got?" he asks. He must be fronting for some of the girls again.

"You got it," I say.

"Looking for a bud," he says and pushes two bills under a beer to me. Everything is cool, the usual. What he likes, some weed, maybe some coke. Same thing most nights unless it's for the girls but F is staring at him like Keith is gonna go nuts and try to boost.

"You guys are drawing attention."

"Here?" F says looking around the half-empty Mexican restaurant/dance club.

"No. I was at Peppers and these Oxnard Dairy Boys were talking about it in the parking lot."

"Yeah, what they said," I ask but I don't know why F is so concerned, just a small humbug.

"Chewie, he's a real asshole. He's the one who's upset. Says it's about prices. You're undercutting them."

"That's it, huh?" F says. "Thanks for letting us know. Never know what a creep might be up to. Tommy'll straighten you out."

Me? What's he doing telling somebody I'm gonna straighten them out. He works for me. I don't work for him.

"Those guys aren't very reasonable. They just have to find something to get into a fight over."

Now Keith's happy, all excited cause he found some way to get F to talk to him.

"What do these busters look like?"

"Chewie is short with muscles and his homeboy is this truly huge individual."

"How come they don't show up here? If they're so loc'd up why don't they come in here and try to punk us?"

"Oh, they never come here. They don't like the crowd, too gay for them."

"Oh, so they're pissed because somebody's working someplace they don't want to go?"

"Well yeah, they're real assholes."

"Not assholes, fools," F says like he's ready to throw down. Keith finally gets up and takes his swishy ass back to the girls. If F was taking care of business he wouldn't have to worry. He'd be strapped so if some bad-assed cholos wanted to squab he'd be able to deal. Anyway, the club's not even jumping and I already pulled 150, how much I got to pull to satisfy his ass? Cowboy's just a bug. Be sweating me over nothing. Anyway I can't be sitting here letting the night go by watching him stare at the bootees on the dance floor not saying a damned thing. Don't know what he thinks, why don't he go out there and mingle, mack to a chick or something, stop this dumb-ass moping. See, I gonna enjoy myself. That's why I'm here. I get going without a word to him. Soon as I put some distance between us everything is cool. Slip into the crowd and work it, through the smoke and noise and the crush of the people I get seen and that's the point. Some chubby brother dressed too casual is slow-dancing with this expensive white chick, like Catherine Oxenberg or something. He don't know what to do with all that. I slide up to them and scope, let her see where I'm at cause I know he ain't ready to do anything about it. She sees me and takes her head off of his shoulder and stares at me, assessing the situation, then she laughs, says something to him and he looks, looks at me and nods. I don't nod back cause it's not like that. He laughs at me and nods again and they move away. I oughta show him who not to fuck with. A hand's on my shoulder. I turn to see that homely chick who's always pulling on me.

"Tommy, can I talk to you?"

Don't even want to see what she wants. Blow jobs don't pay the bills. Aw shit. Keith's coming up, know he wants a freebie like he's entitled. He better get that from F cause I'm not giving up a thing. Fuck this nonsense, need some air. There she is . . . bout time she got here. But she do look good. Spandex body suit, that'll work. Just about shove my way to her, friend she's got with her is done too but she is kind of chunky but maybe F'll go for that.

"Hey, who you looking for?"

She don't even hear me so I slip up to her and wrap my arms around her and she turns like she's forgot who I am. Then she relaxes—so close our noses touch and she's not complaining. Now I know, first I thought nothing might come of it. Just jeffing, playing me for a knucklehead, but now I know she wants a piece.

"I'm sitting on the other side," I yell to her but the music is booming louder than before. All she does is shrug. I take her hand and roust my way back to the table. He's still minding it, got a beer so you know he must be getting down cause I haven't even seen him drink a wine cooler since Margot hung up on him.

"Yo, F. Got somebody I want you to meet."

He glances up and you know he's an alright-looking brother and if he wasn't so sprung on Margot he'd be pulling the freaks. When he gets to looking like that, like a pissed-off bean pie salesman ready to go off cause nobody wants a goddamn bean pie. F's getting to be bad for business. Have to ditch his ass if he keeps this shit up. I can feel Giselle's hand in mine, tense, pulling back like maybe this isn't such a good thing. I pull some chairs out without the brother cracking a smile.

"This is Giselle. The beautiful woman I was telling you about."

Nothing, he's as blank-faced as a baby's ass.

"F?"

Both girls are grinning cause they're just about ready to be scared. Pissing me off. Think the brother would have the sense to act decent so I could get some even if he don't want none.

"Hi y'all doing?" he says and smiles.

"This is Mandy," Giselle says.

"Nice to meet you . . ." Change up! He's going to act right. Yeah . . . bout time. He introduces himself to Giselle, has her spell her name. Sits there thinking with her watching him like he's a big fat hamburger.

"I haven't heard that name before. It's pretty," he says.

"It's French like yours."

Shit, she likes him . . . stupid, just cause most of the time he acts like a psycho. Finally comes out of it and she acts like a freak in heat.

"All right, hold down the table, keep Mandy company. I'm gonna take Giselle to the floor."

Guess she don't know what I'm talking about cause she looks startled but I take her hand and lead her.

"Thought you wanted to dance," I say yelling so she can sure in the hell hear me over some stupid Latin racket that ain't getting nobody moving but I don't care—least I don't have to elbow space on the floor. She steps back and starts that stuff, that aerobic dance shit white girls do. But I manage to corner her between a couple slow-moving pootbutts and she's mine, hands around her waist whispering, "Slow down . . ." caught. She lets go, lets me guide her, pull her closer. She relaxes, rests her head on my chest. Wanna do something—"Let's go outside," I says and don't wait, lead her off the floor to the big white-haired guy working the door. He stamps the backside of our hands yellow and we go into the cool air where a gang of people are waiting to get in. Cold salt air freezes that sweat against my skin. Feels fucking good.

"Hot in there!" I say pulling her around and against me. But she don't say a thing, just looking at me like she sees something.

"You brought me out here because you're jealous. Isn't that true?"

"What?"

Is she crazy? Mouth's hanging open just looking at her. What does she think this is? I don't want to hear this.

"You overreacted. You thought I was attracted to him but you thought I was going to act upon my recessive mind. You have to get beyond that."

Might as well go back in, ditch her out, thought it was gonna be lovey dovey but it's more of that nonsense.

"Hey dude, yo!"

It's that big jock-looking white boy. What's his name? Freddy. "How's the herb supply?" he says shaking my hand slipping rolled bills into my palm.

"Yeah, yeah. I got it. Talk to me inside."

"Cool dude. See ya."

The big doofus gets back in line. Glad these turnips listen.

"Is that what you do?"

"What?"

"You know."

Bet she's going to give me more of that nonsense.

"I know?"

"See, that's what I mean. Your life's unrealized."

I know she's gonna say something else, more of the same so I kiss her ear, her neck. She tries to pull away but she ain't going nowhere.

"You-should-stop," she says and runs her lips against my cheek.

"Stop talking," I say and keep kissing that long white neck.

"Who?" Trouble and I don't even have to look for it. See them under the light with the big doofus and he's pointing at me. Got to be the guys Keith was talking about. The fat one and the short one. Oh yeah, here they come. Better keep their fucking distance.

"What's wrong?" Giselle asks as I push her toward the club.

"Tell F to come out."

"Who?"

"François," I say and shove her to get her past the white-haired doorman but he makes her wait and I don't have time to tell him to step aside because they're coming up on me. I kneel down and pull up my pants leg and unstrap it and put it in my pocket. Now let's see who's gonna get punked. The little guy takes the lead. He walks up to me like I'm smaller than he is. He must be strapped too and I get a chill. I don't want to get shot. I hate this shit.

"Who you?" the little guy says.

"What?"

"Who you supposed to be? You ain't from around here."

"Why I got to be from around here?"

That's not what I wanted to say. I wanted to say "Get the fuck out my face, talking that nonsense!" But the big guy is backing him up with his hand in his pocket.

"You gotta be from this hood."

"Yeah. And if I ain't?"

"You gonna get static."

I want to tell these pootbutts to get the fuck out of my face but I don't. I don't say nothing. This isn't me. This isn't why I came up to Santa Barbara. F oughta be out here dealing with this.

"See people come up from L.A. and think they can run our show but we don't go for that."

The little guy is sliding up to dragging his back foot like he's some kind of boxer. Then everything stops. I'm standing there like I'm frozen with my fingers around the butt of my jammy. What they want, to see me pull it out and pull a trigger? Just gonna stare at me till I blink? Don't want to shoot nobody but if they think I'm gonna let somebody beat my ass . . . The big guy got his arms folded if he unfolds they both get shot. And the little guy better keep his hands in his pocket or the same thing goes. Maybe I won't shoot. Maybe I'll just get my ass beat. I oughta back up before they stare me to death.

"Where you going, *puto*?"

I turn back to see if they're rushing me but they're still rooted. It's F who's moving. Comes out of the club striding like he's trying to make a bus without running. He heads up to the big one and without a windup unloads big time on his jaw. The little guy turns to see his homey stumble, arms out to the wall to catch himself. F hits him again in the ribs and that's it. He's down. F turns with his left low like he's gonna hook the little guy. He's trapped between the two of us flipping his head like he don't know which way he wants to get his ass clocked.

"You *putos* better step back," he says backpedaling, almost tripping over his buddy for the wall. Wants to keep us in front of him. Guess he's got a big finger the way he's got his hand in his pocket.

"You got something," I say and flash mine. Clinches his teeth like a smile or something. Got his elbows around his head ready to get unloaded on. Right through that weak shit, bam! François snaps his head back with a right and he's faded, stumbles by me like a crab, sideways, still grinning, wonder if he's got all his teeth. The other guy's trying to rise. F lifts his coat, pulls it over his head and knees him in the ribs. Lets out a *oop*! and gets up stumbling. Boots his ass and lets him go. "Told you, what you need a gun for? Bunch of jokes."

Not going to say anything. He ain't for real. Fuck it, I don't need to hear that static so I go back into the club. Gonna get the girl and get the fuck out of here.

Another beautiful day in Santa Barbara. Look at him bored because he don't have a damned thing to worry about, because it ain't him that's got to worry. It ain't his problem. He don't have to pay for that iced tea or the lunch or the view, none of that. Definitely got the best end of the deal. Bet he don't know he's on the Riviera or that this restaurant is class, that sitting out on this veranda with a cold-ass ocean view is class. But he don't know or he don't care.

I'm hungry but I can't eat. See he don't have to worry about that. It's free ride time for his ass. Now if Cowboy comes strolling out here with an attitude and sweats me is F gonna think he can play it off? Don't work like that.

"What you thinking about?" I ask his weird ass. "Nothing," he says lying with a straight face.

"You wondering about why Cowboy's late?"

He shrugs with that I don't give a fuck attitude.

"If you got it together what you got to worry about?" he says.

That's what happens when you don't know your ass from up because he's too sprung to realize he's messed up. Don't even want to understand.

"It's money. If it's about money you got to worry."

"Yeah," he says acting like he's too good to waste any words.

If you drink three fucking Long Island iced teas you don't worry so much because they get you so fucked up. Not like I'm worrying because I don't have to worry I got it under control. Gotta get a fresh refill. Where's that fucking waiter?

"Give me another one of these iced teas." Acting like he don't hear me. Wants me to go over there and shake his butt.

"You really need another one?" François says.

"Yeah, I do. What's wrong with that?"

"You oughta get something to eat."

"Why I got to eat. I ain't drunk. You think I'm drunk?"

Shaking his head and muttering he gets up and goes into the restaurant. What's he gonna do spend my money to make a call, beg her to come back like he's been doing, probably talking to a dial tone. He's letting love make him silly. Oughta get it under control. Waiter comes with the drink and puts it down under a cute red napkin then stands there, eyes at his shoes, waiting on me to come up with the five dollars. It's too goddamned much to be paying for a drink like I got cash to burn. Better learn to like waiting there.

"That's five-fifty."

"Yeah." He better go ahead and have a sip. "Why do I have to pay you now? Why can't I run a tab?"

Looks shocked like he's never heard of a fucking tab. Guess he don't think I deserve a tab.

"Do you have a credit card to open a tab?"

"Credit card? Here, take one of these." Slip a note from my shirt pocket. "Now, run me a tab and bring me more of these cause I'm thirsty. Be quick."

He takes his silly butt back on inside. So what if I want to get buzzed sometimes. A brother got to relax. Nice out here with the sun and a breeze, out here enjoying the view, nature, beautiful . . . ocean and everything . . .

"Here's your drinks."

"What?" Must have fell asleep. Setting up the drinks like bowling pins. And he gets out of here before I tell him I don't want the drinks. Then I see F and Cowboy and his boy walking onto the veranda. Shit. Just like François' piss ass to bring them right to me when I'm feeling like shit. Stand up and turn around and straighten myself out, get presentable. Jerome gets to the table first and pulls a chair out for Cowboy, gives me the eye like he does, like he knows I'm soft. Cowboy's still talking to François about something but it's not like he's schooling him like he does me, it's more of a conversation—finally they come up to the table and Cowboy pats him on the shoulder.

"You oughta go to S.C. I went to S.C. for two semesters— would have played if my knees had held up."

He says it to Jerome and Jerome nods cause that's what he does. F takes it like he always takes it acting like he's not listening.

"You oughta apply. It's a good school. Did you apply?"

"Naw. I want to cool out. I'm sick of school."

He wouldn't ever get admitted. And what's this with Cowboy? He's ignoring me.

"See? He's the kinda brother who gets it together when he's little older. I was like that but nobody could see."

Look at him staring at F like he's a girl. Finally he turns to me. "Man, how's business? Got drinks for everybody? How nice."

What the hell he means. Probably just runnin me down. But he takes the tea and sips it.

"Normally I don't drink but that drive up here got me thirsty. So, how do you like Santa Barbara, been up here a month?"

"It's a classy place. It's happening, a good place to do business."

"Yeah?" he says to me pressing the frosty glass of tea against his forehead. He's dressed like a typical tourist, baggy shorts, cotton shirt, sandals. Jerome's pretty much the same, cept he's got a clutch, just know he's got something in there.

"Why is it a good place to make money? You been making money and keeping track of it?"

"Yeah. I been doing it. Taking care of business."

"I hope so. I explained to you what you needed to do to do this right. *No shortcuts, no fuckups.*"

"I got it going on. It's under control." He turns from me and looks at François like he doesn't believe a word I said.

"What do you think, François?"

Gonna give that blank look like he don't know.

"It's all right but it ain't like nobody's working it. Last week we got into it with some cholos from Oxnard but they were just pootbutts, fronting."

"What happened?" Cowboy says to him like François got all the answers.

"They got beat down. Wasn't a big thing, but some real gangsters have been checking us out. Even got some Jamaicans up here but they ain't interested in us."

"That doesn't sound like what I want to hear. See, I'd like to move up here. I like the atmosphere. I don't want attention. Just enough capital to ease me into real estate. I like this laid-back beach life."

"Yeah, I like that too," I say, but I see it, him rolling his eyes like I'm silly for saying something.

"See, that's why I wanted y'all to work this, low key. The money isn't the bottom line, it's about how I'm living. If it's too difficult to make it here like I want it to work I'll leave it alone . . . work my L.A. thing a little longer."

Cowboy finally shuts up. Looks at Jerome, checks his Rolex, big-time businessman. Worrying about a little static and what F's doing. Running us out of a job?

"So, Tommy, you keeping track of the dollars?"

"Yeah, got it down on paper."

"See, if you two can work it here—make a little room, move product and keep it quiet—I'll let y'all run it. I'll front you and it'll be your thing."

"Cool," I say. "I'll take care of it."

"Naw, it's not cool. It's business. You're a pretty boy. You're smooth but that's not all it takes. You got to have somebody to watch your back, keep it together. I see F doing that even if he don't want to handle money. You need a partner like that."

"Yeah, guess I do."

"I'm not joking you need him."

"I know."

"All right. Look, I got to look at some property. You got the books?"

I hand him the notebook and he takes it and props it open like I'm some half-assed schoolboy squinting at my numbers.

"How I'm supposed to read this? Looks like chicken scratches."

"Want me to do it over?"

Just glares at me like he knows I'm stupid. What did I do wrong? He keeps flipping through it, shaking his head. Jerome's looking at it too, didn't know he could count. F's sitting sideways so he can't see.

"Told you to put sales in this column. You're writing things all over the place. Don't make me work, make it hard on me."

Gotta nod cause that's what he wants.

"This is what you got, units, and this is what you moved. That's your gross. It's easy. You're not one of them knuckleheads from the projects. You can learn how to do it the right way."

He spins it across the table to me like a Frisbee, knocking a tall glass of tea into my lap.

"Sit in it," he says and gets up to go, looking over his shoulder to see if I'm still sitting. When they're gone I stand up and head for the restroom and F's still sitting here looking at the ocean like he ain't seen a damned thing.

*   *   *

Cooling it on the balcony, sipping wine coolers trying to relax, and he has to come up and interrupt me. Business talk and I don't want to hear it. He drops an envelope and stands there like I got to mind it.

"So, how much is that?"

"Ten G's."

"He wants it Express Mail."

"I got you the four cashier's checks. You can mail them." He's lookin at me like he expects me to thank him for doing what he's supposed to do.

"Cool. If you want me to mail it."

More like I'm tired of having him complaining about everything.

"Is Giselle gone?"

"Why you asking?"

"She's here all the time. I'm thinking about getting out of here so y'all have some privacy."

"Oh, that ain't it. Be for real. You think she's up to something and you want to get your ass out of here."

"You putting words in my mouth. I didn't say nothing like that. I'm going that's all."

"You going back to L.A.? You gonna go with Moms to Atlanta? You gonna work for Cowboy? Gonna sleep on Margot's porch? Really, you oughta consider your options. They're not what you think."

F looks like he's gonna get mad but he don't. Instead he shrugs, reties his sweatpants, checks his watch, squats down and laces a sneaker. Finally he stands up and looks at me.

"Don't know why you're talking to me like that. I could see if you thought you could correct me or beat me down but you know it ain't like that. You've got nothing to correct me about and you ain't beating me down. So all of this ain't worth my while." He turns around to go but I say it to see if it'll stop him.

"You think I'm coming up short so you're bailing on me. Ain't that it?"

He turns around shaking his head.

"You . . . whatever you think . . . It don't matter. It's your show. I don't got nothing to say about it. You and Cowboy can work it out."

"What do you mean me and Cowboy? If I'm in the shit so are you."

"If Cowboy wants to talk to me he'll be able to find me."

"So, you gonna go back and leave me hanging? What kind of partner are you?"

That got him mad he pulls the shades off and steps up.

"It's you! You're the one who don't know how to be a partner. Got that girl counting money, doing your books . . . But that's you . . . this ain't my business it's yours. I'm going. You work it out."

"So, it's gonna be like that? Gonna just go. Load up the bug and take your sorry ass out of here. I don't need you."

He stands there twitching like he's gonna leap but that's not him, he's not going to lose control. Naw, he's too together.

"Don't come running back to me cuz it ain't gonna work. You out of it."

Don't even slam the door, just gone.

Why shouldn't she take care of the money. What's she gonna do? Bump my head and chance the kind of beating I'd give her. I don't think so. She ain't stupid. White girls give respect. They know better than to be trying to stick a brother like some bitches do. But he can't see that . . . too complicated, acting like Margot is the salt of the earth. What he knows? He knows but a woman who won't do nothing for him. Here he is with all these white women, and what he does, goes back home. What's he doing, being some kind of pussy-whipped kind of a faggot. Should have taken advantage of opportunities when he had them. Don't know what he passed up.

She better be home. Where the fuck is she! Car ain't in the back, nobody answering, oughta bust her fucking window. Damn neighbors what the fuck are they looking at. I don't care, I'm gonna go in there and pull her ass out and get my money. Think she can take my money and dog me like that? No joke.

Get over there in no time, park in the red, not time for that,

throw open the door and go in—not stopping for no fucking receptionist.

"Hey!" she says and I roll by. The door of Giselle's cube is
closed, locked. Give it a quick kick, the whole thing shudders. The
stupid cubes. Kick it again, this time it gives. She's not hiding,
none of her stuff either, everything cleaned out. I got to go. Know
that bitch receptionist called the cops. So I head over to her and she
tries to stand. Got her scared.

"Look, I'm not interested in you. You tell Giselle I want my
money!" I turn and cut out, get into the 5.0 and make a quick left
going up Chappala a police car passes me, going down to lower
State. Bitch. Thirty thousand short. And she think she's gonna get
away?

"Yeah, he took off. Said he don't want to be involved but when I
checked the books it came up short."

"How short?"

"About thirty grand."

"About thirty grand?"

"Yeah."

"And you think he took it, ran back to L.A. with thirty grand
of my money in his pocket to live with his moms a couple miles
from me?"

"Yeah, it might not sound right, but that's it."

"That's it?"

"It's the truth."

"Tell you what, I'll get a hold of François but you better bring
your ass down here so we can straighten this shit out."

"When?"

"Tonight."

"Tonight?"

"Yeah, get in your car and drive your no-thinking ass down
here."

"All right."

"Hurry it up! All right my ass! I don't want to have to call you
back."

"I'm on it. See you in a couple of hours."

*   *   *

So that's it. I'm done. Think I'm stupid enough to go back to L.A.?
Cowboy's got to be stupid. Load the trunk, my clothes, TV. Glad
I got one of them compact sound systems. Least I can get that in,
but all my other stuff, the bed—paid bucks for that big-assed water
bed—and the furniture, the leather couch, all that stuff, got to stay.
I lock the door and head out. Everything shot, all that money.
Wonder if Cowboy would take all this shit instead of the money—
at least cut me some slack? Yeah, fat-ass chance. Guess I oughta
get a map, haven't driven to Sacramento in a long time. Pick up
101, always liked long drives, trips too. Stay the fuck out of Dodge
until I come up with that. Got a ten-grand nest egg, that'll keep
me until I can pay him off. Don't need no cigarette burns in my
forehead. Maybe Daddy will spot me the cash, something. Don't
want to end up like F's gonna end up when Cowboy gets a hold of
him. Gonna be like a pit bull catching a cat. There's nothing back
there but a bullet to the temple. He oughta know. I feel sorry for
him. I really do.

11
Ann

■

Red and blue lights flashing against the wall. What's going on? Is he out there? I roll out from the bed searching for my slippers, robe. Not even time to think, running out of the bedroom, into his room, turn the lights on. It's empty, bed untouched. In the dark, out of the range of those strobes, in the living room, I see Mary standing at the picture window, spying through the blinds.

"Mary, get away from there."

"It's him, Mama. They got him facedown."

"What?" I say and push her out of the way and look for myself, knowing full well she's telling the truth. I feel it before I see it. Chills all the way to my feet. Silhouette of a man, a policeman straddling someone, his face pressed in the lawn. Another policeman is at the side of him, gun drawn, pointed at the head of the man . . . François' head. I flick on the porch light and turn to Mary.

"Do not come outside!"

She shrugs like she had no intention to. "Sorry," I say and open the door and walk outside with my hands in front of me palms forward as though I'm a priest blessing the Mass. Home for only a month and already . . . trouble.

"Is there a problem, officers?"

"Stay on the porch!" the one with the gun says. The other one is finished cuffing François and goes through his pockets.

"That's my son. What has he done?" I say to the nearest policeman but he doesn't respond. The other policeman searches François and pulls him up by the handcuffs and jerks him to the patrol car. What was he doing walking the streets this late at night?

After they put him into the backseat the policeman walks over to me, like they do, as though everybody is a problem, baton still in his hand, he stops at the edge of the steps.

"François Williams is your son?" he says like he doesn't trust me.

"Yes, I'm Mrs. Williams. He's my son. What has he done?" I wait for the answer but he looks through me as though he's going to ignore me but I insist, stepping down from the porch.

"We saw him running and followed him to this house where he tried to enter through the side window."

"That's the window to his room."

"Well, it looked like a break-in. Usually people don't break into their own house. You sure he lives here?" The cop seems amused at his own question and takes a moment to shake his head. "We're checking for warrants. Is that his name? François Williams? If he's clean we'll release him to you."

He says it as though he's doing me a great favor. What's he going to do, take him for nothing? I see François' silhouette in the yellow of the streetlights in the backseat of the patrol car. Are they going to take him away? The policeman leaves me and returns to the car and says something to his partner who's at the radio. The radio crackles voices, broken sentences, colored lights still flashing. Why do they leave them on, waste of the battery. What are they trying to do? Call people out of their houses to see somebody get arrested? The policeman who talked to me is leaning against the patrol car, relaxed, chatting. Good sign? Then he comes over to me with that I'm-all-business walk.

"Miss Williams, sorry, we're going to have to keep your son. There's a warrant issued for his arrest."

"What?" I say as he walks away. I touch his shoulder and he whirls as though I've burned him.

"What did he do?"

"It's a warrant. You'll have to wait till he's arraigned."

"Oh," I say. And the policemen get into the car and drive off with my son. I wonder who's watching, seeing him get carted off like that. I'm out here like they've had to be out here when it was their son. Never thought it would be me having my business in the street. It's cold. I should go in. Mary's still there wanting to come out so badly, does she think that there's something else to see? Soon as I go in she'll start with the questions. She must know everything, all the details, details I'd just as soon forget.

"Mama?"

"What," I say and turn to see her in the doorway, why does she want to come outside, to see for herself the spot they took her brother?

"I told you to stay in."

She comes out anyway.

"Why are you standing on the porch? Everybody's gone. There's nothing going on."

"I'm thinking."

"Somebody might come by."

She stands there watching me as I hold my face, pressing my eyes, I don't want to start. She's pulling at my robe scared to be alone, and worried somebody's going to drive down the street and think I'm . . . What is she thinking? What am I thinking?

"Let's go in," I say as I allow her to pull me into the living room. But in the living room, she always has the heater too high, and dark, so she can see outside. I lead her to the coolest room, my bedroom, she's crying now, so many tears, heaving like she's going to vomit. . . .

"It's not serious. They're going to release him."

"Mama," she says and something else, mumbles maybe "Us, just us?"

"Lie down," I say and push her to the bed and start redoing the long, thick braids Margot worked just recently.

"Like Daddy."

"No, honey, he's not going. It's not like that at all."

But yes, it is, it's just how Earl was, the whole thing . . . police, the lights, always worried what was going to happen next.

"I'm going to get him out tomorrow. He hasn't done anything. They just do that, you know how the police are, young black kid late at night. It's routine."

I wonder if she believes me. Does she know I have no idea what I'm talking about? This is what I never wanted to have to deal with. What I raised him not to be, a product of this, what he's in, what's out there. I did everything within my power and it didn't work. Maybe I could have done differently, something, everything.

"Why's he acting like he's acting?"

I shrug, not answering. How to answer?

"I don't know. He's going through something."

"He's losing it. That's what it is. He's like one of them . . . baseheads."

"No, he's not! I'm not going to listen to you talk about your brother like that. He's going through something, that's it."

I move to the other side of the bed. I don't want to leave her but I want her to stop talking. I can't stand it. I really can't. How bad is it going to get? I turn off the light and pull the covers high. Please let her go to sleep. Please.

I'm never getting to sleep and she snores. Nothing helps and I'm not going to start with cognac. What is it? Ever since he returned from that supposed job in Santa Barbara he's been this way. Secretive, paranoid, more unresponsive than he usually is. I should have done something instead of what I did, ignore it. I didn't want to know, I didn't want to find anything or find out he's dealing or smoking or just cracking up. What I wanted to do was to plan for a move, get us out of here, the solution. I figured whatever he was doing wouldn't last and he'd follow and see what it is like in Atlanta. With the money I'd get for the house we'd have a start, make a better go of it, a better neighborhood. He'd see it wasn't a step down but a step up from L.A. That's another thing I can't understand. Why does he think this is it? I thought coming back from Santa Barbara with nothing good to say about it would have changed him. How he acted, wanting me to sell his bug. Never thought I'd see that day, and refusing to leave the house, not answering the phone, just staying in the room. I should have said more than what I said. Let him know that I didn't think what he was doing made any sense. That if he wasn't going to school, he'd have to work. What did I say, nothing. What did he say, nothing. And everything just got worse. When I asked him what was he going to do when escrow closes, he just put the pillow on his head. I should have made him answer. I didn't because I couldn't. So, now everything is messed up. We're leaving and who knows what's going on with him.

"They took him last night. They said it was a warrant."

"Are you going to bail him out?"

"I want to but . . . What do you think?"

"I don't know. It's different. He's your son."

"Maybe it's good for him to be away from here. It might shock him into realizing what he's doing to himself."

"I don't know, Mrs. Williams, county jail isn't a good place to be even though you might want to leave him in there."

"I know it sounds cruel, but what else is there to do? The way he's been acting, it's impossible. Before he left for Santa Barbara he seemed like he was about to snap, but I thought he'd get over it."

"If you want a bail bondsman, my daddy used one in Compton when my brother was in trouble. I can go with you if you need me."

"Thanks, Margot. I appreciate that."

I hang up the phone, ready to get started with something else, making boxes, cleaning the walls, wondering why I hadn't heard from him. He's supposed to call to ask me to bail him out like Earl used to do. Two days and still nothing. I'm going to have to do it. This is not going to work. He wants to be an adult. He expects me to treat him like one and yet I'm supposed to do everything for him. Can't even ask me to post bail. He's going to sit in there till he rots? I knew he needed help, but I couldn't make him go get help. I couldn't bring myself to force him and isn't that what I do, encourage patients to do what's best for them, but I couldn't persuade him. I could find a position for an RN at a decent salary and sell a house, a house I've had ten years, and I could get a good price for it and plan a move to another state and arrange to stay with an aunt I'd just as soon never see again. I've already found a real estate agent and told him what I'm looking for, and I've found the school I want Mary to attend. I've even got a gardening book on that region to see how to landscape the property I'll eventually buy. I did all that, that wasn't a problem, the problem is what I couldn't do. Face facts, understand what's obvious, he's so deep in it.

Compton always seems so long and flat. And it always seems you're crossing railroad tracks and that you'll run out of everything, buildings, roads, lights, people and you're still on Compton Boulevard. Stuck by the tracks at some dead end. She's sitting there filing her nails. I hear the *shik, shik* noise of the file, grating against nail and acrylic. She's led me to where I never wanted to go, the backside of Compton. And we're supposed to wait till the bondsman calls. No reason to be in there unless I want to breathe air so thick with cigarette smoke it looks like fog. And the people, they're the same people in the emergency room, the girlfriends, mothers and fathers, relatives waiting just like at the hospital for work or attention. Prepared to wait forever. Patient because that's all there is, red eyed, puffy faced, looking as though they were dragged from warm beds. And when they do reunite with the one in trouble then it'll really start. They have to believe them. Your house is on the line, your money, everything. Like I had to believe Earl even though it was obvious what he was doing. But I had to be a true believer, and accept whatever story Earl had to tell.

"Pretty crowded in there," Margot says looking up from her filing. The fog lights make her eyes dark and yellowish. How long have we waited?

"It's been a while. Should we go?"

"No, I'm okay. I'll check the number they're on."

She opens the car door and slips out. She's wearing a very thick jacket, hides the overly snug jeans and T-shirt. So confident, the way she crosses the parking lot and enters the bungalow, the stupid broadside painting, big red letters 24-HOUR BAIL BONDSMAN, EDDIE BLOCK. Guess they're trying to draw off street business, but the only reason anyone would be in this depressing, deserted part of town would be for a bail bondsman. Why am I going through with this, putting up money, money that I need, to get him out for what, what if he does the same thing? I don't know what he's done. I should know what he has done before I have to put money down to get him out for who knows how long. Doesn't make sense. I could hurt myself and Mary, throw off my plans, ruin them. I shouldn't care. Let him figure it out for himself. He should, he has to be responsible for himself.

Margot comes out of the office and down the steps moving faster than she usually moves. She waves for me, I get out and follow her. Inside, no one is talking or moving. They're looking at me. They see me in the door, a tall black woman in a nurse's uniform. They know I've been crying. They know I'm mad. They know I'd just as soon leave. Look at them, women with curlers in their hair, unshaved men, unwashed, falling asleep, sleeping already. I shouldn't be here.

"Over here." I turn and she's behind the counter, where we're supposed to do paperwork. I'm at the counter but I don't see a way around it but Margot lifts a hinged section and I follow her into an office where a bald-headed fat white man sits behind a desk and next to him a black uniformed security guard.

"What can I help you ladies with?" he asks and lights a cigarette. More smoke in a smaller space. He's greasy, he's sweating and he's smiling.

"My son's in the county jail for armed robbery. There's a ten-thousand-dollar bail."

He thumbs through my three-page application and looks up.

"You have proof of home ownership?" he says, glancing at his watch. I fumble to open my purse and pull out a canceled mortgage check and last month's bill. He leans over his desk and almost snatches it from my hand. Margot's to my left smirking.

"This is last month's bill."

"Yes."

"I charge a ten percent nonrefundable deposit. Plus a lien on your house for the balance in case he skips town."

Margot's walking around the office refusing to sit in the hard folding chairs. She leans against a grubby wall and from out of a pocket comes the emory board, and she starts again to file her nails, concentrating like they are the only things in the world. The security guard is following her with his eyes. Mr. Fat Man is looking at me, expecting me to start signing these papers but I can't. I jump up shaking my head and manage to say "sorry," and walk to the door and turn to see Margot yanking my paperwork from him. She catches me at the bottom of the stairs in the dark of the poorly lit parking lot. I unlock the car door for her.

"I don't know if I would have . . ." she says.

I'm glad to be driving out of this industrial alley. It's so dark out here. Typical for someone to shoot the streetlights out, more bullets than bulbs. The radio's off. I turn it on to drown out the *shik, shik* of Margot filing her nails in the dark.

"I would . . . put up my house, the money, that's not the point. It's everything I have up on the line for him and I don't know what he's going to do. He doesn't listen. I told him not to go to Santa Barbara. I told him not to drop out of school just a couple of months before graduation. He's not listening, how do I know he's going to listen when he gets out? And it's everything, everything I have."

"You don't have to explain anything to me. I don't understand why he does the things he does. I don't think he understands."

He called me and said they'd release him at the end of the weekend. I called to see if they could release him earlier but they don't discharge on the weekend. I was told I could pick him up early Monday morning. I thought maybe I could have asked Margot to go but it was a school day. I had to go by myself. I figured it would be horrible after working Sunday to have to sit for hours waiting for the paperwork to be handled but he was already in the waiting room when I arrived, sitting there in those black sweats looking bored. So glad to see him. Not what I imagined, that he would look bored like a kid waiting for the bus. I imagined he'd be angry, his face twisted like Earl's ready to fill my ears with stories of fools who took advantage of him, who set him up, planted it, took it from him, abused him, humiliated him. I don't want to be emotional, ready to burst into tears, make him feel pressure.

"Ready to go?"

Did he hear me? He doesn't turn so I'm left to look at the back of his head. I wait until he cranes around at an awkward angle to look at me.

"Hi, Mama. Yeah, I'm ready to go." He stands up and walks ahead of me toward the exit where the guards stand, at the metal detectors. Outside, it's ugly, much uglier than when I walked in from the parking lot. I know it was because I wasn't paying attention to the grunge and the panhandlers. It was just a Los Angeles street, something to walk on to the county jail. Maybe everything seems worse because I'm having to hurry to keep up with him and I'm the one who knows where the car is.

I call ahead to him. "What happened?" I say to his back. He slows his pace but doesn't stop.

"Nothing happened."

"They arrested you."

"Yeah, they did, but that was just humbug."

Left turn into traffic, stop. Don't look at him. The light's red, go. Lurch forward, turning, cars riding my bumper. I look at him, he's looking at me but his face is calm, near bored.

"You almost got hit."

"I know that."

I hate downtown, the traffic, the one-way streets. It has been rebuilt since I last had to go there for Earl.

"It's no big thing getting arrested? It doesn't seem to have bothered you."

He sighs. Is that the first sign of remorse, guilt, whatever?

"It shouldn't have happened."

"What does that mean?"

"I . . . I was in the wrong place."

"That's not saying anything."

"I gave somebody a ride. They had just robbed some place."

"You could go to jail. I should have gotten you a lawyer."

"For what, waste of money. They don't have no case. I'm not on a tape. They've got no witnesses."

My hands are trembling, wanting to reach across and choke him.

"And it's overcrowded. They let me out because it's humbug. They'd rather use the cell for a real criminal."

So that's supposed to cheer me, that he got out because of overcrowding. Thank God I didn't put my house on the line.

"I gotta go back in two weeks for the arraignment. It will probably get dismissed." He says it like it's nothing, nothing for me to hear, nothing for him to say.

"You drive."

He shrugs and gets out as I slide over.

"You all right?" he says as he guns into traffic making an RTD bus hit the brakes.

"Margot said to tell you she'd call."

"Margot? You've been talking to her? What she's been saying?" He makes a left without once taking his eyes off mine.

"I'll tell you when we get home. Just keep your eyes on the road." When we get close to the house he slumps low in the seat and drives right into the alley and maneuvers our car around the trash cans and garbage to our garage.

"Okay, Mama. You can drop me off here. I'll go through the backyard."

He pops out of the car, leaving the engine running, and heads to the sagging fence and swings himself up and over as easily as skipping a puddle. It's trash day and the trashmen are down the alley coming along in the garbage truck. I watch the crew, a Latino driver and two heavy black men, handling the cans with contempt. If François . . . a garbage man. My son a garbage man, is that what I'm hoping for? He'd work and pay bills and get married and I would never have to worry.

The house is almost hollow. It looks so much prettier cleaned out of all the clutter of living for so long in one place. It really is a beautiful house even though it's small; wood floors, high ceiling with moldings and built-in bookcases. It could have been prettier if I could have uncovered the hardwood floors under these tired carpets. I wanted to fix everything, my own *This Old House*, and landscape the yard like in *Better Homes and Gardens* but I ended up putting bars on the windows. Still though, it was mine. I didn't

want to move up to Baldwin Hills or Windsor Hills or Ladera
Heights. This was mine without Earl or anybody else. Even if the
neighborhood was slipping but I know now I was wrong. I should
have got out a long time ago like everybody else. Now he has it,
the disease, like all those kids coming to the hospital with bullet
wounds but that's not what's killing them.

He dropped out of the window, landed softly and crept away. He'll
be gone for hours. First time I noticed what he was up to I felt I
needed to confront him, wasn't that why he was arrested, creeping
around like a burglar or something worse? Who is he seeing, what
is he doing? Is there a reason for not leaving the house until after
dark and then not by the front door? Instead he's sneaking out and
disappearing. Maybe he's seeing someone, some girl. It's not Margot.
She said she hadn't heard from him. Sometimes I get out of bed and
go to the side window and search for him, but if I do catch a glimpse
of him it's only for a second. Running across the street, lit by the
streetlight then gone, into the darkness. I can't worry about him. I
refuse to drink myself to sleep yet here I am in bed with a brandy in
my hand trying to imagine what he's doing. I know he'll come back
in about two hours, climb through the window and head for the shower.
Then he'll go to his bedroom and the light will be on till daylight. He
doesn't want to leave that room. Mary's packed up, most everything
is packed up for the movers, her room's not empty but just about bare.
But his, I've told him he'd have to start packing, even if he isn't
coming. He listened, nodding, on his bed in that stupid sweatsuit.
More and more and more withdrawn. We'll be here till his arraignment
but after that we're going with or without him.

"Something is really wrong with him. He's totally to himself. He
doesn't leave the house unless it's in the middle of the night and
then he goes out of the window."

The phone line is quiet except for music in the background.
That stupid "Sex you up" that you don't have to listen to but you
can't help but hear.

"We're leaving in three weeks. I don't even know if he's
coming with us."

"It's not what you think. I'm not saying he isn't flipping out a little but there's more to it than that. He is trying to protect himself and you. I can't get into it. You have to talk to him," Margot says reluctantly.

Again silence. So she's finally done it, brought everything into the open. She knows I know or if I don't I should. "Okay, I'll talk to you soon," I say and hang up. I go to his room like I've gone almost every night since he's been back and knock on the door. And he says that same "what" like he's busy. I open the door and go in. I ask how's he feeling, as usual. If there's something he wants for dinner. When he's going to pack. But it's been going on for too long.

"Is somebody after you?"

He's looking at a magazine, *Sports Illustrated*, Magic Johnson's on the cover. He puts it down on his stomach and turns his head toward the window.

"I don't know, maybe."

"You don't know? Is it about Santa Barbara, what you were doing there?"

He sighs and sits up, his hands folding and unfolding the magazine. "I don't know," he says, looking at the floor.

"Is that why you're here all the time? Is that why I see you cracking the door and looking out before I leave to go to work?"

He shakes his head, wrinkling the magazine, twisting its glossy pages till they fray.

"Do you owe money? You owe somebody?"

"No. I don't owe anybody anything. I just want you to be safe." His eyes look dull, as though the conversation is wearing him out.

"Where do you go at night, that late?"

He smiles, one of the few smiles, pulls the hood off his head and runs his hands through his hair. It's longer now, like the nubs of what those reggae singers wear.

"You know I've been going out at night?"

"I knew before the police picked you up."

"Oh."

"So, where do you go?"

"I don't go anywhere. I run."

"You run?"

"Yeah, I run to the beach."

"But that's fifteen miles up and back."

"Sixteen," he says as though it's more than a fact.

"Why?"

"I don't know."

"That's so far. Don't you worry you might get into trouble?
There must be all kinds of nuts out there. And the police too."

"I've . . . managed to avoid all that. Most stuff I outrun."

"Oh." I don't know what else to say. He seems so reasonable,
as though he worked it all out.

"Don't you want to see Margot? Your friends, and if you're
going to stay in L.A. shouldn't you be looking for a job and someplace to stay?"

"I'm not thinking about Margot. That's dead."

He picks up the magazine again and unfurls its twisted pages.
Guess I pushed the wrong button.

"Shouldn't you be thinking about a job?"

"Don't worry about me, Mama. I got it."

He's got it? What does that mean? He's got it together? That's
a lie. "What are you doing to yourself? What if they send you to
jail? Do you know what that means?"

"I know, Mama. If it happens, it happens."

"Call Margot! Maybe she can talk sense to you. Maybe she
can get across to you what you're doing to yourself." I'm almost
out of the room and I hear him say, "Mama, don't worry about me.
Shut the door please."

I hurry along the breezeway to the classroom hoping he'll have the
time to talk. What if he's in the middle of something and I interrupt
him? The door of B-2 is marred with the typical scrawls. I knock
probably too quietly and wait, hoping that someone will hear me
and open the door without me having to knock all over again.
Footsteps and the door opens and there's Michaels' sleepy, pale
face.

"Mr. Michaels . . . I'd like to talk to you about François."

He stands there in the doorway blinking as though he's trying to remember me.

"I'm François Williams' mother. He was in your composition class last year."

"Yeah," he says. He must have been sleeping, not even bothering to cover a yawn.

"Maybe I should leave."

"No. No! I'm okay. I was napping on the table."

He steps back and gestures for me to enter. The room is completely empty of students.

"That's why I fell asleep. This late in the semester, sometimes nobody shows to my creative writing class and I get a break."

"Really?" I say and I guess I must have frowned. He looks embarrassed as though he said the wrong thing.

He walks to his desk and pulls a chair out for me. The room is neat but depressing. One bulletin board is covered with mug shots, something to do with the number of people killed with handguns. Comic book posters of Dracula and Frankenstein, "Sex Outlawed in the Future Fahrenheit 451," and a very big safe sex sign. He sees me looking at everything and he looks too. Even more concerned as though I'm going to say something about it.

"I like how you have your room decorated. You have more things since last year."

"Yeah. I like finding things they'll pay attention to."

A long pause. He starts to fidget with the edge of his newspaper as though he wants to open it and end my visit.

"My son liked your class. He said you didn't act like most teachers."

"Well I gave him a B."

I made him defensive. He opens his roll book as though François is still in his class. I couldn't have made him that nervous that quickly.

"Is something wrong?"

"No," he says and looks away. "You know, I have your son's girlfriend as my service worker."

"Margot?"

"Yeah."

He looks nervous. Guilt? He's not married if I remembered right, no ring. Somebody like Margot must be trouble.

"She told me about François' problems. It was a daily thing. What she thought he was doing. What he was doing. And about what happened after his friend was killed."

That's it. He doesn't continue. Looking off into space, then into that rollbook.

"What did she say?"

"Oh, she was angry with him for taking it so hard. Then she started to worry about him, really worry like she thought he was going to lose it. But now when she gets around to coming to service she doesn't say anything about him. She talks about her father."

"What do you think about him?"

"About François? I don't know. It's pretty obvious he's going through a hell of a lot."

"Could you talk to him?" I finally get around to asking him but he's smiling like he can't possibly do what I asked.

"Why me?"

"Because you're a teacher he likes. He's not even going to graduate because of all this craziness. Last couple of months everything's just fallen apart."

"So you want me to try to get him back to graduate?"

"Yes."

"I like François . . . but you know these things hardly ever work out. I've tried it, students just have their reasons. They go through things. I've tried but . . ."

He shakes his head as though he's remembering many conversations.

"It might help. Margot said he might talk to you."

"Well, maybe she's overestimating my powers of persuasion."

Michaels turns around to check the clock. The next class must be about to start.

"I should go," I say and he looks relieved. I walk to the door.

"When would be a good time?" he asks.

I shrug. "Today?"

"Today? You're going to bring him around after school?"

I shake my head. "He will not leave the house."

"Why? Is he trying to avoid somebody?"

"I don't know. He doesn't talk to me about it. I don't know what he's going to do but he's a man now, I can't spend my life trying to take care of him."

"Oh, you want me to come by and talk to him, see what's going on with him, his plans?"

"Yeah, that would be great, if you could, but I don't expect much."

"I'll stop by on my way home. That'll be around five-thirty."

"Thanks," I say and walk out hoping he'll show.

.12

Michaels

■

How do I get myself into these things? I should have a sense of dedication, should be ready to spread the light of education to all of my students but I don't want to do this, get this much involved in François' life.

They see me drive up, the door is open. She has her back to me, instructing her beautifully brown and pigtailed daughter in the Catholic uniform on what dishes to pack. The house is quite empty, the room seems almost huge without the clutter of the TV and stereo. I bet there's real wood underneath that tacky carpet. Fresh paint, enlarge some windows and if it was moved ten miles west it would go for a lot. Finally, she looks at me, she's a handsome woman, hair under a scarf, but she's still wearing crisp hospital whites. Must feel very comfortable in a uniform.

"You made it."

"So you're about ready to leave," I say.

"Yes, and it's about time."

"Is he home?"

"Yeah. He doesn't leave his room. May I get you something to drink?"

"Thanks, but I'm fine."

She leads me to the rear of the house and knocks at a door with a poster of Michael Jordan on it. Looks positively inviting.

"François, Mr. Michaels came to see you."

"Who?"

"Your English teacher."

Nothing. Silence, she shrugs, I shrug and she turns the handle and walks into the room. He's sitting on the edge of the bed with his hands folded between his legs, black sweatsuit with the hood over his head. Maybe an executioner or someone about to be. Doesn't seem half happy to see me, even if I am his favorite teacher. This isn't such a good idea. And now she's standing between us as though she's changing her mind about how good an idea it is. He's scowling. I can't tell at whom but I want to leave, follow this up over the phone. She's talking to him in a soothing voice, almost whispering.

"Mr. Michaels wants to talk to you about graduating. He says there might be some hope."

That's not exactly what I said. Actually I said I didn't think there was hope but if deception gets that scowl off his face I'll go along. Now, this room looks a mess, clothes on the floor, books scattered all around and records, lots of socks, more socks than anything else.

"So, I'm going to let you two talk." She smiles at me and slips out. He's still in the same position, frozen hostility.

"So how's it going?" I ask because it's a very dumb thing to ask. He'll probably ignore me. Leave the smart questions to the psychiatrists.

"How's Margot doing?" he asks.

"Huh?"

"Margot, how's she doing? She still ditching service?"

"Yeah, she comes once a week, but I don't say anything. You know how she is."

"When she's leaving?"

"For where, college?"

"Yeah."

"I don't know. I think she says it depends on whether or not she gets a job and a place to stay till the quarter starts."

"Yeah? Thought she'd get out of here soon as she graduates."

I shrug, lying with a straight face. He's right. She's leaving June 25. "Getting the fuck out of Dodge," as she says, but I'm not telling him that. Don't need to be carrying tales and give him something to obsess over.

"She's seeing anybody?"

He pulls the hood off his head, I guess to make eye contact. The clean angles of his edge cut are gone. He's going natural like they do these days—beginning dreads.

"I don't know. She hasn't said anything."

"Yeah."

Now's the time, otherwise I'll be here for the rest of the evening shooting the breeze.

"So what's up with school? Are you planning on going back? Summer school maybe?"

He laughs and he looks like the young man in comp. The one I wasn't nervous about, scared of, who seemed to be perfectly normal, more than a good student, did all I asked, a good athlete.

"I don't know. I'm not thinking about that now. Things are . . . I got to handle things."

"How's that. Your mother said she's moving in a couple weeks. What are you going to do? You got something lined up?"

His face blanks totally. Almost placid like Juan's, the cholo in my first period. Mr. Deathmask. Oh yeah, he's right on the edge about ready to roll off.

"She don't understand. I can't think about that now. I got something to do and that's what I got to worry about. Taking care of business."

It's about money. He owes somebody something and he thinks they might be ready to collect.

"You've got to watch out for yourself and you've also got to think beyond that, have a plan. Otherwise . . . it'll get crazy."

Spoken like I know what I'm talking about.

"I got one. Don't worry, when they're gone it'll be all right. I'm going to take care of myself. You don't got to worry about me."

I don't believe him in the least.

"I got it together."

Yeah right. Well, I've done my duty. I've talked to him. Helluva lot of good I've done.

"So look, I'm going to leave but give me a call about this school thing. If you need some help, let me know."

"Okay," he says and stretches out on the bed. When is he

going to pack? I see why his mother's so upset. I open the bedroom door but he calls to me.

"When are you going to see Margot?"

"I don't know. I guess when she comes to service."

"Ask her if she's going with somebody to your wedding."

How does he know that unless I was talking about the wedding like I talk about everything? Too fucking much.

"I'll take her if she needs a ride."

"Okay, yeah, I'll tell her."

He nods goodbye and lies back and covers his eyes with his sleeve.

I leave the room sure he's coming to the wedding, my wedding, because I couldn't, didn't keep my mouth shut, like Tina says: "Keep your personal life *personal*." Back in the living room Mrs. Williams is sitting in the one remaining chair by the picture window.

"How'd it go?" she asks.

"I don't know. He wants to come to my wedding. That's about the only thing he seemed interested in. He wants to take Margot."

"Margot? Why doesn't he call her, see her or something?"

I shrug. Maybe he didn't have anything to say. From the way Margot told it, he fucked up and that was that.

"You invited them to your wedding?" she says, almost accusatory, suspicious.

"I got pretty close to them. We did the yearbook. Some of them asked to come so I made a general announcement. But he's the only one to bring it up."

"Maybe it's good, he'll start acting more reasonably if Margot talks to him."

"Yeah, sure." I wave to her hoping she'll keep sitting and rest her feet, but like the polite woman she is, she pulls herself up and follows me to the porch. She has a more pained look than before.

"I want to take him to this therapist. He works with teenagers. Young men with problems."

"François's going to see this guy?"

She rolls her eyes. "I've got to try something. What's going to happen with him when I'm gone? Is he going to stay with one of his friends? Rent a room? But he's of age. I can't keep worrying about his problems.''

I'm looking at her with my parent-conference face. Warm smile, concerned demeanor, concealing, masking a mind already on cruise control, already breaking and inching toward home.

''Order pizza,'' she says. The couch is mine, the Lakers are on in five minutes and she's on the phone making those wedding plans. Talking, hour after hour. Plotting and pricing while I avoid and ignore and when cornered do what I'm told. How does she do it? All the logistics . . . and her job! All day at work making decisions and here too. Me, I can't think. It's TV, newspapers and bad books. She's off. She's coming my way. Probably another opinion needed about something I probably have no opinion of.

''You're going to have to bring your father to get fitted.''

''Okay.''

''Saturday.''

''Sure.''

She looks at me with too much interest like I'm some kind of gadget spread out on the couch.

''You'll need new shoes. We'll have to go to Bullocks.''

I nod and she turns away and goes to the kitchen table to her receipts and more books of plans. She's wearing one of my comic book T-shirts, Maggie on a scooter from ''Love and Rockets,'' as a nightshirt. She looks so slim. It's like she's given up eating for the wedding.

''How much we have in checking?'' she shouts. ''Two hundred? That's it?''

''Yeah. Till payday.''

What does she expect? So far we've probably spent four grand of our money. It's a nightmare. What did they call that in anthro, a potlatch? Give everything you have away so everybody will know you made it. I'm quite happy being unadmired and tight.

The game's starting, Chick and Stu are smiling faces and moving mouths. Unmute the TV, pizza will be here in oh, less than ten minutes or it's half-price time. Wonder how much we're going to get in wedding gifts? Maybe some big bills to pay for all this excess. No, I'm not going to worry about that, it isn't my show, Tina wants it and that's okay. School's almost out for the summer. I'm getting married to a beautiful, hardworking, educated woman. I have no complaints. Phone's ringing. Hope it isn't for me. Tipoff time. Of course it's going to be for Tina. Another soror with some complaint about a dress fitting. Tina comes up carrying the phone at arm's length as though it's disgusting her.

"For you."

"Who is it?"

"I have no idea, one of your students."

"Yeah?"

I sit up and take the phone with Tina staring at me like I'm really bugging her.

"Don't stay on long. I'm expecting a call."

Don't want to argue, say something to get her started. "I won't." She leaves giving me the evil eye.

"Michaels, you there? What you doing keeping me waiting. This is a toll call."

"Margot?"

"Yeah, who else it's going to be? You knew I was gonna call."

"What's going on?"

"Don't sound like you don't know. You're the one who talked to him. What's all this about? I'm going with François to your wedding? Don't I got something to say about it?"

"Huh?" I'm in it. Knew this was going to happen. Pulled into the middle of this nonsense. "Look, Margot, I'm not the one you . . ."

"Wait! You listen. I get a call, it's him and he tells me about how we're going up to your wedding in Santa Barbara. Two hours riding with him. Be for real."

"I didn't know you, what was happening, I didn't say . . ."

"Listen! See, I was looking forward to coming up, you know, going to your wedding but I wasn't planning on going with him. That's a dead issue."

"Margot, wait a minute. You think I set you up to do something you didn't want to do? No, I didn't do that . . . He . . .''

"What?! He called and said you wanted us to come up together like we're still some kind of couple but you know, you know how I feel about him. Why you set me up like that? You're supposed to be some kind of a friend and you do that?''

"It's not like that, Margot. I . . .''

"He's the one who did stupid shit. I told him what I'd do.''

"But you should listen to me. It didn't happen that way at all. His mother was worried about him and asked me to come by to talk to him and try to get him to finish school and graduate. When I was there he brought it up. I didn't encourage him.''

"Yeah, right. You just sat there nodding. Now I got to deal with this shit. It's on me.''

Dial tone.

"Hey, y'all keep the noise down. I'm doing grades! Don't play with the door! Stay in the room.''

Stand up for the fiftieth time and go to the door and they scatter around the classroom like rabbits. Don't know half of them.

"Maricela, tell your friend to leave the door alone.'' She nods and her friend, a really tiny guy, grins like I'm going to chase him.

"What are you all doing here!''

"Party day,'' Maricela says.

Who would have expected this. In all the years I taught at Bolt the last few days before summer my class was always empty. But that was when the school was all black. Now, with so many Latino students, suddenly the demographics have changed, and I guess I have to expect a different game. A knock. Some kids going for the door. Might be the principal.

"Wait. I'll get it.''

The kid just smiles and turns the handle. The door swings wide and it's François gesturing for me to come outside.

"What up, Michaels?''

"Nothing much. What's up with you?'' I ask. He looks . . . tense. There are bags under his eyes, and his face looks tense. But he's just been running, that's obvious. His T-shirt is soaked, and his face is stained with whitish tracks of sweat.

"So you're leaving, finally getting out of here. What you gonna do, teach at a white school?"

"I'm going to law school."

"Law school? Where?"

"UCLA."

"Oh, so I guess you've made it. Going to have it all."

What is this? Why am I the one always getting analyzed.

"I just want to have options."

"Yeah," he says, shaking his head, "I like to have options."

"But you do. You're young. Nothing's written in stone."

"Yeah . . . it ain't written but it's clear."

Oh no, I hope this isn't going to be dramatic or anything, but he doesn't look as if he's going to say something so moving I'm going to be moved to try to get my ass out of here. He looks more amused than anything but that makes me more nervous . . . uneasy, too close to the source.

"What do you mean it's clear?"

"If I don't do what everybody is doing, getting the fuck out of here, I'll get done too like everything gets done."

I swear he sang the words he just said. I guess I'm staring too intensely at him because he looks uneasy, steps back and puts his hands in his pockets.

"You gonna see Margot?"

I knew it. Messenger service.

"I hadn't planned on it."

"When you see her, tell her it's no big deal. I just want to spend some time with her before she goes."

"Why don't you ask her?"

"Cause I can't call her."

He blurred the bit about Margot. It's like he's got a routine down, what he has to say. "You can't talk to her on the phone?"

"You got to call her for me. Tell her I, you know, messed up. I just want to see her before she goes."

Everybody has a ball they want me to carry.

"So you want me to get her to see you. That stuff rarely ever works."

Damn, now I know he's going to follow me right to the steps. Then he veers to the fence and begins a quick climb up to the twelve-foot-high chain-link fence.

"Tell her for me. Please."

No one ever says please around here.

It's a good excuse to leave. Maybe that's how it works. You stand there long enough and they're bound to see you. So I remain there. The sun doesn't set early this time of year. Where are those stupid dogs? Everytime I drop her off from school they come howling. Maybe somebody poisoned them. The gate is unlocked, but fat chance going into the yard so those dogs can show up and rip me to shreds. Then I remember Margot in one of those outfits, the black leopard one with the go-go boots. I throw caution to the winds and open the gates, enter the yard and walk quickly to the porch. Nice porch, kind of ranchero rustic, nice benches and flower pots. What's that rustling? I turn to see one dog coming from around the side of the house, along the driveway. I'm not going to make it. Both of them snarling, snapping and frothing and going for me in a big way.

"Ali, Tyson! Stop! Come here!"

She's there suddenly, blue scarf on her head, and shorts. Bare legs. First time I've seen her bare legs.

"What are you doing?" she says coming off the porch with her arms akimbo. "You know I got dogs."

"I didn't see them. I thought maybe you had them in the house."

"You're lucky," she says rubbing her hands together as if to say I would have been dust. "And anyway, who would keep these fuckin' dogs in the house?"

Soon as her attention slips from them, the dogs start inching up on me, both pairs of reddish dog lips curling back to show yellowish teeth.

"Better do something about them," I say, not so sure that she won't turn back and leave me to them.

"Tyson, Ali, come!"

She claps and runs off the porch and they follow her into the backyard. She runs quickly. Never saw her hurry, seems silly to assume she can't. She returns a couple minutes later winded a bit and the scarf is off, her braids around her shoulders flipping in the breeze.

"So what you came by for?"

"I thought we could talk about something. I need your opinion."

"What, your marriage is off? You want me to tell you what to do?"

"Naw, it's not that. It's about François."

"I'd invite you in the house but you don't want to go in there. Señor Dickhead ain't home and he always has a shit fit if I have people over."

"Hey, I don't want to get your father mad," I say with too much conviction.

"Let me change and we can go somewhere."

"Okay."

I head for the gate and the security of being back in the driver's seat.

Short wait? Hoped she'd be a few minutes and I'd only be reasonably late but it's going to be another one of those situations. Boring, listening to the oldies stations. So it's NPR. Listening to those soothing voices. Change, money rattling around. They're really big into sound effects. Some young gangsters stroll by, really small fellas. I try not to stare but I do. One of them sports a ski ball, catches me looking. I nod. He nods. The sun is starting to set. I've been in this car too long. I do the stupidest things. I know how to say no. François was just an excuse so I could do what I really wanted to do. If I believed in psychology, I'd think I was setting myself up. If I'm in her presence long enough she'll take care of everything. Give me the reason to not get married. To fuck up everything. Is that what I'm doing? But I don't believe in that stuff. I'm doing what I want to do, making a fool of myself over Margot. I should just go back to the door and let her know I'm going home. She'll have to understand. From the porch, the door opens and she comes out. She stands there, arms away from her sides, poised as though she's going to step down and come to the car but she hesitates. Is she going to change her mind? Then she turns, slams the door as though she's mad and comes running to the car. She's in a sweatsuit that looks like something Emma Peel would wear, snug and ribbed with leather strips. That's why I do this, all the trouble is no trouble because I've got a clothes fetish.

"So where you want to go?" I ask as soon as she gets in. I hope I don't look too excited. Don't want her to get the wrong idea.

"You asking me? I can pick it?"

"Well, I mean . . ."

"The Marina. I want to go there."

"Yeah, sure," and we start out.

"It's spooky along Jefferson at night. When I was a kid we were coming home from the beach. My father had on the radio. He always listens to the news. I was sitting in the backseat next to my brother and there's this news flash. Charles Manson had slaughtered Sharon Tate and all the people at her party. The police wanted everybody to keep their doors and windows locked and we were in my father's beat-up Ford and the locks didn't even work. Suddenly I'm hanging on every word coming out of the radio. I wanted to be home behind locked doors with bats in our hands, instead of driving on a lonely dark road."

"So you were scared," she says, unimpressed as though being scared is something she disapproves of even in ten-year-old boys. It's not really dark. The orange fog lights do the trick.

"Let's go to Friday's," she says.

I don't say anything. It's a pickup joint with bad appetizers.

"Shouldn't you be home with your fiancée?" she says with some heat on it.

"She's out with her girlfriends doing wedding things."

"She's got a lot of girlfriends?"

"Yeah. She has friends from her sorority who live in L.A."

"So, she's into sororities . . . I don't know if I like that."

I drive till Lincoln waiting for her to explain the not liking Tina in a sorority comment but she's quiet, content to flip the stations.

I turn sharply, cutting against traffic into the parking lot of a Vons.

"It's not here. Where're you going?" she says, sounding alarmed. Is she worried I'm going to force her to watch me shop for vegetables? I just drive faster and after a few turns . . . "Here it is, a little shortcut."

"Yeah. I thought you were lost."

Like that's the worst thing I could be. I park and she reaches up and puts on the dome light and checks herself in the rearview mirror. Puts on lipstick and blots it and drops the tissue on the floor and turns to me.

"You ready?"

I'm out already, walking around to open her door, something I don't normally do, but it satisfies my need to be useful.

Inside it's noisy and crowded. The meat market with that quaint Americana feel. Expect to see a wooden Indian, but this sad-looking black guy with a ski ball and a striped shirt and vest comes up and with a throaty "Smoking or nonsmoking?" leads us to a section of the restaurant mostly populated with blacks. At a table by the rest rooms a couple of guys in blue sweatsuits, one with corn rows with the cute little blue rubber bands on the tips and the other with a messy Jheri curl, are sharing a pitcher of beer and a plate of Buffalo wings and they're deep in conversation. But other than them it's mostly black women at the tables. They look to be young professionals out for an early dinner, sharing a drink with a friend and hoping to come across some interesting young men. Certainly not those raw businessmen behind them.

"What are you staring at?" Margot asks.

"Nothing, just looking around."

"Yeah, sure you are," she says smirking. "You just checking out those cows. You better not be doing that. You're getting married."

"I'm just curious. Even married people look around."

"Oh, excuse me. I don't know what that's like."

"Margot, you really need to stop with that being pissed off

thing. I don't understand why you're always trying to get the drop on people.''

Now I've done it. I've criticized her.

''Me? You think I'm pissed off? Man, Michaels, I think you're trying to call me a bitch or something.''

She stands with this stagey flourish and walks noisily away, her boot heels clicking against the hard red tile. Well, I hope she isn't going to call some boy to come pick her up. That's what I deserve getting mixed up in these situations. If she does leave maybe I'll try a line on some girl. I'd probably catch some action if I hadn't worn a stupid Bolt windbreaker with a yellow lightning bolt down the back.

Here she comes. She doesn't look mad. She's walking crisply but she stops. Those gangsters are talking to her. She says something, nods at them and walks on.

''They said something to you?'' I ask because her face is set, frozen in a sneer.

''Yeah. How'd you know. From how happy I look?''

''Don't take it out on me. I didn't say it.''

She rolls her eyes and almost turns to glance at them but doesn't. Instead she shakes her head. ''Niggahs,'' she says.

''What did they say?''

''Nothing.''

''They said something.''

''Why you worried about it? What you gonna do, go over there and slap them?''

''All I want to know is what they said to you.''

''You know they're watching me.''

I know they are but it's funny how her saying the obvious makes it even worse.

''So what did they say?''

The sneer turns to a weak smile.

''They wanted to get with me.''

''That's it.''

''That's enough. If I could get away with it I would have turned that table over on them.''

We should go. That's what I want to do.

"So what are you going to do if they come up to the table and ask again?"

"Why ask me? You usually have something to say."

"Oh, so you'd leave me hanging?"

"No. I wouldn't let anything happen to you," I say, sounding way too sincere. But I guess sincerity has a good effect on her. She smiles, another rarity, and opens the menu. She skips the light dining stuff on the first few pages and goes straight to the serious eating section.

"So you're gonna do it. Go and get married?"

"Yeah, all the invitations are in the mail."

"Good. You'll get more presents that way."

"Sometimes you sound like Lauren Bacall in one of them old movies where she has a name like Mike and she's always got something smart to say."

"I don't know what the fuck you're talking about. But I want the crab and steak."

"I don't have that kind of cash."

"You have credit cards. And anyway you didn't get me a graduation present."

"You haven't graduated yet. But I guess this is a good present."

"Oh, you know you've got to get me a gift too. Dinner don't count."

Those gangsters don't know how close they came to getting shredded. The waiter comes and takes our order. I get soup and a beer to economize and she orders a strawberry margarita as an afterthought. Wonder what she's going to say if she gets carded. Yeah, I can imagine. The waiter looks at her for a second and then turns for the kitchen.

"You do as you please," I say, sounding like a teacher.

"I don't get carded. I look old enough."

"It's more than that. You look like trouble."

"I'm a bitch *and* trouble?"

"I didn't say that."

She's looking at me so hard. I can't tell if she's angry or what.

Luckily the waiter comes with the drinks and she turns her intensity to the margarita. She takes a sip and frowns as though it's too cold.

"I don't see how you could do that," she says still frowning.

"Do what?"

"Get married."

"Lots of people do. You get a ring. You get a license."

"Lots of people cheat. Just dog each other saying they love each other."

"We're not like that. You've got to have trust."

"But you're out with me."

"Wait a minute. We're out to talk about François."

"You coulda done that on the phone."

"It's not like that . . ." I say staring at the yellow bubbles floating up in my beer.

Thank God the food's coming. Soon she's paying so little attention to me she could just as well be alone with the surf and turf. But even though she seems to be enjoying cracking crab legs she's waiting on me to say something. Make a gesture of surrender.

"Maybe you oughta to think about what you're doing," she says between bites.

"Yeah, I guess I should. Somehow though, it sounds like you're trying to talk me out of going through with it."

"Maybe I am."

"Why?"

"Maybe I like you," she says without looking up from the plate.

"Like me?" I say replaying the words. Air is rushing through my head, I hear it whistling through my head, hollow as a drum. Picture sleeping with her every night, waking up to her every morning. Explaining Al Green songs to her as we sit in front of the fireplace. But above all else her naked, dark body floating on white sheets.

"Maybe you oughta take me home."

She pushes away from the table and heads for the exit. Attention follows her. The eyes of the gangsters, the waiter wondering if she's slipping out on the bill, but I bring it and the money and follow her.

* * *

The drive to her house is quiet except for the many stupid songs she finds on the radio. Her house is lit up like a police station. Floodlight coming from the driveway and the side of the house. Her old man has the world looking like cutout targets in a shooting gallery.

"Thanks for dinner," she says.

"You still plan on coming to the wedding?"

She slowly turns around as though she's weighing the offer.

"Yeah, I'm going to come. I'll go with François if it means that much to him."

"Thanks," I say and watch her unlock the gate's dead bolt. The pit bulls look like big black waterbugs dancing around her feet as she walks to the porch.

The light's on upstairs. She's still up. Thought she might have gone to bed. The security gate slips out of my hand and bangs against the metal fence, making a horrible racket. Now, she's got to know I'm home. Yep, the door opens. She's in her robe, curlers too.

"Hi, hon," she says and kisses me.

"Sorry I'm late. I should have called. I had to see François. It was kind of an emergency."

"I figured something like that happened. Come on in the kitchen, I'll warm up dinner."

"How's François?" she asks as I follow her.

"He's doing okay. He's coming to the wedding with Margot."

"All the way up to Santa Barbara?"

"Yeah, they're looking forward to it."

She's calm now. The wedding is all systems go. She puts a plate of chicken and rice into the microwave and stands at the sink with her arms folded, absent-mindedly staring at the floor.

"How's studying?" I ask.

"It's going okay. Another hour on contracts and I'll be ready for bed."

She smiles and brings the plate over to me.

"Want a beer?" she says and brings me one before I say.

"Need any wedding errands run?"

"No . . . yes. If you could pick up the seating cards from the printer."

"Yeah, sure. On Green Street?"

"Unhuh." She kisses me. "I'm going to bed. Don't stay up too late."

I watch her walk up the stairs. She comes back down suddenly as though she's forgotten something.

"Is everything okay?"

"Yeah," I say, forcing a smile.

Finally, she shrugs and goes up to bed. I realize how much responsibility I put on Tina for these changes. I guess I wanted to believe Tina is the reason I'm leaving, quitting teaching, aspiring to have a big paycheck. But it's me. It's what I want to do.

13

François

■

Cowboy comes rolling up in a black Cherokee with his boys cara-
vanning behind him in a money-green Bronco. He pulls into one of
the stalls sporting a white Stetson to match his sweatsuit. Like he's
gonna wash it, making a big deal about picking up a hose and
pointing it at the Cherokee. Some hook-head guy comes out of the
car wash office and rushes over, laughing and nervous cause he
knows who runs the show. Hook-head gets some Mexican guys to
take care of it. Cowboy stands there watching the Mexicans hose
down the Cherokee like it's something to see. Finally he walks to
the office.

Guess I should get it over with and follow him in. Don't want
to be late. Was he smoking just now? Can't remember. He don't
always be sucking on a cigarette. Would go in and get it over with
but for that cigarette. Can't stand that. I just as soon drive away and
say "fuck it." Mama's going. Don't got to worry about her and
Mary. Just me, but I can't keep living like a fucking mole. I can't
come out in daylight. Can't get caught slipping. Can't keep this up.
Always worrying bout where it's gonna come from.

I get out the bug and beep on the alarm. Might not need to
worry about the bug if this don't go good. Before I get near the
office Ball comes out and blocks my way like he's setting a screen.
Wonder where he gets jean jackets to fit his long-ass arms.

"Hold down, little man," he says and slides one of his long
arms around me like I'm his girl. Pats my ass in public, right out
on Martin Luther King Boulevard.

I can't keep from grinning.

"Ain't nothing funny. Why you smiling?" the big Kareem-looking fool says.

"I ain't smiling," I say smiling.

"Come on. He's waiting on you."

He walks behind me but he's so long that he can reach ahead and open the door to the office before I can get there. From the outside the office looks like a concrete box, except for a spy hole in the center of the heavy metal door, and the inside don't look much different. Just about bare except for a desk and a huge safe taking up most of the room. Cowboy's in a big leather chair watching a tiny color TV and talking on a cellular phone. His other boy, Biz Mac, the football player, is sitting in a little folding chair that looks like it's just gonna cave in under all that butt.

"Sit here," Ball says pointing to a chair in a corner.

Cowboy keeps talking, something about point spreads. Then "Big doofus muthafucka can't play no ball. You keep his ass." He lights a cigarette. Fuck. I can smell that shit already, burning, sizzling on my skin. He gets off the phone and turns the swivel chair to me.

"Yeah, bout time you called. What took you?"

"I don't know."

"You know."

He looks at me and takes a long drag on the cigarette till the tip's cherry red.

"I was scared."

"Why was you scared. Did you do something to be scared about?"

"No," I say wondering if it's a trick question or something. He laughs and his smooth, rubbery face wrinkles.

"What? You owe me something like that knucklehead Tommy?"

"No. I never stole from you."

"But you knew Tommy was?"

The ashes hang from the end of the cigarette ready to fall.

"Biz, get me an ashtray," he says.

"I thought he might be. That's why I quit and came home."

"Yeah, that was intelligent. Cause you know Tommy's going to get his ass smoked. You know that."

"Yeah, I figured."

"See, he tried to set you up. Blame everything on you just so he'd have a little time to put some distance between me and him." Cowboy pauses like he wants me to say something.

"I thought he might do something like that."

"See, Tommy figured I'd be ruthless and take you out cause I was pissed off about getting burned. See, he just set you up from the get go."

"Yeah, I guess so."

"But you didn't play him out and call me to tell what was happening."

"No. I guess I messed up."

"Yeah, you messed up."

He leans back in his big leather chair and smiles at me and the room gets tense. Biz and Ball act like they not paying attention but they're bout ready to rock my world.

"It was you who was mailing the checks to me."

"Yeah."

"Thought so. Tommy writes like grade school kids. It was stupid what you did but I like the fact you didn't drop a dime on Tommy, and, you can count, and, you mail the checks the way I wanted them mailed."

"Thanks."

"Always be straight with me, cause if you ain't . . . ."

Biz gets me by the shoulders and Ball's got my wrist, twisting it so it's palm side up. Cowboy comes over, knocks the ash off and takes a drag till it's glowing red and he grinds it out on my wrist.

"Glad you aren't screaming. That's for your mistake. It's like what them Japanese gangsters do, what they call them? Yakuza? But they cut a finger off. When you work for me you get one mistake. You've made yours."

I can't keep the tears from squeezing out.

"I got something for you. Something for a honest young man who's got some sense. Let me tell you about it. Sit down."

*   *   *

Not going to do it. Don't want to look at that fool or those two
stupid dogs. She sees me sitting in a new ride. Just making me sweat
cause I wanted to see her more than she wanted to see me. When
she's gone for good, never driving down this block again. The door
opens, here she comes. Canary yellow miniskirt. Guess she don't
want people looking at the bride. She strides down the steps and
through the yard like she's mad as hell. I go around to open the door
for her. Not a word about the Jeep. She just gets in frowning.

"What's up with sitting in the car?"

"Didn't want to see your daddy," I say trying to look at her
but I turn to check for traffic instead.

"So you leave me hanging?"

"I thought you would see me."

"Oh, it's my fault. You're the one who wanted to go to this
thing. I was just going to mail them a toaster. It's no big thing
to me."

Shrug it off. This is what I've been missing? Still though,
she looks good. And what happens to me, being with her makes
me . . .

I drive down Imperial to the Harbor. Shouldn't be traffic at
eleven.

"Which way you gonna go to Santa Barbara?"

"Thinking about taking the coast," I say.

"Yeah, I suppose you would know."

"What's that supposed to mean?"

"You were working up there so I guess you should know how
to get there."

"Yeah, I guess I should."

"So how that turned out? You get rich or did you get left
holding the bag?"

"I don't want to talk about that. I didn't want to see you to
argue about the same old shit."

"Oh, I see. You don't want to listen to me. Don't want to
listen to what I got to say. So why did you want to see me?"

All I can do is shake my head. I forgot what it was like and
we just started driving.

"Admit it. You love me and you can't live without me."

"Why you want to hear that. What does it do for you?"

She smiles and starts to go through the radio stations trying to find something she likes.

"You seem to be doing all right for yourself. When you get the Jeep?"

"Last week."

"Thought you said you didn't have that kind of cash."

"Things have changed."

"So that's why you don't look so crazy. You ain't working for a fool like Tommy. You got a real boss."

"You don't know what's been going on with me. Maybe I got a good job."

"Yeah, okay."

She thinks she's so fucking smart. How did I get myself into this . . .

"How's it going with your mother moving and all that? You got another place to live?"

"Yeah, I got something lined up. I'm glad she's going. Ain't nothing out here for her and Mary."

I catch her sighing. Her fingers drumming on her purse looking like she needs to say something she don't want to say.

"Why ain't you going with her?"

I thought it was going to be something like that. Worrying about me.

"What I'm going to do in Atlanta? I got things going finally. I'm doing right for myself."

"So what you got going?"

"I got a job at a check cashing store."

"Oh, that's it. You happy about working at one of those places?"

"I'm going to be running it. Once I get trained."

"And starting pay is enough for you to buy this?"

"I had some money saved."

"Bet it ain't legal. Who are you fronting for?"

"I'm not fronting for anybody. Why are you worried about my business? Not that long ago you wouldn't talk to me."

"Yeah, that's true. But that's because of how you're living."

"We already talked about that."

"Yeah, I'll say it again because you need to hear it. I might love you but I'm not going to be with you. I am not going to be with you when you get shot. Or when you start hitting the pipe. I shouldn't even be with you now."

Love me? So she admits it.

"I don't understand you. You came back from your big-ass business trip and you were tapped out. People were talking about how you were acting, saying shit like you were smoking or crazy. Your mama was asking for advice about what to do with you. She asked me. She asked Michaels."

"That's the first time you said that, about being in love with me," I say. And now she's getting mad that she said it. Words, that's all. Empty. But they make me want to believe that she does, she did. I look at the beach rolling by, the girls, the cars. The road going around the hills.

"That's the last time I am going to say it. And that's all I'm going to say about your job and you cause I know you don't want to hear it. You got yourself a new life, something you think you can handle."

"I'm gonna be okay. Don't worry about me."

She rolls her eyes.

"Don't tell me what to do."

"You don't have to worry."

"Maybe I can't stop."

Have to hold on to the wheel. All the traffic, bumper to bumper. She goes into her purse and comes out with a tissue, and leans over to wipe my face.

"So stupid. Crying."

"I'm not."

I try to stop but I know I can't. Can't even drive. I pull over to the shoulder and open the door and get out. "Watch out!" I hear her yell. Truck blows by, kicking sand. Sprint across PCH dodging traffic to the beach. She's out of the car now on the edge of the highway with her hands on her hips, dress flipping as the cars pass. She yells, "Not running after you," as I run to the water. I want to stop at the edge but I'm going too fast and the surf gets my shoes and cuffs. It don't take long for me to get myself together. Walking along the beach a little ways does it. I go back thinking about what happened, how she just says anything and I'm falling apart when I thought she couldn't do that to me. I cross the highway and she's waiting by the Jeep.

"Let me drive," she says holding her hand out for the keys.

"I'm okay."

"Yeah, but I better drive. I'm not going to wreck your car."

"You know how to drive a stick?"

"Yeah," she says and gets in.

She pulls out and after popping the clutch a few times and almost getting us rear-ended she gets going.

"Don't be looking at me like that."

"I'm not looking at you. I was looking at the cars behind you."

"Men always got to drive. Like it's some kind of right."

Guess I oughta just sit back and enjoy it.

We get to Santa Barbara in an hour and a half. I tell her where Garden Street is and we find the church. It's a big church, bigger than most churches I've seen. And it's on a big hunk of land with the mountains behind it.

"It's a pretty church," I say and she wheels into the parking lot that's almost full.

"Come on. We're late."

We walk up the steps and I try to open the door for Margot but it's locked.

"See, we're late. If you would have taken your dead ass out of the car and come and got me . . ."

I see some people come up and head along the side of the church, got to have another entrance so I grab her arm and lead her that way and yeah, there's a whole line of people waiting to get into the church. An usher, some guy who looks enough like Michaels to be his brother, is keeping the crowd back. In front of us is a tall blond-haired guy holding hands with a fine black female. She's dressed kind of weird like that MTV announcer.

"So what you think of that? Black woman doing that to y'all,"
Margot whispers. Knew she had to have something to say about it.

"I don't know. That's her if she wants to."

Margot lets her mouth hang open.

"It's you saying that? Guess living in Santa Barbara changed
you."

Finally that guy steps aside and lets us into the church. We've
got some latecomers behind us so at least we ain't the last ones to
arrive. I see why they decided to get married here. Church looks
like it's worth a whole lot of money, marble and gold, big stained
glass windows. Michaels is lined up near the altar and his woman,
Tina, is there at the end of the processional like something out of
father of the bride; veil and a long train, and flower girls tossing
rose petals. She looks pretty. Prettier than I thought Michaels would
be with.

"Is that what you want? Somebody to walk down the aisle
with?" I ask.

"Be quiet and watch the wedding."

Michaels looks sort of silly in a tux but maybe it's him. He
don't act serious enough. Grinning and looking at the ceiling like
he's having a good time. It's the end though, that's it for him if he's
going to be true.

Margot grabs my arm and puts her nails into me and pulls me
close.

"I want somebody who'd do it if I wanted it done," she says
in a hard whisper.

"You don't think I'll do it?" She doesn't answer, shakes her
head and puts her hand up to end it. I know she's thinking that's
what she gonna do one day. Michaels and Tina walk up the steps
to light candles and Michaels hits a step and almost stumbles.

"Is this supposed to be beautiful? You think it's beautiful?"

"I think you ought to be quiet."

"It cost a lot of money. I know that."

She looks at me like I'm the biggest fool in the world. Then
she almost smiles.

"Stop worrying. Nobody's gonna drag you to the altar. Least
of all me."

The minister, a cool little man, finally gets around to "You may kiss the bride," and they do, but they do it so quickly that if you blinked you missed it. Then they parade back out. It's a done deal.

The reception's next door. We file in and a light-skinned guy who's got to be another one of Michaels' brothers seats us at a table with folks. At least half of the people coming into the reception hall are white. They've got a lot of white friends.

"Where's Michaels and Tina?"

"Posing for photos," Margot says like I should know. Then she looks over at the table where the gifts are being stacked.

"Did you bring the present?" she asks me.

"Naw, I left it in the car. I'll get it," I say cause that's what she wants to hear. I get up and walk the long way around the room trying to avoid all the people hovering around the buffet table even though nothing is even out. All that just to eat. I go through a side door and end up on the other side of the parking lot near the picnic tables, almost like a little park on the church grounds. They're there posing for the wedding photos in front of great big rose bushes. Michaels and Tina look happy like they've really done something. After going to the car and getting the present I stop and watch them go through the poses. Having to kiss and hold hands, to look like they're the happiest couple who's ever lived. Don't make sense to me cause it ain't gonna last. Nothing lasts.

"Where you've been?" she says glancing at the black female with the white guy. She's got a glass of champagne. Half the plastic glasses in the center of the table are now empty in front of Margot.

"I was watching them pose for pictures."

"You? Didn't know you was interested. You should have been here, think I've got that Oreo freaked out. She won't even look in my direction."

"Let's go outside," I say.

"For what?"

"It's pretty."

"That's a good reason?"

"It's good enough."

She shakes her head and stands up and carries out two glasses
of champagne. Outside, I lead her to the picnic tables close to where
Michaels and Tina and their families are still being positioned for
another shot. Margot stands there, waiting for me to wipe the bench
before she'll sit. I do and she hands me a glass.

"Yeah, you're right, it's pretty out here."

"How many glasses is that for you?" I ask her but she smiles
and looks away.

"If I drink too much nothing's going to happen. I'll just be
buzzed and you'll drive."

"You want to spend the night here?"

"At the church?"

"No, in Santa Barbara. I'll get us a room close to the beach."

She rolls her eyes, smiles again and looks like she's considering it.

"Sometimes you remind me of one of those Al Green records
my daddy listens to. You want to feel bad cause it makes you feel
good or something."

"I don't know what you mean."

"You can see the ocean too. It is pretty here."

"So?"

"So, what?"

"You want to stay or what?"

She slides next to me, puts her arms around me and looks at
me, her lips inches away.

"Think about it. Can't you picture it. Us in a motel room after
we've done it. Then what? You getting mad because you really
wanted to make that baby. And me feeling bad cause I've done
something else I didn't want to do."

"So that's it. We can't enjoy ourselves? Spend a night together?"

"I am enjoying myself. Being with you without you acting like
. . . how you've been acting."

"But we'd have something else to . . . remember."

"You know we should go on in and dance. You ought to have
some champagne."

I take both her hands and hold them, keep her here.

"Don't look like that."

"Like what?"

"If I did what would it mean to you?"

What to say to convince her?

"I'd be with you . . ."

"For the last time. It would be for the last time," she says.

"It don't have to be like that."

"It does. It would be like that. It's up to you."

"I don't know."

"Think about it. You decide."

Michaels don't know how to dance. Don't know how at all. Got Margot by the waist all wrong. But she looks happy, talking to him like she's the one who's marrying him. Stupid to get jealous. Even after the song they stay out there, talking. Tina isn't even looking at them like you think she would. Instead she's dancing with a boy, making him put his hands on her waist, guiding him around the dance floor, just enjoying teasing him. The music stops and the DJ, this tall white guy wearing polka dot pants and a red striped shirt and a straw hat, is looking for another cassette. People start to leave the dance floor but Michaels and Margot stay out there still talking like they've got a lot to say. I step to the DJ and go looking through the tapes.

"Want to hear something in particular?" he asks.

"Yeah, a slow dance."

"Slow? I have 'Reasons.' "

"By Earth, Wind and Fire?"

"Yeah."

"You listen to that?"

"Oh yeah, they're happening."

"Cool," I say and intercept Margot before she gets off the dance floor.

"Too tired. Feet hurt," she says pulling away from me.

"Come on. It's a slow dance. You ain't going to have to do anything."

"All right," she says but she takes her heels off and runs to our table to leave them.

"Nobody better steal them."

"Nobody's gonna steal them," I say and we stand out there the only people on the dance floor, waiting for the DJ to cue the tape. I'm looking at her but she's looking at her feet. "Man I hope I don't ruin these stockings but I know I am."

She really is buzzed. The music starts, and I step up and put my arms around her and she relaxes like she usually doesn't and we go around in slow circles. Her head is snug on my shoulder, feel her against me . . . soft like she will . . . "We oughta go." She doesn't look up. The song ends, and I lead her off the dance floor away from the guests and we leave through the side door.

"Hey wait. We didn't thank them and say goodbye," she says all alert.

"We've got to do that?"

She don't answer. So we go back in, Margot leading the way trying to walk like she's not buzzed but she is, stumbling a little every couple of steps. She beelines straight for their table but they're gone, everyone, all those dozens of people who were so interested in stuffing their faces are crowding to see them off.

"We missed them. They're going."

I catch up with her and try to nudge her back the way we came but she follows the crowd, going after them to do what, throw rice? I go through the door looking for Margot but all I see is a big-assed crowd and little kids jumping up to see what's going on. Michaels opens the door of his tired Sentra for Tina to slide in. Wouldn't be having all that trouble trying to get that long train of Tina's to fit in the front seat if he would have sprung for a limo.

"See, they're going so we can go."

Margot shrugs and watches them drive off. Guess it was a good time for them to go, with the sun setting and all.

"Come on, let's go," I say sliding my arm around Margot. She lets me lead her inside and through the almost cleared-out hall and over to the other parking lot. She holds on to me when I unlock the door for her. I kind of have to lift her up and lower her in because she really is helpless. The Jeep kicks over with one crank and I drive off a high curb to avoid all the cars leaving through the one exit but even the bouncing of the car don't wake her. She was flinging

around a little so I stop again and lean over to strap on her seat belt.
We stay on State down until the cruisers jam up a whole block so I
cut across till Bath and take that down to the beach to that new hotel
they just built. I park and turn off the car and check her out. She's
sleeping for real, almost snoring. So I get out and go into the lobby
of this big hotel right on the beach and go to the clerk to see if they
got rooms available. At first he looks at me like I might be up to
something but when I show him my credit card and a wallet full of
ducats he gets on with it. I go back outside and drive us over to
where our room is, and it looks good. The room is straight across
from the pool, lots of palms like it's an oasis. Margot is just about
dead weight, got to carry her to the door. She's slipping out my
hands as I try to get the door open. I do and carry her inside and
lay her on the bed. It's kind of a small room but it's nice with a big
TV and it has a bar. She's on her side, the yellow dress is all twisted
up showing her ass all the way up to the waistband of her stockings.
Get out of my clothes, down to my shorts, toss that shit into the
corner. What I'm gonna do with her? Get them stockings off first.
I put my hands under the waistband and try to slide them, but they
don't come. I try again, but she just rolls over. So I straddle her ass
and try to work them down.

"What are you doing!" she says rolling me off of her. As soon
as I'm off she pulls a pillow over her eyes and goes back to sleep.
So I slide alongside of her and lift the pillow up and say to her,
"You oughta get outta your clothes. You can't sleep like that." She
don't say anything, just breathing deep and steady. So I say it again,
louder.

"I heard you the first time," she says pushing me away.

"Let me help you . . ."

"Here," she says and sits up pulling her skirt off over her
head. She twists out of her stockings and hands them to me.

"This is what you want."

She sits there cross-legged, shaking her head. Then she looks
at me like I've done something too stupid. The bra she got on, she
never wore those when she was with me. See right through it. Don't
see how that's supposed to hold anything. Then she falls back on
the bed and twists the covers around her.

"Margot . . . I thought . . . we were gonna . . ."

"Okay, okay," she says and tosses the cover off of her. Now that's it. Bout time. She's leaning over me. Feel them nipples on my chest. Yeah.

"Where is it."

"What?"

"The rubber. You know . . ."

"I know."

Reach over to the dresser and grope around in the dark till I feel the package. She takes it from me and slips it on. She leans over and takes my wrists, her nipples brushing against my mouth.

"This is what you want?"

"Yeah. I want it."

"This is it," she says and works it till it's done.

She's gone when I wake up. I look around the room, in the bathroom, then I notice the sliding door's open. She's outside. Back in her miniskirt, and her hair fixed up. She's sitting at a table near the pool, eating a croissant and drinking orange juice with her legs crossed, not even noticing the guys checking her out. After I hop in the shower I go on out into the bright morning sun and it's so beautiful. I walk to her table and it's like it never was when I was up here.

"Nice morning," I say and sit down.

"Nice hotel," she says. She holds up her glass of juice. "They got a breakfast buffet. On the other side of the pool. It's free."

"Yeah," I say and walk over and get my breakfast from a spread of fruit and rolls and stuff. I come back with a load and she rolls her eyes cause I took too much but she takes a croissant and strawberries right off my plate. After we eat and we go back into the room I try to kiss her, but she slides away and kisses me on the cheek.

"We got to get back. I don't want him to nut up."

So we get on. Driving along the coast, with the ocean on one side and hills on the other. Margot going through my CDs, playing that slow stuff she likes. It's like a movie.

*   *   *

Soon as we get off the freeway on Imperial, it's over. It's overcast, like it's going to rain. And Margot is quiet. Bet it's her fucked-up pops.

"What you going to say to him about last night?" I say a few blocks from her house.

"I told him I might stay up with some girlfriends."

I pull up to her house and reach down to cut the engine but she grabs my hand.

"Don't cut your engine. Thanks for the trip. It was fun," she says and slides out with her dress sliding up. She gets to the gate, unlocks it, then she comes back around to my side, leans in and kisses me. "Goodbye," she says and this time she goes on in.

That's it? Yeah. She's just fronting. She'll be calling. I got it together. Got it going on.

14
Sally

■

Mama stayed with this church and she ain't gonna ever leave. I haven't been here since I was in high school. They don't do much to keep it up. They still have that black Jesus mural behind the altar. I used to stare at that. A black Jesus among a flock of white-as-snow sheep with a happy lion looking on. That lion, I knew he was going to eat those sheep soon as Jesus turned his head but that was before Mama told me it was a good lion.

They really can sing. A nice big choir and Mama likes it. Her rocking is rocking me and that ain't easy to do. The minister looks like an old bear with the white head of hair and white beard.

It's a really nice old church. People still come here even though Vermont ain't the nicest street anymore. Now, it's nothing but Latinos and they got their own churches. What's that they're singing now, "God Has Smiled on Me," never heard it like that before.

"Mama, what you think of that."

"Huh, baby?"

"What you think of the choir?"

"It's sweet." She don't bother to look at me cause she's enjoying it so much.

The minister stands smiling like he's got a choir that rocks the rafters but the singing stops and we sit down. Mama needs to catch her breath and so do I. Got me sweating. Out comes the baskets.

"May we have a moment of prayer before the missionary offering," the deep-voiced minister says. Mama comes out with a dollar. The baskets are passing through the pews like they trust you. Not like that storefront church I was going to last year where they have the baskets on long poles like somebody is ready to slip a bill out. Then a skinny minnie gets up there, wearing one of them expensive wigs.

"Hello and welcome to Hill Church of God in Christ this beautiful Sunday morning. Please stand if this is your first visit to our church."

Mama nudges me like I should stand but I'm not a guest. I used to come here. But she pulls me to my feet. And they go around to each of the new people and finally they get around to us.

"This here is my daughter, Sally. She used to belong but now . . ."

"Oh," the church secretary says. "Well, I hope she comes back to our family. She is always welcome to return home."

Mama nods and gives her a warm, toothy smile and we sit down. It is good to be here and the people do seem nice but Mama shouldn't be joining me up. I belong to Price Chapel.

After the general offering the minister stands up and begins his sermon but I can't bring myself to truly listen. Instead, I think of breakfast.

Church ends and we file out to have fellowship in the bright Sunday morning sunshine. Mama sees the minister shaking hands, a whole lot of hands. Mama tugs my arms and gets me in the line. Takes a long time before we get to him but as soon as he takes Mama's hands he's smiling like she's the best thing he's ever seen.

"I do expect to see your lovely daughter visit our church again."

Mama smiles and turns to me and they both eyeball me waiting for an answer.

"I'll come again."

"I'm glad to hear that," the minister says.

"I took your sermon to heart. We've got to start sacrificing for what we believe in."

"Well, maybe you could help out with our homeless program. We bring them in and feed them and give them a place for a night."

Mama nods, and says "yes" for me.

"Sounds good to me," I say and we leave. All the way home
Mama talks about the sermon.

I got the kind of job that wears you out but you're not really doing
anything. Data entry ain't bad work but it's so boring it has your
mind tired and that gets your body tired, maybe that's why I got so
big but when I come home from work and see that boy sitting on
the steps looking like who knows what the cat drug in with a beer
between his legs and a beanie as low on his eyes as he could get it
without blinding himself it makes me more tired just to see him and
I thank the Lord I don't have no kids because I know I don't have
the strength to raise them in this day and time. Plus, what if I came
out with something like Ollie. I'd be sorely tempted to send him
back where I got him from even though it's wrong to even think
like that.

"What's up?" he says drawling like he been slurping beers all
day. I walk by him ignoring whatever he's got to say and go on into
the house. From the living room I can see Mama cooking up a storm
in the kitchen like she ain't done since Doug. Cooking like she's
got to feed plenty plus she's got someone over I've never seen
before. A hard-faced, youngish woman helping stir the big pots.

"Hi, baby, you home from work. This is Bea from church.
She works with the homeless. Helping me cook for tonight."

"Pleased to meet you, Bea," I say shaking her rough hand,
missing teeth, woman's lived a life.

"Tonight?" I say to Mama.

"Yes, child. I told you it's my turn to take food to the church."

She's looking at me with pleading eyes. She must need a hand.
I really do not feel like offering. That's the kind of church she goes
to, where you've got to lend a hand when all you want to do is
climb in bed and turn on the TV.

"You gonna change or are you gonna come like that?"

"Give me a couple minutes," I say and go on to my room to
put on sweats and get out of my dress. Bed looks inviting. I could
crawl right in and not even eat dinner. But they need me and I guess
I got the strength. When I come out the bedroom Bea and Mama

got big pots in their hands, and Ollie's got the biggest pot and skinny as he is he can barely hold on to it.

"Need some help?"

"Naw, I got it."

I make sure the stove is off and follow him out, swaying with that big pot like a sailor on rough seas. We load the food in the trunk and Bea gets into the backseat with Mama. So I guess I'm supposed to drive and then I see Ollie holding his hand out.

"Boy, I'm not giving you money. You capable of getting a job."

"The keys. Mama said I could drive."

Shake my head and hand him the keys. Boy is so pitiful. After getting his behind kicked up and down the street by every thug who had the time to do it, he comes home to be the family chauffeur.

"But you've got to take off the beanie."

"The beanie? Why you always sweating me about my beanie?"

"Boy, don't act dense. Take it off and let's go."

He pulls off the beanie and stuffs it into his baggy back pocket and gets in. I kind of hate driving with him cause he acts like he has got no home training. Soon as he gets in, the radio comes on to the station he knows we're not going to listen to. Then he got to lean so low in the seat he can barely see over the wheel. And every time he comes to a signal he looks to check out the world. Looking for trouble in a '68 Rambler wagon. Think he'd be embarrassed. And if he sees a thug he knows he's in heaven, says, "Oh yeah, I'm rolling. Back on the set," to just about everybody. Sad to see. Least he don't drive fast, easing us out in traffic. I guess it's good for him, close as he's going to get to a church.

"Reverend says they feed forty of them and they stay all night, sleep on cots in the auditorium," Mama says. She's really into the spirit of this church.

"Sounds like they're making a true effort to do good work."

"Yes, they are. Bea here used to be homeless, now she helps the program."

"Yes, ma'am," Bea says and I hear that Mississippi accent.

"Where you from, Bea?"

"Bay Saint Louis, Mississippi. Been living in L.A. too long. Ain't been no kind of luck for me."

"Bea stays at the homeless house. The reverend and his wife got a few families living next to the church," Mama says.

"You've got a baby, Bea?"

"Two. Mary Anne, she's four. Nicole Marie, she's six."

Hear the music in her voice, how they sing what they say down there.

"Bea's doing good. The reverend says he's really proud of her."

Bea doesn't say anything, must be embarrassed. It ain't easy. Sometimes Mama don't know when not to say something.

"Hey, where's the church, where I go, left?" Ollie shouts.

"On Adams."

"Man, I hate to go around there. Got them slobs around there."

The boy irritates me when he talks like that. It's like he hasn't learned nothing.

We come to the church and Ollie pulls into the parking lot that's half filled with cars. People really do help out. We get out and go around to the tailgate and unload the food. The security guard comes up. "Need help?" he says. He's worried about Ollie. So that is what that is. Thinks Ollie's off the street looking for a purse to snatch.

"Naw, we got it. Unless you want to carry this pot of beans," Ollie says, offering the pot to the guard. The guard, a little Latino man, looks molded, and steps back. "No, that's okay," he says but Ollie don't let it go. Steps up with the pot and forces the guard to take it.

"Thanks, doc. Gotta watch the ride."

Ollie gets back in the car and cranks the radio and the rest of us follow the guard into the church.

We walk in the back way through the storage area, only one light so it's kind of dark and smells of ammonia. The guard turns around to open the double doors with his butt. Inside, the auditorium is filled with women. Women with kids, young kids, babies, cots stretched from one side of the room to the other.

"Kitchen's on the other side," the guard says and we walk single file through the narrow way separating the beds.

"Looks like more than forty," I say.

"We only take women and most of them got babies."

Through another set of double doors and we go into one of them big industrial kitchens with a huge stove and lots of burners and long rows of folding tables covered with butcher paper. Lots of people are in the kitchen setting up plates and dishing out food. The reverend's wife's there at the stove, sweating up a storm in front of all them pots. She comes over to us smiling like she didn't expect to see us.

"Glad y'all could make it. I never seen so many children looking for a place. Need all the food and help we can get."

After that we just work our behinds off, taking turns feeding them kids, lines of them wanting to eat. Kids who haven't had a bath in days. Want to make a person just cry. And we feed them, beautiful little girls whose braids need doing and boys whose hair needs to be cut. At first it seemed quiet, seeing all those faces, kids' eyes watching us serve them. Guess I was too tense to hear the racket going on in here but now with babies crying, and some of the mothers doing the same thing, loud talking, arguing over who's got to take the trash out, it's too loud to think. Maybe I'm just getting tired and that's why it seems louder. Soon though, with everybody helping we get things done.

First I thought it was because I was tired and seeing things. I step up and around to make sure and again I see that face, blank now. Like there's not a thought going on inside that head.

I want to drag her off that cot. Shaking like I'm possessed, possessed with the need to tear into her, beat her till she bleeds. She's got on something like a bluish hospital smock, it's dirty, but she isn't. She's clean, scrubbed and fresh like she just got out of the shower. But it's like I don't want to see what's there in front of me, her lying there, the skinny minnie she is with a beach ball coming up from under the smock. She must be seven or eight months pregnant. Should I say something? Should I say you killed him. You should be in jail. You should be in the mental hospital. You should be dead. What if she sees me and tries to run? What if something happens and it's on me. Back off, that's all I can think of. Kids playing around me, little guy running from his sister. I move away careful not to step on him. He falls, splats on the floor, so I pick him up and send him on his way. Douglas' flesh, his blood, our blood is in there. Douglas never did understand a thing . . . sowing the seed . . . but not tending the soil. It won't stop, it won't stop with him, or her, or Ollie.

The reverend's wife, Jo Carole Alexander, is so worn out she's sitting on a stool by the door, like she's trying to get the strength to drag herself together to go home. I pull over a stool and sit next to her.

"Tired, Mrs. Alexander?"

"Oh yes. This always wears me out and I'll be back in the morning to do it all over again."

I shake my head in amazement. "That pregnant woman in the other room, what's her story?"

Her red eyes open for a second and she shrugs. "Honey, there's lots of pregnant women in there."

"The white-looking one. With the long hair."

"Oh, that one. She been with us a little bit now. Usually we don't . . . you know keep them around too long but she's . . . you know . . . There's so little we can do. We want to get her in a hospital under care but that's so hard."

Poor woman rubs her hands together like they're bothering her. "I admire how much you're doing here."

"Just come back. We need people like you."

I turn to tell Mama we should go but she's not leaning on the table anymore. She's gone out of the kitchen. I go into the auditorium and she's not there either. Here she comes and Ollie's with her. Must have got him to help with the trash or something. This is what the devil does. Plagues us with moments like this where the whole world stops and waits for the worst possible thing to happen.

"What are you standing there like that for," Mama asks. "Ollie's gonna take the trash bags and we can get the rest of the pots. Are you listening?"

"Yes, just thinking."

"She's tripping off one of them homeless people. What you gonna do bring one of them home?" Ollie says looking where I'm looking so I turn away. Head to the kitchen hoping he don't see what I see.

"If you do she better be good-looking cause I ain't having no ugly homeless girl around the house."

He goes and we get the pots and help with the trash and I make them go out another way and we have to walk on the street to the parking lot and Ollie complains cause he doesn't want slobs to see him.

If I do anything it's got to be for the baby. She's made her bed she's got to sleep in it. She and Doug, that was their hell on this earth. He lived it and now she still has to. The Lord works to test us. See if we have the strength, the understanding to live righteously. She took my brother but I won't judge her. I must help her but I can't love her. Just as arrogant and possessed as Douglas. Urging him on, think he'd know where they were heading, where she was dragging him. What should I do? They're doing what they can for her and I'm in no position to do anything. House is off limits and I can't tell Mama. I don't know how'd she take it. Not that she know. Ollie had sense enough not to go screaming to Mama like he did to me. He didn't have to tell me, could see that coming too. The devil brought them together and took them apart. Maybe Rika's gone through enough to give it up. Let me raise it cause she can't.

I call the church and get the address of the homeless house and go over there on my lunch hour. Soon as I get there I don't think it's such a good idea. I mean it's just not the kind of street a woman wants to be walking down. Men sitting on the steps of run-down apartment buildings or hanging around the curb just looking at me like they've never seen a black woman walking down a street. I get there. It's a small house that needs a paint job and it has dry dirt for a lawn. It's got a chain-link fence with no gate like they don't have the money to finish it. I go up to the door thinking for some reason they'd all be outside on the porch watching the day go by. I listen at the door cause it seems no one's home but I hear something, a

radio. I knock and the door opens and it's Bea and she's in that
same sweatsuit as yesterday but her short hair is in curlers. She
don't look happy to see me.

"Hi, Bea, how you doing?"

"Fine," she says and we stay at the door. I smell bleach, like
someone's doing serious cleaning.

"So, how's it going."

"Okay."

So she's not going say much. Comes out with a cigarette. She
fumbles to light it, gets it lit and looks at me like she giving in.

"You want to come in?"

"Thanks." I follow her in and I see why she looks so irritated.
The house looks like a junk sale. Living room is crowded to the top
with boxes, worn-down furniture and secondhand clothes. I follow
Bea through the mess into the kitchen. The kitchen is clean and
white with an egg-yellow breakfast table. It's a nice kitchen.

"Doing a lot of work?"

"Yeah, getting this place together but you know it's a lot of
trouble. Some of these women never had nothing so they don't know
how to take care of nothing."

"Sounds like it's too crowded."

"Yeah. We got four other kids here and two women. One's
got a burger job so I don't mind helping her out. She do her share
but that other thing, what's her name, Mary. Now that woman gets
on my nerves. Just sleeps or sits out in the backyard watching the
grass grow. Never lifts a hand to even cook for herself. And I do
resent cleaning up behind her."

"You think she's right in the head?"

"Who that, Mary?" Bea laughs and puts on a pair of rubber
gloves.

"She's crazy. Cocaine crazy. Her lips are cracked and she's
got that look. But I guess she deserves some credit. She might be
burned out but she ain't been doing it long as she's been here."

"Is she outside now?"

"Oh yeah. Soon as she's up it's outside. What, you think
you can do something with her? She's not on this planet. See for
yourself."

So I go into the backyard, down rickety steps, and see her sitting on a folding chair. Still in that smock, looking ripe and peaceful as a peach.

"What are you doing here?" she says to me without turning her head.

"Me?" I say sounding stupid. "Just want to see how you doing."

I see why she sits in the yard. It's a jungle, overgrown vines covering the broken-down fence, and moss is coming up through the brick patio.

"Really," she says like she's truly bored.

"You going to have a baby."

"Oh," she says rubbing her worn sneakers against the bricks. The soles are about gone, flopping.

"Maybe I can help you."

"Really," she says and turns toward me. She just is a pretty girl even after all what she done to herself.

"You need things. And your baby is going to need a whole lot of things."

"Don't worry yourself. Who knows if this thing," she pats her big belly, "is your brother's."

She's smiling. Calm, like seeing me is nothing to her, water off of a duck's back.

"What about your family. Do they know where you are?"

"No," she says and shifts around so she's facing away from me.

"It's up to you. I'm not going to cause problems for you."

Her hair got long. Long and almost blond.

"You can leave because I don't need help. I'm fine."

"What is it? You think I'm going to tell somebody I know where you are? What's done is done. And Douglas, what happened to him was going to happen to him sooner or later."

"Yeah, that's a fact," Rika says.

"Just thinking about the baby."

"Baby? You keep talking about a baby. Maybe I'm not having the baby."

"That's the devil talking."

She stands up, swaying a little cause she's off balance, and starts for the steps and she's gone into the house.

Bea's on her knees scrubbing hard the yellowish tile on the tub.

"Bea, could you do me a favor?"

"Thought you had gone," she says and pushes herself up and looks at me.

"That Mary. Could you keep an eye on her for me. Here's my number."

I hand her a slip of paper and a twenty.

"If something happens, if she leaves let me know."

"That's that important to you?" she says taking the money and the number.

"Yeah, it is."

She sits on the edge of the tub and smiles but it's not a smile, it's pity.

"You're in for a hard road caring about that woman. You know she'd be on the street if it wasn't for the fact she's pregnant and you know she. . . . The reverend thinks she's pretty but he's a good man. Not like some of them ministers."

I nod. "Yeah, I know it's not easy . . . but it's important to me. So . . ."

"Oh yeah, that's easy enough." She goes back to cleaning and I go on to work.

Ollie's on the porch, sitting with his legs stretched out blocking the steps. I'm supposed to ask him to move, but I refuse and step over him.

"Girl, you don't have no kind of manners."

All I can do is keep walking cause I don't want to say nothing profane. Mama's resting on the couch, the smell of fried chicken comes floating in, but I can't eat.

"Honey, you hungry? Dinner's ready."

"Isn't it Tuesday?"

"Yes it is, child. What of it?"

"Shouldn't we be at the church? I thought you liked this church."

She's not going nowhere, just sinks a little lower into the couch. Nothing to say . . . She got every right to relax, done her share of scuffling. I might as well go on and tell her about Rika but I can't do it. Not today, can't face talking to that . . . Rika. It's like that kid in *The Exorcist*. I've got to find a smooth rock to deal with her.

"Gonna watch TV with me, baby?" Mama asks.

"Sure, Mama. I'm too tired to be going out anyway."

"Fix yourself a plate to eat. You gonna get weak."

"No chance of that, Mama, big as I am."

So I sit in the soft chair where I usually sit but it's not comfortable. And I don't want to eat. What I want is to not worry about that girl. Been a week but it feels like less than a day, thinking I oughta drop by to talk sense to her. Pray for her. Get her to pray with me. But I don't have that kind of strength.

Boom, boom, boom . . . keeps up that noise those boys call music.

"See about that," Mama says.

So I go to the door and crack it and just as I expect, Ollie's hanging in the window of a lowrider. I step out onto the porch and call to him.

"Ollie, tell that boy to turn that noise down."

Turns around, all ugly like he wants to curse me. He knows better than that so he just waves me off, sticks his head back in the lowrider and continues even though cars got to stop and pull around them blocking the street, cause that don't matter.

"Go on in! Mind your business," he says. Boy is going to hell. Think he might have learned something. God took him so low not just as a sign but a blow, just a fool not to see. Beat him so good, whoever that was that did it meant to kill him. That was his chance to find Jesus being that close to death's door but he didn't do nothing except mend. Still acting a fool, using them drugs, drinking. I'd rather throw him out and let him kill himself on his own but Mama . . . she don't see it that way.

"Go in!" he says. I stay right where I am. I got every right to watch him consort with sin. Stare down the devil, cause the devil don't want to be watched, exposed to the light.

"Baby, phone." Mama's at the door, so I go in. "Bout time,"

I hear Ollie say. Inside, Mama's back on the couch, pointing to the phone. "Got a call."

Who's this?

"Hello?"

"Sally, this is Bea."

"Hi, Bea. What's going on?" She probably can't even hear me, whispering like I am cause Mama can sometimes hear what you don't expect her to hear.

"Mary, you wanted me to call about her."

"Yeah, something happened?"

It's coming, hanging out there big as a balloon. What I could have done?

"She's sick. You know, vomiting, staying in bed all the time. I'm thinking about that baby. She ought to go on to King but she won't. See, I don't know how to talk to her."

"I'll see what I can do."

"Baby, who was that?"

"Bea. She wanted to know if I was coming to help."

Mama frowns. "See, I don't like that, people taking advantage of you. Do something and they want you to do more."

"She just called, that's all," I say but she's not paying attention no way, watching that show she likes *In the Heat of the Night*. But me, I don't like seeing that man, Tibbs, his lips are too blue, another one with that cocaine thing.

"Good night, Mama, too tired to watch TV."

"All right, baby."

So I get in bed, try to sleep but I'm thinking. Thinking about that girl and that baby she's going to have, do something for it, get her to a doctor, how much that'll cost and would she go?

Put on my robe and go into the living room to the door. Mama's so into that show she don't pay no attention to me. Bet he's sitting in that car smoking weed. No, he's on the porch with his friends, two of them, I put on the porch light and all their faces turn to the door. "Turn it off," I hear Ollie yell. I open the door and call for him to come.

"What you want!" he says and his friends, one of them's Smoot, haven't seen him in a long time, laugh at me. Bet I look like Aunt Jemima, scarf on my head, hiding big curlers. Ollie skips up too quickly must be cause he wants something. All three have big bottles of that malt liquor. Ollie's eyes are BB's. Takes a second to focus on me. His breath stinks.

"Buy me . . . ninety-five cents."

"What?"

"Ninety-five cents."

"You know François' number?"

"Who?" he says with his eyes bugging out.

"François."

"Why you want to talk to that fool for. He's too young for you and you're too big for him."

All right, that does it. I slam the door, let him stay out there and want a beer.

"What's wrong?!" Mama asks sitting up, startled by the door.

"Sorry. Arguing with Ollie."

"Go easy on him. He's doing better."

The door opens and there's Ollie, smiling toothy like he does when he wants to have his way.

"Got that ninety-five cents?" he says.

"Come here," I say and make him follow me into the kitchen. I turn to face him but he's got his head in the icebox and comes out with a cold pork chop and bites into it like he didn't eat tonight and I'm sure he did. It's the weed.

"Look! Don't you come in here, high like that and get Mama upset."

"What?" he says and opens his arms, smiling that stupid smile with his eyes squinty like a Chinaman's. I grab him by the shirt and fling him into the sink. Bounces off, and starts to say "Hey!" and I do it again and grab him by the throat and take hold of his hand and force him backwards till his head's touching the windowsill.

"Don't do it again," and I let him go after another shove.

"Think you can do that cause you big!" he says rubbing his neck.

"I told you, Ollie. I ain't going to put up with nonsense. Bad enough what you do but don't bring it in here."

His eyes go darting around the room like he's looking for a frying pan to bash me with.

"You," he says.

"What?"

"You mess with me!"

"That's because you deserve it. Now what's that boy's number?"

"Gonna get me a beer?"

I come out with a dollar and show it to him.

"The number?"

"767-7673," he says and I write it down and give him the money. He turns on his heels and rushes out of the kitchen. I call the number. I should have known, disconnected. Bet he made up the first number that came to his little mind. Feel like going outside and snatching it out of his hand. How much is this going to cost me?

So the next day I go over there, knowing it's next to the Pattersons' house. I find it all right. It's the cute green and white one. Then I see the FOR SALE sign on the lawn and a smaller orange sticker with SOLD on it so I guess Ollie wasn't lying like a dog. Still though, I go up to the door and knock and almost as fast it opens and there's that boy, François, looking good. Too good, expensive jacket and fancy shades.

"François, y'all moving?"

"My mama's moving."

"She's moving, really? Where?"

"Atlanta."

"Atlanta, Georgia?"

"Yeah. That's where they're going."

"Oh, is she home now?"

"Naw. She's running around town doing things. You wanted to see her?"

"Yeah."

"What about?"

"I got a problem. Thought she could help."

"What kind of problem?"

"I wanted her to look in on somebody bout to have a baby."

"Want me to have her call you?"

"Yeah, here, let me give you my number."

"I know it. I'll tell her to call."

"Thanks," I say and start down the steps. This just keeps getting more complicated. Drive, that's all I do. Driving around thinking about this mess.

Just when the house gets quiet and Mama's in bed and Ollie's out the house doing something and I get a quiet moment the phone's got to ring like it knows I don't want the trouble.

"Hello, may I speak to Sally?"

"This is she." It's her, sounding proper and white like at the hospital.

"Hi, this is Ann Williams, François' mother."

"Thanks for calling. I got this friend and she's in a bad way. She's pregnant. I don't think I can get her to go in to see a doctor so I was wondering if you'd go with me to talk to her."

"Me?" she says sounding put out. Guess it's too much to ask with her moving and all.

"Don't worry about it. Really I'll get her there myself," I say.

"I don't know if there's anything I can do but I'll go with you."

"Thank you. Your help is truly a blessing."

"How far along is the girl?"

"I think she must be eight or nine months pregnant but I don't know."

"Okay, so when do you want to do this. It'll have to be soon because we're leaving this week."

"Tomorrow, around twelve?"

"That's fine."

"I'll meet you at your house."

Hang up thinking at least I'm doing something.

The next day I call in sick cause I can't worry about this and do that typing. Mama's worried cause she thinks I've got the best job in the world. But it's not a good job, it's a stupid job. Word processing, work slaving, typing, typing, that's all it is and it don't stop. So, first thing I do have my Bible study. First Corinthians, Chapter 13, the strength of love. Then I try to fix some breakfast and eat something but I can't. Least I'm losing weight. I get to Mrs. Williams' house early so I sit in the car listening to the gospel station. Some of that music they play serves the Lord but I'm glad I don't have to listen to that every Sunday. Their front door opens and there's François looking good as before. This time he has on a suit.

"Hi. My mama wants you to come in for coffee," he yells to me.

"How's your mother?" he asks when I get to the porch.

"Oh, she's doing good. She's grieving but not like at first." He leads me into the kitchen through the bare house and pours the coffee for me. Guess she's still getting ready. The kitchen is as empty as the rest of the house except for a folding chair he opens for me.

"So, how's Ollie?" he asks me as I sit down.

"Oh, you know. He's doing better than what he was doing. All that trouble he was getting into. Now, he's getting along."

"Good," he says and his face is blank so I can't tell what he's thinking.

"How are you doing," I ask him. He smiles all uncomfortable.

"I'm doing all right."

"Are you going south too?"

"No. I'm getting an apartment."

The way he talks, his mouth moves slow like he's really thinking about what he says.

"If I were you, I'd go. This place, all it does is ruin people."

He smiles, his lips curl like he's going to say something but he doesn't.

"My brothers . . . they were never good. Not like a mother would want her children. They could have found the work like I did but they didn't. Still, it isn't just them, something about how people go bad here . . . you know, getting by like people do, then they just go crazy, possessed with evil."

"Is it different anyplace else?" he asks and I wonder with all the problems we've had around here how he could ask that.

"Oh yeah. It was different in Mississippi. Where we're from. People . . ."

"People didn't do stupid things there?" he says and I know I must be sounding silly, but I know I'm right.

"Did you ever hear from Rika?" he asks out of the clear blue sky. I must look shocked cause he looks surprised.

"You heard from her?" he asks again.

"Yeah, but that was a long time ago. Just said she was sorry about Doug."

"Oh," he says and runs his hand across his near bald head.

"She's a real case that girl. I hope she gets help."

"She needs more than that," he says.

"She needs the Word of God, but she isn't likely to hear it unless through the grace of Jesus."

"I don't know all about that but I don't think she can get what she needs. After all she done she still don't know what it is." Looking away from me, like he's being disrespectful. I know François isn't familiar with the Word or none of that, but how he talks about her and what he say . . . what is he thinking?

"It doesn't make any difference what she does . . ."

He's not talking to me. I don't believe he's paying attention to me. Talking to himself like someone who's not right. Thinking that way makes a person crazy.

Ann comes in and I'm glad to see her. She doesn't have on nurse's white. Instead she's in a nice green dress.

"Hi," I say and reach for her hand. She smiles and takes mine. I wish I could be more like her, slim and pretty.

"Ready to go?" she says. In her pocket. I can see her stethoscope. If I could be like her, good job helping people and to be able to leave with the family, just go.

"I really appreciate you going out your way like this."

"It's no problem," she says. "But we should go."

François watches us walk off the porch, but he don't say goodbye to her. It's like he's angry but he doesn't have the energy to be. Then, for some reason, I feel like I should open the door for her.

"You don't have to do that," she says like she's embarrassed but she gets in all ladylike. But I've already done it, embarrassed the both of us.

"Are you glad to be moving? I'd be. This place has really gone to hell," I say as we get going.

"I don't know." She's got a troubled look. It's got to be the boy.

"Is it your son? You worried about him?"

She takes her time. We pass through three intersections before she says something.

"Well, it's beyond me worrying. I try not to think about it. Ever since your brother . . . he's been going through it. He never was the most communicative child but now he hardly says a thing. I don't know. But I can't keep worrying like this. It's up to him. And now he's got a job so that's good."

I say a prayer for her. Children might be a blessing but . . . It's so much easier not having them.

We get to the homeless house and I feel like I should tell her everything. That's she's pregnant with Doug's baby and that Ollie thinks she's the one who shot Doug. But I don't. I park and run around and open the door for her.

"Really, you don't have to do that."

"Sorry," I say feeling stupid. I don't know what I'm doing. I give her space to get out of the car and walk ahead so she won't think I'm tripping.

I knock on the door and Bea answers still in her sweats but at least she don't look like she wants to kill somebody; still though, she ought to put a scarf on those curlers.

"Bea, this is Mrs. Williams, she's a nurse."

"It's Ann. Pleased to meet you." She shakes Bea's hand and looks so polite. Pretty and young even though her hair is getting a little gray. I really like her.

"So you gonna take a look at her. Somebody needs to. The reverend drove her to the hospital but it was gonna be an all-day wait if she got seen at all."

Bea turns around and leads us through the living room which is much neater now. The boxes make an island in the middle and the newspaper is off of the windows. They got curtains somebody must have given, worn and white turning yellow but they keep out prying eyes.

Bea knocks on her door, and nothing, she don't say a thing.

"Hey, Mary," she says and rattles the door. I get nervous and so does Ann. She fidgets with the small leather bag she has with her.

"Maybe we should go in?" Ann says.

"Mary!" Bea says and jiggles the knob once more. "We're coming on in."

We walk into the room, all three of us trying to get through the door at once. And she's standing there naked as a bird, long and skinny but with such a swollen belly, so round, makes her stand like she's trying not to topple over.

"You should give somebody a chance to get dressed," she says.

Bea leaves the room muttering to herself and I'm more embarrassed than I should be, flushed in the face. But what do I expect. She's always been off. Ann is calm and helps Rika get into her underwear. It's a struggle with that stomach. Ann tries to fasten the bra for her but Rika pulls it up over her head and flings it on the bed.

"They're prodigious now. Too swollen for that thing," she says cupping her breasts.

"Why were you naked? Were you hot?" Ann asks.

"Yeah, hot," Rika says. Not one straight answer inside of her.

"Do you feel dizzy? Are you still hot?"

"No, I feel better."

Ann opens her purse and comes out with a digital thermometer.

"I want to take your temperature."

"Isn't that a lot of bother and I don't even know you."

"That doesn't matter."

"It matters if you want to get paid."

"This is a favor to Sally."

"Oh, really? She is something else, that girl. And you know, I've met quite a few Christians in the last few months but this Sally, she just takes the cake. The way I can act the fool and bringing a nurse to see me.''

Ann is calm. Slips that plastic piece in her mouth without missing a beat.

''Keep it there,'' she says and holds Rika's chin until she does. I feel calm around this woman. Just watching her smooth Rika's soul is something. It's close to a miracle. The stuffy room with the moldy carpet don't seem so stale, so uncomfortable. God is in the room, acting through Ann. She is a very special woman. A beep and a light flashes on her machine. She takes the thermometer from her and checks it.

''It's 101. You're running a temperature.''

''Oh.''

''I'm going to take your blood pressure.''

''How thorough of you,'' Rika says. ''For Sally to do all of this with all of the rumors about me.''

What is she going to say? Aw no.

''You know what her brother thinks?''

Ann doesn't respond just continues tightening the straps around her arm.

''My baby is her brother's baby. But her brother, you know got kilt, as they say.''

Ann stops pumping the little black football and stares at her but her face is unreadable like her son's. She starts pumping again and then lets the pressure down.

''It's elevated.''

''How elevated?'' Rika says imitating Ann, eyebrows raised like she's some cartoon character.

''It's elevated enough for you to see a doctor.''

''I really don't care for hospitals. I like to stay away from institutions.''

''Why do you talk that way?''

''Which way?'' she says shrugging it off like she has no idea what Ann's talking about.

''You talk as though I'm not listening to you or that I'm an idiot.''

"Well," she says rolling her eyes and covering her mouth, "are you accusing me of being offensive?"

Ann laughs and it's a heavy laugh not how you expect it to be.

"Do you have insurance?"

Rika laughs, high and stagey.

"That was a dumb thing to ask," Ann says still laughing.

"My family isn't around. I'm alone . . . terrifically alone in a cold and cruel world," Rika says.

"You are very theatrical," Ann says and stands up.

"Thank you," Rika says and I want to kill her. Making fun of people trying to do something for her.

"I'm going to get some iron tablets out of the car. It's very important that you take them."

"Sounds like a plan," Rika says in a stupid TV show voice.

Ann taps me on the shoulder and I follow her out of the bedroom through the living room and onto the porch. There Ann stops and lets out a laugh, laughing like it's a good joke.

"I'm used to working the psych wing. She fits in."

"What do you do with somebody like her?"

She laughs again.

"You do your best."

"What do you think?"

"She needs to get into hospital at least for an evaluation."

"How do we do that?"

"Talk to a few people. Maybe we can get her into someplace." Ann shrugs, goes to the car and comes back with a couple of pill bottles. Her face looks blank again.

We go back into the room, Ann first, and she hands Rika the pills.

"Take two a day. The baby really needs it. And I'm going to bring some other things if that's okay with you."

"But that's so generous of you. To do all of this for me and me being the psychotic bitch that I am."

Ann doesn't blink, just has a little of a smile on her face. The woman's patient. Rika's working on my last nerve. Sitting on the edge of the bed with her belly to her nubby knees, smirking at Ann.

"You are a very reasonable per—son," she says stretching the word till it sounds like a joke. "You know I'm not. Opposites attract? I saw you once when Douglas dropped François off and you were leaving. You were blocked in because Douglas had business he wanted to discuss but you waited calmly. Waited till Douglas pulled away. I thought this is a very reasonable woman. But what does that get you?"

"It's how I am. I don't think about it."

"See, I always think. That's my problem . . . I t-h-i-n-k . . ." She stretches *think* out. "I think too much. It makes me . . ."

"That's the way you are. Maybe you can't help that, but I might know some people, they can help you."

"Help me, huh? Oh yes, that would be nice to be helped, solve my problems, my thinking lifted away off of me like a white sheet I've somehow found myself wrapped in."

"You're making fun of me," Ann says without anger in her voice.

"Well, I was being metaphorical. There's nothing wrong with being metaphorical. It's supposed to be clever."

"I know you're being clever. But this is important. I don't want to see anything happen to you."

"Nothing's going to happen to me, I'm fine."

Ann sighs and looks like she's tired for the first time. Rika's finally starting to wear her down.

"Maybe we should go?" I say.

"Soon," she says without taking her eyes off of Rika.

"There are people who could help you. There are treatments, programs . . ."

Rika stands up suddenly, making Ann back up.

"Maybe what I need is an exorcism. I suspect it's beyond medicine anyway. Did you ever see that movie *The Exorcist*?"

"Yes, I saw it."

"Great movie, huh?"

"I don't know, it scared me," Ann says and I think that is what Rika wants to hear. Gets all nervous and comes up even closer to Ann, in her face practically.

"That's what I need because what I have, it's not germs or chemicals or something misfiring in my head . . . it's poison."

Ann takes Rika's hand and leads her back to the bed where they both sit. Making me nervous, the way Rika is getting. Ann's bringing it out, getting her to talk.

"Rika, it's not poison. You might think it is poison but it's more complicated. Whatever it is you know you need help. You understand that. And probably because you're so intelligent it's worse. You know how you are. You know that things are wrong."

Rika smiles sweetly, runs her hands through that good hair, getting longer and with that baby it's even prettier.

"Well, thank you for the compliment. Being bright certainly does have its drawbacks."

Ann holds both her hands and seems so sad. "It's hard what we live with but you have to . . ."

Rika looks down at her knees.

"I want you to talk to a friend of mine. We might be able to help. I don't know how but . . ." Ann stops, waits for Rika to say "Yes, I'll do it," but nothing. She just smiles like she ain't heard a word.

"Sometimes it's not good for me to talk to people," she finally says.

"But you need to. You're pregnant. It's not just you. It's more than you."

Rika laughs low, shaking her hair as pretty girls do.

"I'm supposed to feel something about this," she says patting her round belly, "but you know, it's so common being a single mother and all. And you know Douglas and I didn't get along all too well."

"Regardless," Ann says firmly. That always confuses me. Regardless, I always say irregardless. Ann's right I know. "When you give birth to a baby, when you're carrying it, you're changed. If you don't accept it, it will never work. You'll never be . . ."

"What?" Rika asks like she's truly interested.

"What it is to be a mother."

"Oh . . . motherhood. I don't think I'm qualified. This state is purely accidental," she says, patting her stomach again.

"It's not an accident anymore. It's here and you are the mother."

"Going to be. It hasn't happened. I'm still free and single. And if I want to run into a doorknob, that's my choice."

"Don't say that. Don't be cruel to yourself."

"See, I don't get all this rah rah about child bearing. How's François? Is he what you were expecting. Not saying that he's the same as Doug but . . . Doug, now Doug was a dog, sorry to speak ill of your brother, Sally. But it's an irrefutable fact. Doug was a dog. And your son? Isn't he somewhat of a disappointment? You sweat and struggle and they just do the wrong thing."

"This isn't about me. My last pregnancy was thirteen years ago. I got through it."

"And François could end up like Doug. Facedown in the street and all of your planning, your effort squandered."

"Really, I'm not the one we're concerned with."

Ann is shaking. This woman's got to her. Made her look tired. So I get up sure of what I'm gonna do. Take her by the arm and whisper but not really caring if she do hear. "Let's go. This was a bad idea . . ."

"No . . . Rika, I'm going to come back. I'm going to take you to the hospital myself and sit you through it. I want you to have a healthy baby. Anything else you say is beside the point."

Rika nods like she is going to act normal.

"I admire your directness. If it means that much to you, I'll go. But say hi to your son. I haven't seen him in months."

"Sure, Rika . . . if that's what you want."

"Well, I guess you guys should go . . . I'm probably keeping you."

Soon as she says that I'm pulling Ann out of there. Rika watches us go sitting on the edge of the bed with that happy attitude.

"Sorry I made you go through that," I say, leading her through the living room and on out of the house. Ann stops on the steps, pulls away from me. She's mad.

"She is going to the hospital. It's ridiculous. So stupid."

"You can't make sense to her. I couldn't, nobody could."

"No. I'm going to get her admitted. The point is I lost it. Got myself involved in her fantasies."

So we get to the car and I take her home. Distracted the whole way, she doesn't look at me. Talking to herself. I know I've got something started. She's involved and that's what I wanted but still . . . I pull up to her driveway.

"It's going to take some time, but I'll call you soon as I have something lined up."

"You don't have to do that. I was wrong, I'll think of something."

Finally she looks at me, smiles that smile, smooths back her hair.

"How do you handle this? She's talking about your brother . . ."

"I'm a Christian, that should be my reason, but she's carrying what's supposed to be Doug's baby."

"What if you have to take custody? More than likely it's going to happen."

"If that's what God wants."

She pats me on the hand.

"Think about it. For the rest of your life you'd have to deal with her. She'll show up, she'll always show up."

"The Lord tries us. It would be a struggle."

I look at her pretty face again so I'll remember it and then she gets out of the car.

Days go by and she just gets bigger. Bea's at the end of her rope. I go over there and she looks so tired. I stop going to the church and bringing food. Instead I go straight to the house and do what I can. Bea, you know she's a hardworking woman but it's a little much to turn that place into something livable and take care of her children and deal with Rika. That would run anybody ragged. So I go over there and sit with Rika, but she don't have much to say, just ignores me unless she wants something particular. Ice cream and chips mostly. Girl won't eat right for nothing. And I help Bea out. Buy stuff for the kitchen, some used clothes for the children. Not a word from Ann and it's been over a week. I was thinking about calling her after I came over and Rika wasn't in her room or the backyard. Got me nervous for real. Bea didn't see her leave. The girls didn't either, just gone like that. Now Bea looked like she was trying to be worried but how could a body expect to be after all she been put through. So I was about ready to go search for her cause it was starting to get dark. I got out on the porch and see the sky looking purple and orange and the streets big and empty and I see her coming up the street swaying and bobbing, white against the dark street like a fat ghost.

"Is that you?" she asked me.

I got her in the house and she said offhand like it was so sensible, "I just went for a walk."

That's when I thought I'd better call Ann even though she said she'd call me. But I didn't. Even though trouble was coming. Somebody does something like that and you know a black cloud's coming ashore. So I waited for the call, for Bea to say she's gone. And that would be it. Be over for her and the baby, ground down like glass and that would be it, back to that hell.

But nothing, not a call from Bea or Ann, didn't hear a thing. The week went by but she must be thinking about it. Ann must be really busy. Getting ready to go. But it's been five days and I know. You know these things. It's gonna happen unless she gets someplace. Got to do something.

I call her house. "Is Ann there?" It's the boy. His hello's so deep it sounds hollow.

"No, she's out. She's working."

"Tell her Sally called."

"Oh," he says and stays on. "How's your mother?"

"Fine."

"How's Ollie?"

I don't know what to say to that other than the truth.

"He's doing the same. Maybe a little better."

"Okay," he says like he's going to hang up but then he stops. "Do . . . you know what's going on? Mama keeps saying she's helping you. You know what she's talking about?"

"Talking about . . . must be the church. You know, helping the homeless."

"Yeah," he says like I should tell him the truth.

"I have to go," I say.

"Okay, bye." And he hangs up the phone. Now that's nice. Got to sneak around with Mama over there on the couch watching her shows. Least Ollie don't stay in the house listening to phone calls. Spends all his time on the porch flagging cars down. Don't need another hand stirring this up. Soon as I get on the couch again, Mama gets to staring at me.

"What was that about?"

"Somebody at the church."

"You running yourself ragged over them homeless people."

"I ain't ragged. Just doing things that need to be done."

She snorts like I'm being silly. Guess I do come home late every day now.

The phone rings. I get up to get it but the metal screen flips open banging the wall and Ollie comes running into the house like a fool, grabs it way before I do.

"What!" he says.

"No way to answer the phone," I say but he turns his back to me. Acts so ignorant.

"It's for you," he says and leaves it dangling off the table and goes on outside.

I know it's her before I pick it up.

"May I speak to Sally?"

"Ann! It's good to hear your voice."

"Sorry I took so long in getting back, but I had to do favors, working a couple of awful shifts to get this. But, it looks like we've got something. There's an opening at a state hospital in Camarillo."

"Thank you, Jesus."

"But we've got to get her there. And she has to admit herself. We can't do it for her. She has to sign the papers."

"What if she don't?"

"I don't know. This is it. I had to go through hell to get her this."

"When is she supposed to go?"

"Tomorrow. There's a waiting list of months to get in. We've got to get there tomorrow in the early afternoon so a doctor can examine her to see if they can admit her."

"Thanks for looking after her. You've done so much."
"Don't mention it. I'll be by at ten so we can pick her up."

In my bed with a pillow on my head I can still hear that car radio
thumping in the street. One of Ollie's friends. But I ain't going to
go out there and get into it with him. Don't want a fight. Something
to upset Mama. When she finds out about Rika being pregnant with
Doug's baby then she's going to have something to be upset about.
A little crack baby. Her first and only grandbaby. And the mother
is looney as a junebug. With a mother like that baby's got a hell of
a chance. Hope they can do something for her. But what? Seems
till she accepts Jesus Christ they won't be able to do a thing for her.
It's the baby that's important. Mama'll understand and Ollie will
have to if he wants to live under this roof.

All night long I thought about it. What's going to happen. The
whole notion fills me up, got me thinking about how I'd do it
differently than how Mama did it. Cause she did her best, she tried
to have the presence of Jesus in the house but the boys, they never
understood. They never accepted it. That was their choice. Maybe
there was nothing else she could do. Mama said they were men and
men got to do what men do. But I don't believe that. If they got to
live like they lived then I think they get to do their living far away
from me. But Mama's not like that. Family's got to stick together
she says, but this family wasn't sticking, it was dying.

Seems like the whole night I spent thinking, so it wasn't hard to
make the call in to work and tell them I was sick. That's okay.
Being a Christian I don't want to lie but this was all right, Jesus
understands choices we've got to make.

Mama's up watching them talk shows. I never see them cause
I'm always working. What's sillier is Ollie being up with her when
he should be spending his morning finding work. Them sitting there
in the dark living room, curtains drawn so the glare won't come in,
keeping out a fine sunny day. Ollie ought to be looking for a job
instead of sitting there in his drawers, showing his skinny chest off

with a plate on his lap. Mama don't want to admit it, but she babies that boy. Just so she'll have a man in the house.

"You want some breakfast? Got some potatoes left and I can fry an egg . . ." Mama says cause it's a commercial.

"No . . . I'm fine. Gotta take care of something."

"Going to the doctor?" she asks.

"No. It's something else I got to do." Guess she got a right to be wondering why I took off since it don't happen often. I oughta just leave the living room go some other place in the house but I don't. I can't sit in that kitchen, the smell of all that bacon is making me sick. So I'll just sit and wait for the knock cause I don't want Ollie answering it.

"So you applying for another job. Is that why you dressed up?" Mama asks and Ollie finally looks away from *Donahue* and grins stupid like he's got something dumb to say.

"Bet she's gonna check in one of them weight loss clinics. That's what she's about to do. All that white she got on makes her look like a big-ass cloud."

"Don't talk about your sister like that. You know I don't approve of that."

I don't even look at him cause I know I'd hurt him if I let him get to me.

"You look nice, baby. Don't let him make you think different."

"Ain't studying him." So I sit there clutching my purse like I'd like to be clutching his neck. But that's okay cause I know he's possessed. It's the devil in him.

"You going shopping?" Mama asks.

"You need something?" That's what she wants me to ask.

"No, I don't want nothing. I got some stew meat for dinner. You gonna be home for dinner?"

"Probably but I dunno."

"She's got a man! She finally got herself a man. I was starting to worry she don't go that way."

See how the Lord works to try us.

"Boy, you ought to shut up. Cause you working on my last nerve."

First he gets ready to open that mouth of his but he takes another look. Sees me starting to stand up and he turns his head back to the TV like he knows he should.

"So who you seeing?" Mama asks straight out. Well that is easy to answer.

"Nobody. I'm doing an errand. I ain't seeing nobody."

Don't see why she got to know, most of the time she don't ask. But that's probably because I don't do nothing like this. Something like take a day off and change their morning routine. Maybe I should just stand outside and wait for Ann but then they'd just comment on that. I hear her, a car door slamming.

"Never seen her move that fast," that fool boy says. All I want to do is open the door and get out before Ann knocks but the stupid dead bolt is stuck and here's Mama wanting to see who it is.

"Who is it, baby?"

"It's nobody, Mama!"

I look at Ollie and open the door wide enough to get through and keep him from coming around me. I slam it shut and there's Ann looking at me like I'm nuts. But before she can say hi, Ollie yanks open the door. His BB-shot head comes craning around. Like to push him right back in the house. He better not come out in his drawers.

"Hi," he says like the word finally came to him.

"Ann, you know my brother, Ollie?"

"Yes, I saw him last at the funeral."

All three of us stand there awkward.

"We got to go," I say and start off the porch. We get down the steps and I see somebody in the car. It's her boy and then I hear Ollie come outside. Turn around to see him with his hands over his eyes squinting at the car.

"You going with that hustler?" he says and looks like he's about to run off the porch and throw himself at the car to get at François.

"*Go in the house!*" I scream and he stops. François gets out of the car. Ann hurries over—"Get back in"—and both of them stand there ignoring us, till finally François ducks his head and slides into the driver's seat.

"Yeah, we'll see about this shit," Ollie says and runs back to the house. Almost bumps into Mama who comes out to see what the commotion's about. We get into the car and François's shaking his head.

"He's a fool," I say. "He's a true embarrassment," but as François's pulling away, Ollie's running outside again struggling into a sweatshirt, already in his baggy jeans. Before we turn the corner I see him running for the station wagon.

The whole drive I'm looking behind me, looking to see that boat of a car, but it's not around, not behind us. We get to the homeless house fast cause there's no traffic and François is quiet but he don't seem upset about what my stupid brother did. I want the ride to go on cause I know . . . I just know, can just feel it, something is about to happen. We get out, me as jittery as Ann is calm. Today she looks like a businesswoman in her navy suit. I probably look silly in all of this white.

"It's okay," she says as we walk to the porch and she squeezes my hand. But it's not right, Bea comes outside. Her hair's done, pressed and oiled for once, with a cigarette in her hand, takes a drag and smiles at us showing off her snagger tooth.

"Girl's ready to go. Got her stuff together. She's wearing one of your things. Something like what you got on but it looks good on her."

"Great, Bea," I say and see Ann's face wrinkle. But I'm sure Bea didn't mean nothing by it. That's just how she is.

"Let me get her, y'all come in," she says and we step inside. Seems like every time I'm here Bea has the place looking nicer and nicer. Her little girl, the dark one with the pigtails, she's on the couch, legs under a blanket. Nose is running, must have a cold. See her watching us, big eyed and curious. Living with Rika must give a child a lot to be curious about.

"Hi, honey," Ann says to her. I say the same.

"You friends of Mary?" she asks.

"Yeah," I say.

"She say she don't have friends."

"We're friends," I say. "That's why we're here."

"Oh," she says like she doesn't trust us.

Then Rika comes out of the rear of the house. She comes into the room like a princess, like she owns everything, wearing my old choir gown and her hair is slick and wet like out of a shower and she must not have dried herself the way the gown is sticking to her ball of a stomach.

"I'm ready," she says and takes a brown bag filled with clothes and stuff from Bea and we start out.

"Bye, Mary," the girl says to Rika and Rika smiles and pats her on the head.

"Thank you," she says and kisses the girl on the cheek. Bea frowns.

"Thanks," she says to Bea but she doesn't kiss her and we go to the door. I hear it going on outside. The shouting, the cursing, the door opens and there's Ollie arms flinging around like he's lost it screaming at François but François isn't doing nothing. Leaning against the car being calm. Ollie's got something in his hand. Not another gun. Gettin' up on François and acting like he's going to hit him but he doesn't. Jumps back and points his gun. But I can't make out what's he saying. Just "Fuck, Fuck" and we all stand there watching. Ann tries to say something, her face is ashy and slack, mouthing words. Maybe I don't hear them. Then Bea comes out the door, sees what's going on. She sees the gun in Ollie's hand and slams the door. Comes out again, "I called the police." She's got a baby, that's what I would do. Then Ann goes down the steps slow like she's stepping into cold water.

"Don't," she says but Ollie's not even looking at her. But I'm coming too, to stand on the edge of the lawn and watch like we're at a movie. Maybe this is it. François is just gonna stand there and let Ollie point that gun at him.

"Think you gonna punk me like that, like I'm a bitch," Ollie says.

Then the noise, Ollie stops cursing. Maybe he's seeing it ain't having much of an effect on the boy.

"Fuck you, Ollie," comes from Ann's boy's mouth so clear and loud. Ollie's arm rises and the little gun is pointing right at his head.

"Wait a minute. Is that Ollie, Douglas' little brother?" Rika says coming off of the porch. "No," I say and step in front of her but she keeps coming with that brown bag in front of her belly.

"Ollie, you not going to shoot that boy? I thought you were looking for me."

"What! . . . you huh?"

"So what's the deal, Ollie? You don't want to shoot nobody. You'll look back at this and laugh and wonder what was all the fuss about," Rika says.

"Bitch, what are you talking about? You the one! You know you shot Doug."

"And if I did. Wasn't he going to be shot by somebody sooner or later?"

Ann is trembling, trying to pull away from me, trying to get to her boy. But I hold her back, she's so thin, it's easy to do. I'm not going to let her go out there and get shot. Ollie looks like he don't know what he's gonna do.

"Think I won't plug you cause you're knocked up. That don't got to be Doug's baby."

"Well, you're right about that. You can never be sure about these things. Could be another baker's loaf in here." She pats her stomach and smiles like she don't got a care in the world.

"Y'all fucked up," Ollie says turning around to look at all of us. Sees François smiling and gets mad and points the gun at him again.

"Just say I won't."

François just smirks. But Ollie looks serious, his lips twitch.

"Ollie, put it down," I say and push Ann behind me.

"Don't tell me what to do," and he shoots in the air. Everybody's diving but for Rika; she slips and lands on her butt, hands on her hips, not like she's scared at all. Ollie's looking satisfied, got everybody else on the ground, crawling away.

"Where you going?" he says to François. "Better get your dead ass down before I shoot it."

And Rika like a fool stands up again.

"You big fucking cow. Think you too good to be scared," and he steps up to her and slaps her across the face but somehow the gun goes flying. François comes behind him and picks him up and throws him down. And for a moment, they look like a jumble of legs and arms until François gets up and kicks him. Ollie gets to crawling to the gun but the boy kicks him again and Rika squats down slowly and picks it up. Ollie's on his knees next to François and both of them freeze.

"You know, Ollie, you shouldn't point a gun at somebody unless you mean to use it."

His mouth is a big hole like he's trying to say something and she shoots him until the gun clicks. Ann runs to the boy. François runs to Rika and Bea comes outside screaming for everybody to go away.

15
Michaels

■

I got the news six months late, but it was new to me. I really didn't expect to hear from her again, especially after how awkward it had gotten. But it was her, sounding just as impatient as if I were the one calling.

"Michaels, you know what happened?"

"No, I don't know what happened. What happened?"

"Ollie got shot."

"Is he all right?"

"He's dead." She sounds more impatient like that's all she wants to tell me and that's all I need to know.

"What else? That's it?"

"Naw. It's crazy. I want to tell you in person."

"You're home from school?"

"Yeah, I'm home. Don't expect you to drive to Santa Cruz."

"When do you want to meet?"

It wasn't a problem to get away. Run some errand for Tina, something I had to do anyway. Took off in a mood of anticipation. So I would get to see her again, something I didn't think would happen.

Even on a Saturday afternoon the Harbor with all of that construction is a mess, and along the sound walls there are all of those inner city advertisements about the hood, colors and culture. I look at it but it never makes much sense—graffiti can be so totally self-referential. Scary though, six months away and already I feel like I'm entering something new, looking at everything with fresh eyes. I get off at Imperial and drive east a few blocks and turn on her street. It's a trip how middle-class it looks around here. Some young friendly-looking kids sit on the porch of a neatly remodeled tract home. There's her house. The garrison hacienda and right down the road the Grape Street projects. That's unusual, the spiked gates of her yard are open. A big man in tight jeans kneels before a lawn mower, tightening something with a wrench. It's her father.

"Excuse me," I say and he takes a moment to turn around. His dark, round shades make his head seem empty. This is one of the reasons I didn't call.

"What do you want?" he says sharply without looking up from his work.

"I'm Garvy Michaels, Margot's English teacher from Bolt High."

"Go knock on the door. She's home."

Glad to be free of him I hurry to the porch, but before I can get there the metal screen door swings open and she comes outside.

"What are you staring at?" she says and I shrug. Her braids are gone. Her hair is cut bluntly, shaved close on the sides and she's dressed conservatively, a black shapeless dress and black leggings. Already she looks ashy from Santa Cruz's foggy days.

"You've changed your look."

"You ready to go," she says walking by me and passes her father without a word on her way to the car.

Leimert Park comes up faster than I thought it would. I follow her into the "Family." It looks much different from the neat and clean soup and salad shop run by a black family I used to go to. It's much larger with dark wood replacing the bright decor and now there are photos of Malcolm, Martin, Miles, Trane and Zora and a large red, black and green flag behind the counter. Back to the sixties. It's comforting. Probably cuts down on robberies and draws college students. The light-skinned woman behind the counter still sports the Angela Davis–like afro but now it's a little gray.

"You want a tea. They got good iced tea here."

"Yeah, sure," and she leaves me at the table without asking for money. The woman behind the counter knows Margot. They talk a bit and Margot comes back with long frosty glasses of tea. I take a sip anticipating the almost syrupy taste of an herbal concoction and lots of honey and lemon. Yep, it's just the same.

"Are you home for the whole break?"

"I don't know. I might not go back."

I was hoping she wasn't going to say something like that.

"You'll go back."

"How do you know I'm going back?"

"I expect you to."

"Oh really, it's like that."

She smirks a smile.

"Yeah, you're right. I'm going back on the second of January."

"So how you like it?"

She shakes her head.

"Talking about me liking something. What about what I called you for, Ollie getting shot."

"Well, I was expecting it."

"Oh, so it's no big thing."

"I didn't say that. I can't be too surprised considering the way he was living."

"Rika shot him."

So I sit there as she looks away sipping her tea liking the fact that I need to know. So instead I imagine how it happened. At the rockhouse, at a club, at a motel. Over money, dope, the usual. Then she turns around and eyes me.

"So you don't want to know?"

"I want to know but I'm not going to beg."

"Hey, you talk differently since you left Bolt. More white . . . 'I'm not going to beg . . .' Law school do that to you?"

"Thanks," I say. And then she tells me everything, all the news, an update—filling me in. François' business, Rika's troubles. Rika's achievement killing two men in one family, a double bagger,

and then having one, a replacement. And Margot tells it hard and
fast and without much feeling like it's the plot of a soap opera and
concludes, "They got what they deserved."

"But you know it's not as simple as that. What happened to
Rika?"

Margot smiles. "She's in some mental institution."

"And François, how's he doing?"

"So, you like law school?" Margot says, changing the subject.

"It's boring but I expected as much."

"How's Tina?"

"She's doing fine. She passed the bar."

"You guys having a baby yet?"

"No, not for a long time. We're enjoying being married."

"Oh," she says. She nods as though she's happy to hear it.

"Do you feel awkward coming home? I did for the first couple
of years," I say.

"What do you mean awkward?"

"You know, nervous, like people know you've been away."

"Why would I worry about that? Who cares about me being
away?"

"People care about all kinds of things."

She shakes her head, just about turns all the way around in her
seat like she's about to say something to Angela at the counter.

"See, I don't know what you trying to say and that makes me
mad like you either beating around the bush or you're talking down
to me."

"Maybe I don't know how to say it."

"Yeah, right."

"Do you know what I'm trying to say?"

She rolls her eyes, really rolls them.

"What? You think I need to be like you or think like you? You
think I'm going to turn white like an Oreo or something. No. It
wouldn't work for me. No way."

"But it's not that simple, after a while you'll change and you'll
understand."

"Getting soft, that's what you're talking about?"

"I'm not saying that. Don't you feel like you don't fit into either place?"

"Maybe. But I never have fit in. I don't worry about what people think."

"So that's what you think I do, worry too much about what people think. Not black enough? Not hard enough?"

"I don't know. *You* know."

I'm looking down at my drink. Getting squashed by a nineteen-year-old.

"Don't be thinking about me. Trying to figure me out like I'm some puzzle. You're making everything complicated."

"Oh," I say and try to force myself to think of the shooting and François and Rika. Somehow that all seems simpler.

"What time is it?" she asks.

"It's about three."

"He's off work if you want to go by there."

"By where?"

"To see François."

"I thought you weren't seeing him."

"I'm not but if you want to see him."

"I don't know if I want to see him."

She ignores me and tells me how to get there.

It's close to François' old neighborhood.

"Slow down, pull over there."

"Is this where he lives?"

"No, this is where the baby lives."

"Whose baby?"

"Rika's. Doug's sister, Sally, is raising him."

We wait for him in the car. I guess he'll be showing up soon. A Hispanic girl plays with her brother in the yard near us. She tries not to look at us but I catch her glancing. Then she picks up the blue-diapered boy and goes into the house.

"This is dumb. I don't want to talk to him if you don't."

Down the street a black Jeep pulls over in front of a big, worn-out house. Margot slides down in her seat. A tall, well-built, well-dressed man gets out. Before he puts on his *X* cap I see his head is shaved. He goes to the door and knocks. After he goes inside, I ask.

"How's he doing? He looks good. New Jeep, hair style. He's in school?"

"He goes to West L.A. and he works at a check cashing business for Cowboy. Same old game. Trying to walk the fence."

"You've been talking to him?"

"Naw, I told you that. I just find out what I need to know."

A few minutes later he comes out again with a baby. He sits down on the porch with the baby cradled in his arms.

"We better go. He's gonna notice us. Go back the way you came. I don't want him to see us."

Back at the hacienda. The gates are locked and the pit bulls are on patrol. I turn the engine off and Margot sits there smoldering.

"He does that often?" I ask.

"Just about every day."

"That's Rika's baby?"

"Yeah, I said that."

"I don't understand. You don't talk to him but you think about him. You know what he does. About the baby. But you won't talk to him."

"What's there to talk about? It's final. Cause I want to know about him don't mean I got to talk to him."

"It must be hard."

"So? Lots of things are."

She gets out of the car, turns around and leans into the window.

"Thanks for coming by. I'll be calling you."

She lingers at the window. She's crying.

"Margot," I say and get out of the car. I walk up to her awkwardly. I put my arm around her as she buries her face in my chest and cries, weak against me. I hold her up. And as she composes herself she starts cursing, "François, Rika, Ollie, fuck 'em all." Then she stops and pulls away from me. Shakes her head as though she's angry at herself. Turns to unlock the gate. The dogs follow at her heel as she walks to the porch and unlocks the front door. Before she goes into the house she waves and calls, "I'm all right! See you!"

I drive back by where François was. But the Jeep is gone. He's gone. I picture him though, holding the baby, Margot crying. It's so much harder for them now than it was for me. At least I had the luxury of being naïve about love. But they don't have it. If they don't want to be ground down to nothing, which is the flavor of the times, they must understand everything.